"For readers who love mysteries more for character development than puzzle solving, the seventh Molly Murphy novel . . . does not disappoint."   —*Booklist*

"Sharp historical backgrounds and wacky adventures."
                                                —*Kirkus Reviews*

IN DUBLIN'S FAIR CITY

"Readers will surely testify that Murphy has become one of their favorite characters . . . This book is a keeper."
                                                —*Tampa Tribune*

"Enjoyable charm and wit."   —*Baltimore Sun*

"Molly is an indomitable creature . . . The book bounces along in the hands of Ms. Bowen and her Molly, and there is no doubt that she will be back causing trouble."
                                                —*Washington Times*

"The feisty Molly rarely disappoints in this rousing yarn seasoned with a dash of Irish history."
                                —*Kirkus Reviews* (starred review)

OH DANNY BOY

"Entertains readers and teaches them about the immigrant experience . . . charming."   —*Tampa Tribune*

"Murder, mayhem, disease, and death . . . reliable period thrills for Molly's fans."   —*Kirkus Reviews*

"Another outstanding mystery."   —*Library Journal*

"Excellent."   —Toronto *Globe & Mail*

BLESS THE BRIDE

RHYS BOWEN

St. Martin's Paperbacks

This is a work of fiction. All of the characters, organizations, and events portrayed in this novel are either products of the author's imagination or are used fictitiously.

BLESS THE BRIDE

Copyright © 2011 by Rhys Bowen.
Excerpt from *Hush Now, Don't You Cry* copyright © 2012 by Rhys Bowen.

For information address St. Martin's Press, 175 Fifth Avenue, New York, NY 10010.

Library of Congress Catalog Card Number: 2010040697

EAN: 978-0-312-54745-5

Printed in the United States of America

Minotaur hardcover edition / March 2011
St. Martin's Paperbacks edition / March 2012

St. Martin's Paperbacks are published by St. Martin's Press, 175 Fifth Avenue, New York, NY 10010.

10 9 8 7 6 5 4 3 2 1

It seems appropriate to dedicate this to my husband, John. You have been the wind beneath my wings.

AUTHOR'S NOTE

I am trying to re-create, as faithfully as possible, the world of 1903. This includes not only the sights, sounds, smells of old New York, but attitudes and prejudices. Some readers may be offended with the use of derogatory terms like "Chinaman" and with the opinions expressed by characters in the book. However much we find these offensive, they were usual for the time and as such, have to be included to paint the true picture.

CHAPTER ONE

I think I may be in a spot of trouble," I said.

Mrs. Sullivan looked up sharply from her needlework. I read a succession of expressions pass over her face—shock, dismay, disgust—then finally she said, "Oh, well, these things happen, I suppose. Luckily you have your wedding date planned and it wouldn't be the first baby to arrive remarkably early."

"What?" It took a moment for the penny to drop, then I started laughing. "No, it's nothing like that. Actually I only meant that I think I've sewn the wrong sides of this bodice together." I held up the offending handiwork.

She took it from me, examined it, then sighed. "Goodness, child. However did you manage to grow up without learning the rudiments of sewing? Did your mother not teach you anything?"

"If you remember, my mother died when I was ten," I said. "After that I had to do my share of darning and patching, but that was about it. I've certainly never had to sew fine fabrics like this."

"Then it's fortunate that we've no bridesmaids' dresses to make as well, isn't it?" she muttered, not looking up as she started unpicking stitches. "Although it's a shame we've no little flower girl. I always think they add something special

to a wedding. I did suggest that we ask the Van Kempers'
granddaughter . . ."

"I don't know the Van Kempers' granddaughter," I said.
"I'd feel awkward having a stranger as part of my wedding
procession. There was one little girl I was very fond of—little
Bridie. I believe I told you about the child I brought across
from Ireland who lived with me for a while. I did send an invitation to her family, but I've received no response, so I can
only assume that they've moved on." I sighed. Or that they
thought a wedding in Westchester County sounded too grand
for them, being the simplest of Irish peasants.

Mrs. Sullivan nodded and looked at me with genuine
sympathy for once. " 'Tis a shame that you'll have hardly any
guests of your own at the wedding, and no family at all—
except those two brothers. Fugitives from the law, didn't you
say?"

"With the Irish republican freedom fighters," I corrected
her, although I suspected she remembered well what I had
told her. "I don't even know where they are anymore." I stared
out across the dewy lawn. A mockingbird was singing its
heart out in the plum tree. It was so peaceful and safe here,
while my brothers were off somewhere, still fighting for the
Irish republican cause.

Daniel's mother and I had been sitting on her porch swing,
enjoying the sweet morning air before the day became too
hot, while we worked on making my trousseau. At least, she
had been doing most of the making while I did a lot of unpicking, each set of removed stitches leaving a trail of little
dots on the creamy white silk.

It hadn't been my idea, believe me. I already knew my
lack of prowess with the needle and would have been quite
happy to have left my wedding gown to a Manhattan dress-
maker. This was Daniel's idea. He thought it would be a great
way for me to get to know my future mother-in-law better
and to learn some housewifely skills from her at the same
time. Actually I knew what his real reason was: he wanted
me safely out of the city so that I wouldn't be tempted to take
on any more detective assignments.

In theory I had no objections to spending a couple of weeks in the pleasant leafy atmosphere of Westchester County while the city sizzled in the muggy August heat. I had looked forward to having nothing to worry about except finishing my trousseau on time for my September wedding. I had had my fill of danger and was ready to admit that had I been a cat, I would have used at least eight of my nine lives. The reality of my current situation wasn't exactly as sweet as I had imagined. While Daniel's mother had welcomed me politely for Daniel's sake, she had also made it perfectly clear that I didn't measure up to her expectations for her only son. She and Daniel's recently departed father had scrimped and saved to give Daniel a good education. They had moved out to Westchester County so that he could mix with the best families. He had fulfilled their dreams by becoming the youngest captain in the New York police. He had been engaged to the daughter of one of those rich families, but then he had broken it off in favor of marrying me—Molly Murphy, recently come from a peasant cottage in Ireland, with no money, no background.

The fact that Daniel's mother and father had come from similar beginnings was never mentioned. From the way she talked, one would have thought that she'd been born with the proverbial silver spoon in her mouth. I had endured her subtle criticisms with a patience verging on saintliness that would have amazed those who knew my usual quick temper, wanting for Daniel's sake to keep the peace and even to make my mother-in-law like me. But after ten days my patience was wearing awfully thin.

She took the rest of the silk from me. "You'd better let me finish this and you stick to the undergarments," she said. "In my young day they always said that if a woman wasn't handy with her needle, her children would go in rags."

"Then it's lucky that I'm going to live in New York City where there are plenty of department stores selling ready-made clothes, isn't it?" I replied sweetly.

She pursed her lips. "Ready-made clothes? You'll make my son a pauper if you start off married life with ideas like that."

"Actually I do know how to use a sewing machine, if someone likes to give me one for a wedding present," I said. "I worked in a garment factory once."

"A garment factory? Did you?" The disapproving look again, as if I'd dropped yet another notch in her estimation. "Daniel never mentioned that to me."

I didn't think that Daniel had mentioned a lot of things I had done while working as an investigator. My profession was a constant thorn in his side. But I didn't want my future mother-in-law thinking that I had been reduced to working in a sweatshop. "I was on an undercover assignment to find out who was stealing dress designs. It was awful. You should see the conditions those poor girls have to work in."

"So I've heard," she said. "Well, I expect you'll be glad that you won't have to do such unpleasant things any longer. A lady detective, indeed. It's not natural for a woman."

"I had to earn my living or starve," I said. "I imagine that it was much the same way that your family had to survive when they came from Ireland in the famine." I paused to let it sink in that I was well aware that her family had come over to America with nothing. "It was either that or fish gutting in the Fulton Street Market, or prostitution." I was attempting to make a joke but her lips were still pursed, so I added, "To be truthful, I've enjoyed running my own business, and the excitement."

"Daniel's been worried about you, you know. He doesn't say much, but a mother can tell."

"I know. But he didn't have to. I've learned to take care of myself pretty well."

This wasn't exactly true. There had been times when I was lucky to come out of a situation alive. Those were the times when I had longed for the peace and security that I was now experiencing. Now that I'd had ten days of it, I was ready to go back to my world of excitement and danger. But I'd made Daniel a promise that I'd give up working when we married. I couldn't go back on that now, could I? My thoughts turned to Daniel and the upcoming wedding and the cold feet returned. Don't get me wrong, I wanted to marry him. I loved him. I was just scared of becoming a wife, confined to the life that respectable wives led: tea parties, sewing and idle gossip, and children soon enough, knowing the way that Daniel and I made love.

"It's too bad he can't join us for Labor Day after all," I said. "I'm sure you were looking forward to seeing him as much as I was."

Mrs. Sullivan sighed. "You'll soon learn that being a policeman's wife isn't easy. Meals at all hours, calls in the middle of the night, and sometimes hardly seeing your man for days. And the constant worry when he doesn't come home on time. I went through it all those years with my husband. My hope for Daniel is that he'll soon leave the force and go into politics. He has the connections, you know, and I've no doubt that Tammany Hall would back him. They'd love to see another Irishman in Washington."

"But he loves what he does," I said. "He's good at it. I wouldn't want him to give it up because I was worried."

As I said it the thought crossed my mind that he was making me give up my job for that very reason. Or was it rather that my being a detective would not sit well with his colleagues—even open him up to ridicule?

"Did he tell you what important case he was working on that keeps him in the city?" Mrs. Sullivan asked.

"We made an agreement," I said. "He doesn't share his cases with me and I don't share my cases with him."

Mrs. Sullivan grunted her disapproval again. I stared out across the back lawn to the row of tall trees that separated this house from its neighbors. In the next backyard someone was mowing the lawn. I heard the *click-clack* of a mower and the sweet smell of new mown grass wafted over to me. There were roses blooming along the fence and the buzzing of bees mingled with the sound of mowing. Truly it was quite delightful here. I should just let my future mother-in-law's criticisms wash over me and make the most of this time.

"I can't blame Daniel for not coming out to see us," she said. "He has no real reason to make the long, uncomfortable journey now that he doesn't have to collect the furniture."

"What furniture?"

"I offered him some choice pieces of our furniture for your new house," she said. "But now that you're apparently going to start married life in that poky little house of yours, I gather there's no room for extra furniture."

My saintliness was wearing thinner. "It's a dear little house. I'm very fond of it. And it's in a quiet backwater." I wanted to add that her house, while pleasant enough, was no mansion. Not much bigger than mine, in fact.

"But the neighborhood," she said. "I know that Daniel wanted you to start married life in a better part of the city, farther uptown."

"There's nothing wrong with the neighborhood." I could hear my voice rising.

"Greenwich Village? My dear, it's full of immigrants and bohemians, not the sort of people you'll want your children to mix with."

"Mrs. Sullivan," I said, taking a deep breath to steady myself, "don't tell me that when your own family stepped off the boat they went straight to the Upper East Side and lived in a mansion. They started off with nothing, in the slums. Daniel told me. And yet I'd say he'd turned out well enough. And in case you've forgotten—I'm an immigrant. I don't want to pretend to be something I'm not."

There was a long, frosty silence during which the lawn mower continued to click away, then she said calmly, "We'd better get back to work if we want these garments to be finished on time. I told you we're expected at the Misses Tompkins for lunch, didn't I? And after that I promised Clara Bertram that you'd come and play croquet with them. Clara is another of Daniel's old friends and she does so want to meet you."

I'll bet she does, I thought. So that she can examine the fabric of my dress and find it wanting. I'd already encountered several of Daniel's friends during this stay. I could see their surprised reaction that Daniel was marrying someone like me when he could have had Arabella Norton and a fortune to go with her.

I picked up the half-sewn white silk petticoat and was about to start stitching when the porch screen door opened and Colleen, the little maid of all work, came out. "The post has just come, madam," she said and handed Mrs. Sullivan several letters. Mrs. Sullivan glanced through them.

"These will be responses to our invitation to the wedding. The Van der Meers," she said, looking pleased. "Oh, and Alderman Harrison. And there's one for you, Molly. That's not Daniel's handwriting."

She handed me the letter. I recognized the writing at once. "It's my neighbor on Patchin Place," I said, then couldn't resist adding, "Augusta Walcott, of the Boston Walcotts, you know."

Mrs. Sullivan looked suitably surprised. "The Boston Walcotts, in Greenwich Village?"

"She's an aspiring painter. Would you please excuse me if I go and read this?" I didn't wait for the answer but went down the steps and across the lawn until I was standing in the shade of an elm tree, out of sight of Mrs. Sullivan and the porch swing.

My dear Molly, I read in Gus's educated, fluid script, *I can't tell you how much we are pining for you. Life seems positively dull without having you around. And New York is beastly hot and uncomfortable, but Sid insists on staying put because of the articles she is writing on the suffrage movement. We imagined you sitting in the leafy shade, drinking iced lemonade and having a lovely time, and we were tempted to hop on the next train and come for a visit, but Sid pointed out that your mother-in-law might not approve of us and she didn't want us to do anything that might cloud your future relationship. Sid is always so thoughtful, isn't she?*

But then she had an equally splendid idea. Why don't we give a small party for Molly, she suggested. All those friends who are not being invited to the wedding. Of course we started planning and scheming immediately. Should it be a Japanese theme, or Ancient

Greek? Sid suggested an underwater motif and wanted us all to be mermaids, but that was really impractical as we wouldn't be able to dance with tails on. So we're still debating the theme but we thought that some time during the Labor Day weekend would work well, if you've nothing planned. Do let us know as soon as possible whether this suits you and we'll go full steam ahead with the plans.

We've seen your betrothed from time to time, although I can't say he has paused to be sociable with us. As you know, he has been having the place completely redecorated. And the other day he stopped by with a load of furniture, presumably from his rooms, since it looked very dour and masculine. We peeked in a couple of times and we must say that it all looks wonderfully brand, spanking new—and the wallpaper remarkably tasteful. I think you'll be pleased.

We do hope you can come for Labor Day. Sid sends her warmest regards.

Your friends Sid and Gus,

P.S. I almost forgot. A man came to your house yesterday and when nobody answered, he rapped on our door and demanded to know where you were. He said he represented a most important man who had an urgent commission for you and left his card with us. He demanded that you to contact him as soon as possible. We told him we didn't think you were taking any commissions at the moment but he said he was sure you'd take this one. He was quite insistent. So you might want to come back to the city a day or so before the party, just in case there is a juicy assignment waiting for you. Naturally we've said nothing of this to Daniel.

I reread the letter, then folded it. An urgent commission from an important man. I had promised Daniel that I would give up my detective business when I married, but I wasn't married yet, was I? And if it was a simple, straightforward assignment, it would provide a nice fee to add to my coffers—so that, at the very least, I could go to a department store and buy ready-made undergarments without feeling guilty.

Daniel's mother looked up as I came up the steps onto the porch. "Good news, I hope?"

"Delightful news, thank you. My friends in the city have planned a pre-wedding celebration for me, to take place next weekend. So I do hope you'll forgive me if I go back to the city for a few days. I fear I'm more of a hindrance than a help to you in the sewing anyway."

I thought she looked relieved if anything, but she said stiffly, "This celebration requires you to be away for more than one day, does it?"

"I know these friends," I said. "Their parties are always elaborate costume affairs, so I'll need to assemble a suitable costume somehow."

"A costume affair—that seems an odd sort of wedding party to me."

"It is Greenwich Village," I reminded her. "And many of our acquaintances are artists and writers. They enjoy being creative in their celebrations."

She went back to her sewing, one neat little stitch after the next.

"With your sewing skills, let's just hope that it's a Roman toga," she said at last.

I laughed dutifully, although I couldn't tell whether she intended to make a joke.

"I'll be back in good time to help you with the wedding preparations and to do the final fittings on my dress," I said.

"And I take it you'll be staying for our luncheon with the Misses Tompkins and croquet with Clara Bertram today?"

"Of course," I said. "I wouldn't dream of missing out on luncheon with the Misses Tompkins."

And this time she looked at me to try and guess whether I was joking.

CHAPTER TWO

As the train gathered speed through the woods of Westchester County, heading south, I felt as if I had been released from a straitjacket (and trust me, I had been in one of those once—not an experience I wished to repeat in a hurry). I found I was smiling at my reflection in the window glass. I was going to be married soon, going to be a bride, and I was finally looking forward to my wedding. It was true, as Mrs. Sullivan had reminded me, that I had precious few guests of my own, but that didn't matter. Those few who were coming were dear to me: old Miss Van Woekem, for whom I had once worked. Mrs. Goodwin, the female police detective, and her young protégée I had rescued. Gus and Sid, of course. I had put my foot down at that. No Gus and Sid, no wedding. But I felt a wave of sadness that I hadn't heard from Seamus and his little family. There had been a time when they had been big part of my life, but I had had only sporadic contact with them after they moved out to Connecticut for Bridie's health. *She would have made such a perfect flower girl,* I thought wistfully. *Better than the Van Kempers' granddaughter any day.* And I smiled to myself, again.

I can't tell you how good it felt as the train rolled across the bridge over the Harlem River and into the upper reaches of New York City. No more luncheons and croquet parties at which I had to watch my words, mind my manners, and put up with what I took to be veiled barbs. Maybe I was being oversensitive, but then, maybe not. And anyone who knows me can tell you that I'm certainly not used to being the demure miss. It had been taxing. And now I was about to be back among my friends with the added prospect of a lucrative assignment. And I might even have a chance to see Daniel—a jarring thought came to me. Daniel would not be pleased that I'd deserted his mother. And of course he couldn't know if I took on that case. So a brilliant plan came to me. It probably wouldn't be wise to stay in my own house if it was newly painted and plastered. Besides, it would hardly be fair if I occupied it alone before my wedding. Sid and Gus's guest room would be a much better idea, I thought to myself as the train went into the tunnel before arriving at Grand Central Depot.

Before I went to Westchester County the city had seemed unbearably hot and stifling and I had longed to escape to the countryside. It was still hot, to be sure, but I saw only the bustling life of the streets—a city that was vibrantly alive. Patchin Place was by contrast a quiet backwater, while city life teemed around the Jefferson Market building and along Greenwich Avenue. I stood on the cobbles, feeling the heat radiating back from the rosy brick houses on either side of me, thinking how grateful I was to Daniel for giving in to me and allowing us to start our married life here. I knew it was a sacrifice for him. I knew he wanted a more prestigious address. I knew he worried that I would be unduly under the unhealthy influence of Sid and Gus. But he had seen how much the house meant to me, and how much I valued my friends, and had agreed to give it a try. I had pointed out to him that the house would probably be too small after a year or two, when the babies started arriving and we'd need a servant. He wanted me to hire a servant now, but there really was no need for one if I was home, doing nothing all day. And frankly I didn't want the intrusion on my newly married life—certainly not somebody sleeping in the spare bedroom.

I hoisted my carpetbag and picked my way over the cobbles to my house, eager to peek inside at Daniel's renovations. I was about to put the key in my front door when I had second thoughts. I should find out first if anyone was inside. I didn't want workmen reporting to Daniel that I had made an un-scheduled appearance. It was hard to see past the net cur-tains, so I decided to go across the alleyway to Sid and Gus first. They seemed to have an uncanny knowledge of what was going on and would surely know if any workmen or paint-ers were in my house.

I knocked on their bright red front door and felt a rush of pleasure at the thought of seeing them again. Eventually I heard the sound of feet and the front door was opened, re-vealing the strangest of apparitions. It was Gus, wearing a robe over what appeared to be a black lace corset and sus-penders, holding up fishnet stockings. Since Gus was the more demure of the two, this in itself was shocking, but the fact that it was topped off with a police constable's helmet made it even more astounding.

"Molly!" Gus's face lit up as she recognized me. "We didn't expect you so soon. How absolutely lovely to see you."

"And you too. But do you make a habit of coming to your front door dressed like that?"

"Oh, dear," she said, gathering her robe about her with only the mildest hint of embarrassment. "I hadn't realized that my sash had fallen off my robe. Thank heavens it was you and not some man."

"Most young women of your upbringing would have fainted dead away by now," I said.

"Most young women of my breeding are currently being good wives and mothers and spending the summer in New-port or Cape Cod. I am already a lost cause in their eyes. But how rude of me to leave you standing in this awful heat. Come inside, do. Sid will be delighted."

She ushered me into the cool darkness of their hallway and then called up the stairs. "Sid, put down that pen immediately. We have company."

Footsteps came down the stairs and Sid appeared, wearing bloomers and an open-necked white shirt. "Molly," she ex-claimed. "How wonderful to see you. Isn't it wonderful, Gus."

Then she noticed what Gus was wearing. "Dearest, did you actually open the front door in that extraordinary outfit?"

"I was trying it on," Gus said. "I thought my robe was securely fastened."

"But the policeman's helmet?"

"Oh, yes." Gus put her hand up to her head. "I'd forgotten about that. You see, Molly, we were trying to decide on a theme for your party. We thought a policemen's and prostitutes' ball might be fun, in honor of Daniel, you know. So I was just trying out whether I wanted to be a policeman or a prostitute."

I started to laugh again. "My future mother-in-law was so impressed that I was going to a party hosted by one of the Boston Walcotts," I said. "If she could only see you now!"

They joined in my laughter. "As stuffy as you feared, is she?" Sid asked, leading the way to the kitchen and taking a jug of lemonade from the ice chest.

"Worse," I said. "My sewing skills are a disaster. I've had to have luncheon and tea with any number of her friends, where it has been hinted that Daniel was expected to make a much better match than me. You would have been so proud of me—I remained calm and demure throughout. Not one hasty word passed my lips. Close to sainthood, I'd say. But I couldn't have stood it much longer. Any moment I was about to scream and hit someone with a croquet mallet. So your letter was a godsend."

They were still smiling at me, as if I was an adored child returned to the fold. Sid led us through to their conservatory at the back of the kitchen and indicated that we sit in the shade of large potted palms that gave the space the feel of a jungle. She brought through a tray with lemonade and glasses.

"So you fled at the first opportunity," Sid said.

I nodded. "It was the excuse I was waiting for. Honestly, I'm not designed for genteel idleness. I don't know what I'll do with myself when I'm married and have nothing to do but cook for Daniel and keep the house clean."

"So you are going to remain true to your promise then."

"I have little choice. Daniel's career must come first."

"Why?" Sid asked.

"Because—because he is the man and the breadwinner, and because he already has a flourishing career," I said with slight hesitation.

"I suppose so," Sid agreed with a sigh. "So you will have no interest in the calling card Gus mentioned in her letter. We should just throw it away, should we?"

They were watching me expectantly. I saw the smile twitch on Sid's lips.

"I'm not married yet," I said. "I can still make my own decisions. And if this proved to be a lucrative proposition—well, I think it's healthy for a bride to start marriage with some money of her own, don't you?"

Sid shook her head, smiling, went back into the house, and returned with the calling card.

"Frederick Lee." I examined it, then looked up. "Is this the card of the important man or his emissary?"

"The emissary," Gus said. "He wouldn't give his employer's name. Rather secretive about it, in fact."

"And no hint of what kind of assignment this was?"

"None at all. I didn't take to him, if you want to know—there was something in his air that seemed to say that you should be honored that he had selected you, and that there was no way you'd turn down the commission."

"Probably a divorce then," I said. "A rich man who didn't want his identity known. In which case I won't take it. I don't care how much he offers me. I find it too sordid sneaking around and trying to catch people in compromising situations."

"Hear, hear!" Sid said. "Our laws are so antiquated. When a couple no longer wishes to remain married, they should be able to shake hands and part amicably, without all this ridiculous subterfuge. If Gus and I ever decided to part ways, I know we'd be most civilized about it. Wouldn't we, Gus?"

"I don't want to think about it." Gus turned away.

"Not that we ever will," Sid said hastily.

I turned over Mr. Lee's card. "His office is on the Bowery," I said. "Hardly the best of addresses. I wonder what his employer does for a living?"

"I agree it's not Fifth Avenue, but it's quite respectable in its upper reaches around Cooper Union. Perhaps the employer is a lawyer," Gus suggested. "I know I've seen law offices around there. . . . So are you going to pay him a call?"

I looked up from the card. "Why not? What have I got to lose? Just as long as Daniel doesn't find out."

"Our lips, as always, will be sealed," Sid said.

"Now you must let Sid show you the wonderful articles she is writing," Gus said. "The history of the suffrage movement. Most edifying and illuminating. Take Molly upstairs and show her the one you are writing at the moment, Sid."

"I haven't polished that one yet," Sid said. "The prose is still rather rough. But she can read the one that was published this week."

"It's her best yet," Gus said, sitting beside me as Sid went upstairs.

I had been the model of calmness for two weeks. Now my naturally impatient and curious nature had risen to the surface and was threatening to boil over again. I was dying to see what Daniel had done to my house and I wanted to find out about the mysterious Mr. Lee and his lucrative assignment. Sid and Gus were dear friends. They had been very good to me, but they had no concept of the word *urgency*. Life to them was one long game to be enjoyed and savored. I accepted the magazine that Sid offered me and read. Actually it was extremely interesting to read about the various states that had passed laws allowing women full participation in the governing process. Unfortunately New York was not one of them.

"This certainly reveals how far we have come," I said, handing it back to her.

"No," she said. "It shows how far we have to go. For every state that acknowledges women as rational beings who can only enhance the political process, there are four or five who think us fit only to scrub floors, bear children, and give tea parties."

I nodded.

"We are hosting one of our meetings tonight," Gus said, "so you will meet our fearless warriors for yourself. If you are here, that is, and the important Mr. X has not invited you to dine with him at Delmonico's."

"Oh, I don't think that is likely to happen," I said. "But I have to confess I'm impatient to find out more now. And I'm also anxious to see what Daniel has done to my house. Have you had a chance to peek inside yet?"

"No, we were not invited to have a look and one can see almost nothing through the net curtains."

"I know," I said. "I tried to look through them myself. I didn't like the idea of going inside, in case someone was working upstairs."

"I believe they are finished," Gus said. "We haven't spotted anybody for the last few days, have we, Gus?"

"As quiet as the grave," Gus said. "And we have to admit to being equally curious. We're dying to see if we approve of Daniel's taste in decoration."

"Then let's take a look, shall we?"

They needed no urging to follow me across the street. I opened my front door cautiously and listened for signs of activity. The smell of new paint made my nostrils twitch, but there was no sound. I stepped into the front hall, followed closely by Sid and Gus. As Gus had predicted, the place looked brand, spanking new. The hallway was light yellow, the parlor, which previously had contained one rather dilapidated armchair, now boasted a new sofa and attractive striped wallpaper.

Sid gave a grunt of surprise. "The man has remarkably civilized taste for a policeman," she said.

"And look, Molly. You actually have a dining room," Gus said, peering through the next door.

"So I do." The dining room now contained a dining set, complete with an impressive sideboard carved with grapevines. I had no idea where it came from. It certainly hadn't been in Daniel's rooms.

"Holy Mother of God," I exclaimed. "I'm going to be the mistress of an elegant house."

We went upstairs and the first thing I caught sight of through an open door was a large new four-poster bed.

"My, but that's a handsome object," Sid commented. "It's clear what's uppermost on his mind, isn't it? And yours too, I expect." And she chuckled.

To my annoyance I felt myself blushing. The young ladies I had been playing croquet with would have swooned at such a remark and had to reach for the smelling salts. Sid and Gus seemed to think it was perfectly natural to discuss such matters, as I suppose it was in bohemian society.

"Well, I say that Daniel has done you proud, Molly," Gus said, wanting to spare my feelings. "I think the redecoration and the furniture are splendid. But you're not thinking of sleeping here before the wedding are you?"

"I don't think I should," I said. "It wouldn't be fair to Daniel when I'm sure he wants to surprise me. I was hoping I could stay with you until the party."

"Of course you can. That way Daniel won't even have to know that you're in town," Sid said. "Come on then. We should make our escape just in case the eager groom puts in an unexpected appearance."

I glanced back at that bed as the other two made their way down the stairs. It certainly was impressive—so high and large that I couldn't imagine how the moving men had carried it up the narrow staircase. For a moment I pictured Daniel and me. . . . I rapidly reined in where that thought was going. I had kept Daniel at arm's length for too long, knowing how quickly the fire between us ignited. And now the waiting was almost over. I'm sure it wasn't proper for a young lady to look forward to her husband's lovemaking. Mrs. Sullivan had tried to give me gentle hints, warning me of men's appetites and how we women must endure it for their sakes. To my credit I had managed not to smile.

CHAPTER THREE

When we returned to Sid and Gus's house, I was itching to seek out the mysterious Mr. Lee, but had to mask my impatience a little longer while Sid and Gus took me up to my room, fussed around making sure that the pillows were to my liking and I had sufficient drawer space, then swept me downstairs to prepare luncheon. In truth I enjoyed eating with them, especially because the meal consisted of crusty French bread and what Sid described as her four-P meal: pâté, Port Salut cheese, pears, and peaches. After Mrs. Sullivan's stodgy and filling meals it was delightfully informal, but that business card was burning a hole in my dress pocket. Fortunately as soon as the meal was over, Sid was anxious to finish her article, so I took the opportunity to escape, making my way southward to the office on the Bowery.

The street number indicated that it would be at the bottom part of the street, where it joined Chatham Square, not at the more respectable northern end after all. So my curiosity was aroused even further. What very important man would have offices in an unsavory neighborhood south of Canal Street?

The day had now become uncomfortably hot and humid, with the threat of a thunderstorm later in the afternoon. I had no wish to walk a step further than necessary and tried to evaluate whether I'd be better off taking the trolley down Broadway and then cutting across Canal Street, or walking from my house to the Third Avenue El and not having to walk at the end of the trip. I decided on the latter and walked in the sedate quiet of Eighth Street, past Astor Place and the Cooper Union building to the nearest El station. I regretted this decision instantly as the train arrived already crammed full, and I was forced to stand between a large Italian woman who reeked of garlic and an equally large laborer who smelled as if he hadn't taken a bath for weeks. All I could think was thank heavens the line was now electrified or we would have had smoke blowing in through the open windows to add to the mixture of unpleasantness.

I can't tell you how glad I was to fight my way to the carriage door at Chatham Square. I came down the iron stairs into that teeming mass of humanity that is the lower Bowery. Trolley cars inched their way up the middle of the street, bells clanging impatiently to force delivery wagons, hansom cabs, and the occasional carriage out of their way. A constable stood on the corner, swinging his billy club in what he hoped was a threatening manner, as crime was rife around here.

I was already familiar with this area and unexpected memories resurfaced. I had stayed in a tenement on nearby Cherry Street when I first arrived from Ellis Island. That introduction to the city had not been the most pleasant of experiences—especially since I was accused of murder at the time and fighting for my very life. Then later I had worked undercover in a sweatshop on Canal Street. And when I was fighting to prove Daniel's innocence after his arrest on trumped-up charges of taking bribes, I had rubbed shoulders with Monk Eastman and his gang, who ruled this part of the city. As I recalled the disturbing memories, a voice in my head warned me that it might not be wise to be entering this dangerous world again. But I pushed the images to the back of my mind, as that was all behind me now. Daniel was back safely on the police force. I had a bright future with him, and nothing to worry about at all. And if I didn't like the sound of the assignment Mr. Lee was offering me, I simply wouldn't take it.

Having sorted that out, I strode out with confidence. Even

in daylight it was not the most desirable of streets. For one thing, the elevated railway ran along one side so that all the businesses beneath it were in perpetual shadow. Those businesses ranged from butchers and grocer shops to flophouses (advertising beds by the week—strictly no drinking allowed) to barbers with their striped poles (offering a hot shave and a haircut for ten cents). And then, of course, there were the saloons in abundance, not to mention houses of ill repute. Scantily dressed girls stood in doorways, their eyes scanning the crowd for likely customers. Their gazes passed me over as if I was invisible.

The saloons were doing a brisk trade, even this early in the afternoon. Drunken men—many of them Irish, I regret to say—staggered out and stood blinking in the strong sunlight as if they couldn't believe where they were. Occasionally a man would be ejected forcibly and come flying out to land sprawling on the sidewalk. Women out shopping would draw in their skirts, grab their children, then step past as if nothing had happened. I remembered those saloons well. I had had to enter one or two on occasion and narrowly missed being thrown out myself, as women were not permitted inside. How long ago this all seemed. Recently my cases had been of a more respectable nature and this part of the city now felt dangerous and foreign to me.

I stared up at the street numbers. Mr. Lee's address had to be around here somewhere. I finally found it next to a Baptist mission. From inside came the sound of children singing. Clearly the Baptists were trying to save souls on days other than Sunday. I went up a narrow, dark staircase and found myself outside a door on which a simple brass plate announced GOLDEN DRAGON ENTERPRISES. I opened the door and went in. There was nobody in an outer office, lit by an anemic gas bracket, but as I entered, a young man came through from an inner room. Not much taller than me, he was slim, fine-boned, and clean-shaven with black hair, and he carried himself with an air of elegance. His dark eyes narrowed as he looked at me appraisingly.

"Can I help you?" he asked.

"I'm here to see Mr. Frederick Lee," I said and held out the calling card. "My name is Molly Murphy. I gather he has a business assignment for me."

His expression didn't change, but he bowed slightly. "I am Mr. Lee. So you came back to town after all. Your neighbors did not think you would be available to assist my employer."

"I have been staying out in Westchester County," I said. "Luckily I came back to attend a function and my neighbors told me of your visit. They seemed to think it was most urgent."

"It is," he said. "We are honored that you have decided to give up your valuable time to help us. Please come into my office, Miss Murphy."

He ushered me inside and pulled up a chair for me. "Please sit down. I hope you managed to find me without too much inconvenience." He also took a seat behind the desk. His flowery politeness was beginning to annoy me, especially as I could sense that he was in no way honored by my presence. "None at all," I said coldly. "I have conducted cases in this part of the city before."

"Ah. That will be useful in this particular matter."

I looked around the room. Apart from the desk and chairs it was sparsely furnished with a large mahogany cabinet on one wall and shelves containing file boxes behind the desk. Suddenly there was a rumble and the whole place shuddered. It took me a second to register that the elevated railway ran by right outside his window. Hardly the sort of place where a rich client would choose to work or even keep an office.

"I understand that you are representing an influential gentleman," I said. "Are you his lawyer?"

"Oh, no. Merely his secretary."

"Then may I ask the nature of this assignment?" I asked.

"As to that, he will wish to tell you about it himself."

"Then please escort me to him." There was only the one door through which I had entered, and I came to the conclusion that this was an outpost of an empire, with Mr. Frederick Lee being among the lower ranks of employees. "I take it he is not in this building."

"Indeed no." Frederick Lee stood up. "I will be honored to escort you to him. He will be pleased that you have decided to assist him in this little matter."

"I haven't decided anything," I said. "I'll need to hear the nature of the case and the fee he is offering before I make any decisions."

"My employer does not readily take no for an answer," Mr. Lee said. "He is used to having his wishes fulfilled and his orders obeyed."

"Then perhaps I should leave right away," I said, "because I don't take kindly to being bullied or ordered around. I run my own business and I'm not anybody's lackey, Mr. Lee." I rose to my feet. "Good day to you."

He leaped ahead of me to bar the doorway. "I'm sorry. I spoke hastily, Miss Murphy. Please forgive me. Of course my employer appreciates your expertise and status, otherwise he would not have sent me to find you. This is a matter of great delicacy and he needs a detective with your kind of experience and finesse. Please at least let me take you to him and hear what he has to say. He is a very rich man and his generosity to those who help him knows no bounds. I can assure you that you will not be disappointed."

I opened my mouth to point out that his generosity to his employee clearly knew quite narrow bounds, if this office was anything to go by, but I swallowed back the words at the last moment. I have to confess that I was intrigued and challenged. The least I could do was to meet this man, and if I didn't like what I saw, then I was free to walk away.

"Very well," I said. "Lead me to him."

He took his derby hat from a hat stand in the outer office. "This way, if you please. It is only a short walk. I hope you won't find the heat too oppressive, but it makes little sense to hail a cab for such a small distance." He led the way down the stairs. Another train rumbled past overhead as we came out onto the street.

"This way. Please watch your step. The street is not the cleanest, I'm afraid." He took my arm, gripping it firmly above the elbow, and steered me across the street, between a trolley and a knife grinder's wagon. When we safely reached the curb he released me. "It's always an adventure crossing the Bowery, isn't it?" he said. "Never mind, we'll soon be out of the hubbub."

I was curious to know where we were going. There was nowhere within walking distance of the Bowery that I could think of as a respectable residence for a rich man, so I presumed we'd be going to another office. Maybe we'd be heading south to Wall Street and my client would be a wealthy banker. Or perhaps he was in shipping, but surely we were walking away from the docks.

"Up here," he said and steered me into a side street. I looked up and read the street name: Mott Street. I also noticed immediately that it was unnaturally quiet and empty after the hustle and bustle of the Bowery. And looked different, somehow. Brightly colored balconies festooned the buildings, which were topped with ornate curved roof gables. Some of the balconies were gilded and carved with what looked like mythical beasts. Lanterns and bird cages hung on them. Then I noticed the names over stores and restaurants. Yee Hing Co., Precious Jade Chop Suey House, On Leong Merchants' Association, and notices pasted up on poles and billboards in Chinese characters. I was being taken into a place I had only heard about until now: Chinatown.

CHAPTER FOUR

A t that moment a door opened in a building to our right. A man poked his head out and looked up and down the street before darting out of the doorway and scurrying fast down the block as if the hounds of hell were after him. He was dressed in baggy pants and a dark blue cotton jacket. On his head was a skullcap and down his back hung a long pigtail. It was my first glimpse of a Chinaman and I watched him with interest.

Then all the rumors I had heard about the Chinese and their habits rushed into my head. They smoked opium. They ate puppies. They stole women for the white slave trade. I glanced uneasily at Frederick Lee. Was it possible that I was being stupidly naïve and was being lured into captivity? My rational brain quashed this instantly. If anyone wanted to capture white women for prostitution, there would be no need to seek out someone who lived miles away in Greenwich Village when there were plenty of girls who were willing and able and already offering their services just around the corner.

"Why do you think that man is running like that?" I asked Mr. Lee. "He looked as if he was in some kind of danger."

"No Chinese likes to be out on the street longer than he has to," Mr. Lee said. "Surely you know that our Italian neighbors on Mulberry take great delight at beating and kicking us, even setting our queues on fire."

"Your what?"

"The pigtails that Chinese men wear. They are a constant torment. Small boys love to tug at them. Larger louts even try to cut them off."

We passed a storefront. What appeared to be scrawny cooked ducks hung by the necks in a row, and in front was a tank full of live fish swimming around. Two older men were chatting at the doorway, both wearing similar long pigtails.

"Then why continue to wear them if they pose such danger? They do make the Chinese stand out as different, don't they?"

"It is a hard decision to make, unfortunately. Back in China any man who does not wear his hair in the queue is thereby insulting the Emperor and thus subject to instant beheading. So a man who cuts off his queue can never go home again."

"That's terrible," I said. "Barbaric."

"No more barbaric than the way we are treated in America," Mr. Lee said calmly. "What about the Chinese out West who were driven from their homes, or locked in their cabins and burned alive? Is that not barbaric?"

"Extremely," I said. "But why would anyone do this?"

"Because we look different, and because we work hard and prosper. Always a recipe for hate."

I glanced across at him. "You use the word 'we,'" I said. "You're not Chinese, are you? You don't look like these men." But as I said it I realized that what I had taken for an arrogant stare was, in fact, a slight difference in facial features—the high, flat cheekbones and the narrower-than-usual eyes.

"I am half Chinese," he said. "I am one of the few of the first generation to be born here. My father had to flee from the West Coast after the Gold Rush when the persecution started. He came to New York and has prospered. I received a good education. I have been brought up between two cultures but consider myself an American."

"I'm glad to hear it," I said. "So do I take it your employer is also a prosperous Chinese gentleman?"

"Extremely," he said. "He owns many businesses, including a large import company. He brings things like porcelain and fine silks over from China. Ah, here we are now." We stopped outside a storefront. GOLDEN DRAGON EMPORIUM was written in golden letters over the doorway and under it presumably the same thing in Chinese characters. In the window brightly colored plates and cups, jade statues, and carved ivory daggers and balls were displayed. "Please be kind enough to wait here for a moment. I will go and announce our presence to my employer."

"May I know his name?"

"My employer is Lee Sing Tai," he said. "You may have heard of him. As I told you, he owns many businesses— cigar factory, importing, this store, that restaurant."

I shook my head. "I know nothing about the Chinese."

"You will address him as Mr. Lee, or Honorable Mr. Lee."

"Oh," I said, as light dawned. "The same last name as you. So that's why you work for him. You're related?"

"Not exactly, but we are both members of the Lee clan. In a way we are all related. This is how things work among the Chinese—we rely on our clan for support. And Lee Sing Tai knew my father when they were still in California. This is why he employed me." He held up a slender hand. "Now please wait here. I will not keep you but for a moment."

With that he darted inside the shop. I heard harsh, unfamiliar words spoken and Mr. Lee emerged again. "They say that our employer is upstairs in his residence and will receive us. This way, please."

He led me up a flight of steps beside the shop. He used a key to open a front door, then we climbed a long flight of stairs before we came to a second closed door. He knocked on this and it was opened by a young boy, dressed in Chinese garb, who bowed to us. Mr. Lee snapped some words to the boy, who gave me a curious glance before he scurried away, leaving us standing in a foyer. I looked around me. Another flight of stairs ascended up into darkness to our left. Ahead of us was a large, intricately carved screen, inlaid with what seemed to be semiprecious stones, depicting a mountain scene with cranes standing among reeds. It blocked my view of the interior of the apartment.

"That's a beautiful screen," I commented.

"Chinese always have something like a screen at the front of their dwelling," Frederick Lee said. "It is to deter evil spirits from coming in. They will not enter if there is not a straight path for them."

"People still believe that, do they? Or is this just for tradition's sake?"

"Of course they believe it." He sounded shocked. "Is it any stranger than praying to a statue in a Catholic Church?"

"I suppose not, although we don't really pray to statues," I said. "Actually—" I broke off as the boy returned. He said something in Chinese to Frederick Lee.

"My employer will receive you now," he said, and led me around the screen and into a large living room. I almost had my breath taken away at the sumptuousness of the surroundings. The furniture was of a black wood I took to be ebony and it was intricately carved, inlaid in places with mother-of-pearl. On the floor were exotic carpets, again with designs of mythical beasts on them. There were bright red silk hangings draped around a large jade statue in one corner and more lovely pieces of jade and ivory on shelves and side tables. On the walls were hung jeweled ceremonial swords and daggers, as well as scrolls of Chinese characters and painted scenes of mountains and flowers. The air was thick with a scented kind of smoke, and I noticed in a far corner little sticks glowing in front of yet another jade figure.

And in the midst of all this a man sat on a high-backed chair, looking for all the world like an exotic emperor on a throne. He was not young, and a long wispy white mustache drooped at the corners of his mouth. He was not wearing a skullcap and his head appeared at first to be bald, until I saw that he had hair at the back of his head, falling in a long dark queue. Although he was surrounded by these exotic objects, he was dressed in a smart Western business suit, with an immaculate white shirt and ascot. He held a cigar in one slim bony hand and puffed on it as we entered the room.

"I bring you Miss Molly Murphy, as you requested," Frederick said, bowing slightly before retreating behind the screen again.

Lee Sing Tai waved the hand bearing the cigar at me. "Excellent. Excellent. I knew you would come, Miss Molly Murphy. I knew you would not let me down. Very well. Sit. Sit."

He pointed at a long bench, piled with brocade pillows. I perched on it cautiously because it looked extremely slippery. Also I was feeling ridiculously nervous and at the same time angry with myself for being intimidated.

"I understand you have a commission for me to carry out?" I said. "I asked your employee about its nature but he was not very forthcoming."

Lee Sing Tai tapped ash into an exquisite blue-and-white dish. "You will take tea with me," he said. He didn't wait for an answer but clapped his hands. The boy came into the room and bowed low. An order was given. The boy disappeared.

"Chinese tea is very fine," he said.

"I know. I've drunk it. It tasted almost perfumed."

"That was Lapsang Souchong," he said. "In my household I prefer to drink Keemun. The king of teas, they call it. I am only one who imports it to this country." He spoke English with a heavy accent, snapping out individual words rather than delivering a fluid sentence. "But important families in New York City come to me for their tea. Rockefellers. Astors. You have heard of them?"

"Of course," I said.

"I supply them tea and silk and many other things." There was a quizzical smile on his face as he said this. "You would be surprised which distinguished people come to Lee Sing Tai to be supplied with what they need."

He didn't even glance up as the boy came in, carrying a red lacquer tray. I noticed that the servant moved silently and was wearing black cotton slippers. He put the tray on a side table and poured tea into two little round cups. Clearly Frederick was not to be included and indeed he had made himself scarce. Then the boy placed one of the cups on a smaller tray and carried it to me, presenting it with a bow. I took it and savored the smoky aroma. It was scalding hot and

I hoped I wasn't expected to drink it yet. Luckily the boy served his master, then came to me with a bowl of little almond cakes. I took one and nibbled politely.

"Delicious," I said. Lee Sing Tai watched me eat and waited for me to take a sip of the tea. It was still very hot and I was used to having milk and sugar in my tea, but I sipped dutifully.

"This assignment you have for me, Mr. Lee. What is the nature of it?" I asked.

A spasm of annoyance crossed his face. "The tea is not to your liking?"

"It's very nice," I said. "Only rather too hot for me at the moment."

"Tea is good for hot days," he said. "You drink tea. You cool down. Better than water."

"Yes, I'm sure it is."

"The Chinese know better how to remain cool in this heat. We have known it for thousands of years."

He went back to sipping from his own teacup. I was growing impatient. "Perhaps we might discuss our business while we wait for the tea to cool?"

I sensed from his expression that I might have committed some kind of faux pas, but frankly I didn't care. I wasn't the one who was looking for a job; in fact I really didn't need one at the moment. "I need to know what sort of assignment you are offering," I went on, my confidence returning, "as I am busy preparing for my upcoming wedding at this moment and actually I am planning to give up my business."

He took a long sip of his own tea. I noticed how he deftly pushed the wispy strands of his mustache out of the way as he drank.

"I should let you know immediately that I don't handle divorce cases," I said.

This elicited the ghost of a smile. "Chinese have no need for divorce cases," he said. "Private life is kept private. Don't your people have a saying, 'a man's home is his castle'? This we too believe."

"So if it's not a divorce case, then what is it?" I persisted.

"Such an impatient young woman," he said. "You would not make suitable bride for Chinese man."

"Then it's lucky I'm marrying a fellow Irishman."

"I know. The famous Captain Sullivan."

I must have shown my surprise because he said, "Do you think I would not have my people do a thorough search on a person I wished to hire? So one thing I have to know before you and I proceed with this matter—do you discuss your business with your future husband?"

"Absolutely not," I said. "My business dealings are entirely confidential. Whatever is spoken between you and me goes no further than this room."

"Ah, so. This is what my spies tell me about you, but I wanted to hear it for myself. I had to make sure you were trustworthy. This is a matter of great delicacy."

By now I was almost ready to grab him and yell, "Tell me what it is, for God's sake!" but I practiced my newfound patience a little longer. I was certainly intrigued by him. Even if we had met somewhere other than in this elaborate room, I would have assumed him to be a man of power.

He leaned back in his chair and folded his arms. "I wish you to recover a precious possession that has gone missing." I noted that he could not say the *r* in the word "precious." It came out closer to "plecious."

I digested what he had just said before asking him, "When you say missing, do you mean that you have mislaid it or that it has been taken from you?"

"Both," he said.

"Stolen, you mean?"

"In a way. Taken. Carried off."

"Mr. Lee," I said, "if something has been stolen from your residence, then surely this is a matter for the police."

"The police?" His lip curled in an expression of disdain. "Do you think that the New York police will help me recover a lost item? Do you think they would come to the aid of a Chinese person, even if that person is as prominent in the community as Lee Sing Tai? They stand by when we are beaten by thugs. We have to pay them protection money if we want them to patrol our streets, to prevent our shop windows from being smashed. No, I could not call upon the police in this matter. Besides, I do not think they could help me."

"I don't see how I could help you recover a stolen object," I said.

"You are a lady detective, is that not correct?"

"Well, yes, that is correct," I said.

"And should a detective not have the skill to pick up the trail of a missing possession?"

"Might I know what is this possession you speak about?"

"To begin with, I will show you this," he said. He reached across to a side table, took a brocade envelope from it, and opened it carefully, drawing out a large medallion of carved dark green stone. "Examine it carefully," he said.

He handed it to me. It felt cool to the touch, almost as big as my hand and carved with strange curling, intertwined beasts. It was attached to a chain of heavy gold by an ornate gold clasp.

"The missing piece is identical to this?" I asked.

"Not identical. The missing piece depicts the dragon and the phoenix—the beasts of good luck and good health," he said. "But it is the same dark green emperor jade and the gold work is the same. You will know it if you see it. There are few pieces of such quality in this country."

I turned the piece over in my hand. It was still remarkably cool. "Do you have any suspicion about who might have stolen it?"

"We will not discuss my suspicions at this moment, except to say that I believe that whoever has taken this jade will try to sell it. You will conduct a search for it in the obvious places first—pawnshops, jewelers—and if it can't be found there, we will take the next step."

He held out his hand and I passed the jade back to him. He sat calmly folding the brocade around the piece of jade again.

I frowned. Something didn't make sense here. I plucked up the courage to break the silence. "Mr. Lee. I am given to understand that you run an empire of businesses. Do you not have employees enough to visit every pawnshop and jeweler in the city?"

He held my eyes with his cold, frank stare. It was like being observed by a snake. "Have you noticed many Chinese men in other parts of the city?"

"None at all," I said.

"Do you know why this is? We are hated, despised. Bullies take great delight in setting upon us with no excuse whatsoever. If we try to fight back, we find ourselves arrested for disturbing the peace, and even deported. Therefore we keep to ourselves as much as possible and do not stray far from this small area they call Chinatown. But there are other reasons I do not wish to hand this task to an employee. It requires a woman's touch."

"You do not employ any women?"

He actually smiled this time. "There are almost no women in Chinatown—at least no Chinese women. The American government does not allow Chinese men to bring over their wives and daughters. And respectable Chinese women are not allowed out in public." He leaned forward suddenly, tapping ash into the little dish. "So Miss Molly Murphy, I require your services for a good reason. I need someone who can be discreet and ask the right questions. I want this item returned to me quickly and with as little fuss as possible. So will you take my assignment or not?" He paused, holding me with that reptilian stare, then added, "I assure you I will make it worth your while if this prized possession is returned to me quickly."

He sensed my hesitation. "Well?" he said. "What is your answer? Do you think you are up to the task?"

"I'll do my best, Mr. Lee," I heard myself saying.

"Splendid." He clapped those bony hands together. "Very well then. Off you go. Good hunting, as they say in your country."

I stood up. Frederick reappeared and came to my side to usher me out.

"You will report back to me tomorrow," Lee Sing Tai said. "Let us hope you have good news for me by then."

I started toward the door.

"And if you find this piece, you will get a description of the person who brought it in," he called after me.

I turned back. "Do you have your suspicions about who this person might be?"

"No more questions," he snapped. "Off to work now."

As I looked back at him I saw the heavy drapes at the back of the room twitch as if suddenly dropped. Someone had been watching me.

CHAPTER FIVE

Frederick Lee insisted on escorting me back to the Bowery, then took his leave.

"I wish you success," he said. "Until tomorrow then. Please come to my office and I will escort you as I did today. I do not want you walking through Chinatown alone."

Since it had seemed a particularly deserted place I wondered why he felt the need to protect me. Surely not the reputed white slave trade? Or was it rather that I was an outsider, did not know how to behave, and might offend with my Western ways? We parted and I stepped into the shade of the elevated railway, trying to collect my thoughts. Why had I agreed to do this? On the surface the assignment seemed simple enough, but something wasn't quite right. Lee Sing Tai had sought me out in order to have a female detective retrieve a piece of jade jewelry. Granted it was attractive enough, but how much could such a piece of jade be worth? Enough to pay me a generous fee for its recovery? Then I concluded it must have some kind of sentimental value—some link to his past life in China. If not, then he could certainly afford to pay a jeweler to re-create it here or even have another one shipped from his homeland. That would make more sense than sending a detective running all over the city hunting for it.

Oh, well, mine was not to reason why. No doubt all would become clear when I found the piece and delivered it safely to him. I mapped out a plan in my head. There were pawn-shops aplenty along the Bowery, as is usual in a place where drinking, gambling, and prostitution abound. If someone had stolen the item for money, then he'd want to get rid of it as quickly as possible, so I should start here.

I paused again at the entrance to the first pawnshop. Why steal that particular piece of jade from a household that was full of treasures? I hadn't asked if other items were missing. Perhaps he had set me on the trail of this one because it was so easily identifiable. I stepped from the heat of the sidewalk into the cooler darkness of the pawnshop. The shop had a musty smell as if a lot of old and forgotten things were stuffed away here. The man behind the counter was an elderly Jew with a long white beard. He listened carefully, but shook his head.

"We don't see Chinese in here. They've nothing to pawn," he said. "You know why? They only came to this country with the clothes on their backs. They left their wives and families at home and they still plan to make their money and go back where they came from. So no jewels, because there are no ladies."

In the next pawnshop I was not treated as politely. "Don't deal with no chinky Chinese stuff," he said. "Who'd want it? And I don't trust those Chinamen further than I can throw them. Slit your throat the moment you turn your back, that's what they do."

I got variations on these speeches from other pawnshops close to Chinatown. As I moved farther away, along Canal Street in one direction into the Lower East Side and then in the other toward Broadway, I faced a cold indifference. No, they'd never seen anything like the piece I was talking about. A Chinaman never set foot in their shops, and if he did, they'd show him the door quickly enough.

I began to see how daunting this task might be. If a rob-ber had taken the jade piece because he needed cash, then he hadn't used a nearby pawnshop. And if he had delivered it to a fence, then I had no way of proceeding. I knew no fences. I had come into contact with the two large gangs that ruled Lower Manhattan between them, and I had no wish to deal with either again. I knew I had been lucky to come away with my life on one occasion and I had managed to seek Monk Eastman's help when I was truly desperate. But I also knew him to be fickle, sadistic, and ruthless. I couldn't count on any assistance a second time.

The obvious thing would be to ask Daniel. He would know every fence in the area. But he was the one person I couldn't go to. Most frustrating. I was rapidly coming to the conclusion that I'd have to appear before Mr. Lee Sing Tai the next morning and admit my failure. And come away with no fee for my labors. But I wasn't about to give up yet. There were plenty of jewelers, especially along Hester and Essex and those crowded streets of the Lower East Side where the Jews had settled from Eastern Europe, bringing their craft as goldsmiths with them.

I began to work my way along Hester, up Essex, then Delancey, and Rivington. Most of the shops dealt in secondhand jewelry or bought gold to melt down, but nobody seemed interested in jade.

"It's not worth that much," one of the jewelers said. "It's only semiprecious."

"I wouldn't find a customer for it," another said. "My customers only want gold."

As the afternoon wore on I was hot, tired, and growing more despondent by the minute. My overriding impression was of an extreme distrust of the Chinese. I was warned several times about getting involved with them. One man actually said, "You haven't gone and married one of them, have you?"

I wondered what had made him say that, until an old Russian, more astute and interested than the others had been, listened carefully to my description. "Dragon and phoenix intertwined?" he said. "That sounds like a bride-piece to me. Dragon for virility and power, and phoenix for fertility and health. I saw that kind of thing when I was in Shanghai, waiting for a ship."

When I looked puzzled by this he added, "We fled from Vladivostok, you know. Our home was destroyed in the war with Japan, and Russia is no place to be right now."

I had had enough for one day. The soles of my feet were throbbing from those burning sidewalks. The thin muslin of my dress was sticking to my back with sweat. I decided to call it a day and make an early start in the morning, although I was already telling myself that I was not likely to be any more successful than I had been today.

Workers were leaving sweatshops, indicating how late it had become. Those girls worked a twelve-hour day at least. I watched them walking three or four abreast, arm in arm, chatting and laughing with the relief of being in the fresh air and free after the long day of toil. The pushcarts had come out too in abundance and I had to thread my way between stalls selling roasted chickpeas, live chickens, pickles, buttons, and lace—in fact anything that could be sold to earn a few coins. Usually I savored this lively scene, but at this moment all I wanted to do was escape from it to the peace of Patchin Place, where a bath and a cool drink would await me.

I was on my way back to the Bowery and the El station when I heard the most improbable sound: someone was yelling my name. I turned around, unsure that I was actually the one being called, and saw two figures running toward me, fighting their way through the crowd. It was my long-lost Irish children, Bridie and Shamey, followed by their father.

"Molly. Look, Pa, it's Molly!" Bridie was shrieking, not caring whom she pushed aside to reach me.

Shamey made it first with his big, almost man-sized strides. He went to hug me, then thought better of it, wiping his hands down his shirtfront instead, but smiling at me delightedly. "We thought you'd gone away," he said.

"I thought you must have gone away," I replied, putting my arms around both of them. "I sent you an invitation to my wedding but I got no reply."

"We came back to the city," Shamey said. "We're living with Auntie Nuala for a while."

"Goodness gracious. What on earth made you do that?" I demanded, as that lady's abode did not hold pleasant memories for me.

Seamus had caught up to us, his round Irish face streaming with sweat. "Molly, it's grand to see you again. We went to your old house, but there was nobody there except for a painter and he said a young couple was to be moving in. So we thought you'd gone away."

"The young couple is Daniel and myself." I stepped aside as there was a shout and a cart full of bolts of cloth came rumbling down the street. "I'm getting married in less than two weeks."

He tipped his cap to me. "Lord love you. God's blessings on you and your husband."

I smiled. "I sent you an invitation to the wedding. Now I hope you'll be able to make it."

"If we're still here in two weeks." Seamus wrinkled his forehead. "Not exactly sure how things will be going."

"Where do you think you might be?"

He frowned again. "I heard they were looking for men willing to take a ship down to Central America," he said. "There's plans to build a canal through a place called Panama, clear through the jungles. When it's done they say that ships will be able to sail from the Atlantic to the Pacific without going 'round the Horn. So I signed on and I'm taking young Shamey with me. We want to be on the spot when the contract gets signed and get first pick of the jobs. They say the pay's good and I reckon it will set us up for life."

I looked from one face to the next, my unease growing. "You're taking Shamey with you?"

"I am. He's a good little worker and almost a man."

"I'll be twelve soon," Shamey said, "and I can lift really heavy things, can't I, Pa?"

There was such pride in his voice that I couldn't yell out what I wanted to: *Don't let him go!*

I turned to look at little Bridie. She had also grown, but she still had that frail and delicate air about her, holding on to my skirt as she looked up at me with those sweet blue eyes. "You're never thinking of taking Bridie down to some heathen jungle?" I demanded, stroking that baby-fine hair.

"No, it would be no place for a young girl," Seamus said. "That's why we came to look for you. I was hoping that you'd find her a position in service. Mother's helper or maid of all work. She's a willing little worker and she learns quickly."

I could feel my anger rising. Bridie was a sweet young child. She deserved a childhood, not starting out as a servant before she'd had a chance to play and learn. I wanted to volunteer to take her in myself, but then I remembered that I was about to get married. I could hardly start married life with someone else's child in our household, could I? And I remembered that back home in Ireland many young girls were put into service when they were not much older than Bridie. I myself had been left with three young brothers to raise after my mother had died. But it wasn't a fate I would wish on anyone else, especially not on a delicate child like this.

"Don't make any plans for her without consulting me," I said, trying to measure my words. "I'll ask my friends and see what can be done for her. I'm staying across the street at number Ten with two ladies while my own house is being decorated to be ready for my marriage or I'd ask you all to stay with me. It must be horribly cramped at Nuala's place."

"Aye, it's not the most comfortable," Seamus said. "But 'tis for only a short while. Nuala's willing to take the girl in herself, having only produced sons, but I thought you'd know how to give her a better future than that. I don't wish a life in the fish market for my daughter and I know my dear departed Kathleen wouldn't want it either."

I took a deep breath. "I will do my best, Seamus, I promise. And I won't let Bridie wind up with Nuala, that's for sure." I smiled down at her. "We'll find something for you, my sweet. We'll stay in touch, and you'll come to my wedding, won't you?"

We parted, my head buzzing with this latest complication. Why was life never simple? I had thought how nice it would be to have Bridie in my wedding party and lo and behold Bridie appears, but now it was up to me to find a way to prevent her from living in that hovel and working in a fish market. Always too many things to worry about.

I made it back to the Bowery and squeezed into a car on the El back to Astor Place. As my straw hat was knocked to one side of my head I reminded myself that at this very moment I could be sitting on Mrs. Sullivan's cool porch, sipping iced tea, and doing nothing more strenuous than stitching my petticoat. Daniel would probably be angry with me that I had returned to the city. I had taken on another case when I had virtually promised him that I wouldn't and I was achieving nothing by it. In fact the thought actually crossed my mind that it might be more useful to have acquired some sewing skills—which shows you how despondent I felt.

I quickened my pace as I walked the shady length of Eighth Street. I turned into Patchin Place. Sid and Gus would have a pitcher of lemonade or some kind of exotic drink waiting, and I could sink into one of those chairs in their back garden. Ah, bliss.

I knocked on the front door. Nobody came. This was something I hadn't expected. They had not mentioned that they might be going out this evening. And I'd left my key to my own house on the dresser in their spare room. I felt tears of frustration welling up as I stood in the deep shade of the alleyway. Now what did I do? They were usually so considerate. Surely they'd have left me a note. But perhaps they assumed that I carried my house key with me and that note they'd written lay on the hall table across the street. With little hope I rapped on their door a second time and waited. I'd just have to go to a coffeehouse and hope that they returned before too long.

I had just turned away when I heard my name being called. I spun around. Gus was standing there.

"Molly, I'm so sorry. We're all out in the garden and we were debating so heatedly that we didn't hear the door. You poor thing, you look worn out. Come in, do. Sid has made sangria. It's divine. And everyone's dying to meet you."

"Everyone?" I asked. My mind went to the party they were

giving for me at the weekend. They couldn't have put it forward, could they?

"Our suffragist group. I mentioned to you that we were meeting tonight. Such wonderful women. So brave. You'll adore them." With that she dragged me inside and helped me off with my hat.

"Come along. Sid's sangria will revive you in no time at all." And she propelled me down the hallway, through the kitchen, and out to the small square of back garden. I had no idea what sangria was and I was too tired to speak or resist.

"Here she is at last," Gus called. "And in serious need of revival."

I saw faces looking up from deck chairs as we approached. A group of around eight women were sitting in the shade of the sycamore tree.

"Molly, what have you been doing to yourself? You look as if you've just walked across the Sahara Desert." Sid jumped up and started pouring a red liquid into a glass, thrusting it into my hand. "Get this down you. You'll feel better."

I was placed into a wicker chair and sipped the drink I had been given. It was delicious—a sort of red wine punch with fruit in it, and it was icy cold.

"Let me make the introductions." Sid perched herself on the arm of my chair. She was dressed in white linen trousers and an open-necked white shirt. The look was dramatic with her black bobbed hair. "I don't believe you've met any of our suffragist sisters."

"I did meet some of them when we marched on Easter Sunday," I said, "but I don't think any of these ladies were among them."

"Easter Sunday?" one of the women asked.

"We were among a group of Vassar girls who joined the Easter Parade. We had banners: VASSAR WANTS VOTES FOR WOMEN. Not a very successful outing, I'm afraid," Sid said drily. This was an understatement, as we'd been arrested and thrown in jail for the night.

"And not exactly wise," an older woman said. She had a round, distinguished face and her gray hair was swept back into a severe bun. "The sort of people who attend parades want to be entertained, not informed. And they don't want the firm foundation of their little universe shaken when they least expect it. I expect they pelted you."

"They did. And we were arrested."

"The arrest was not a bad thing," the woman said, a smile spreading over her severe face. "It gets us a mention in the newspapers. It may even evoke the sympathy of other women—at least it may start them thinking. But you're neglecting your duty, Elena. How about some introductions?"

"Elena?" I looked around the group and then of course I remembered that it was Sid's real name. I had never heard anyone refer to her that way before.

"Of course," Sid said. "Ladies, this is our dear friend and neighbor Molly Murphy. And Molly, let me begin with the most distinguished of our company: may I present Carrie Chapman Catt? She is the current head of the North American Woman Suffrage Association and she has deigned to grace our little gathering tonight."

"Nonsense, you make me sound like visiting royalty," Carrie Chapman Catt said in her rich, deep voice. "We're all foot soldiers in this together, you know. These are my fellow infantrywomen: Sarah Lindley, Annabel Chapman, Hortense Maitland, Mildred Roberts, and Felicia Hamm. I'm delighted to meet you, Molly. I hope you're a fellow champion of the cause."

"She's about to join the ranks of the enemy," one of the younger women quipped.

"Meaning what?" Carrie asked sharply.

"She's getting married in a couple of weeks."

"That doesn't necessarily mean she'll cease fighting for the cause," Carrie Chapman Catt said fiercely. "I myself have been married twice and have never been under my husband's thumb."

"And I don't intend to be under my husband's thumb either," I agreed. "I'll most definitely still be a supporter of votes for women."

"Well said, Molly." The speaker was a beautiful young woman with porcelain white skin and hair that was deepest copper. "I've been enduring the same teasing from our more militant sisters. I'm Sarah and I'm also getting married in a few weeks. So we shall be twins—the two redheads who will defy the odds and remain true to the cause after they marry."

"I'll wager you won't have an easy time of it, Sarah," another of the women said. "Your intended seems horribly conventional and old-fashioned to me."

Sarah flushed. "Well, he has been raised in that kind of society, so I admit that my task won't be easy, especially if we go back to England."

"Your future husband is English?" I asked.

"The honorable Monty Warrington-Chase," Gus said with a grin. "Son of an English peer. Our sister Sarah will be a lady one day."

"She may be able to influence her husband in the House of Lords," Carrie said. "The women of England are having a tougher time than we are, but in spite of it are acting with greater bravery and audacity—throwing themselves in front of carriages, chaining themselves to railings. Foolhardy, but one must admire their courage."

Sid touched my arm. "So Molly, we're dying to hear about this assignment. What could the mysterious rich gentleman have wanted that has wearied you to the point of exhaustion?" Her eyes twinkled as she said this.

I looked around the group. It was somewhat unnerving to have those earnest faces staring at me. "Oh, but I don't think I should interrupt your meeting," I said. "I should go up and change out of these crumpled rags and leave you to your discussion."

"As to that, I believe we've agreed upon everything that we can tonight," Carrie said. "Elena will continue to write her series of articles on injustices to women, and we hope that some may be published in the national press."

"And Annabel and I will try to persuade Mr. Samuel

Clemens to join us at the rally next month," the sharp-faced girl said—I believe she was Mildred. "His endorsement could really give our cause the boost it needs. He has a wonderful way with words."

"Well, he would have, wouldn't he, being a famous author," another of the young women said drily.

"Samuel Clemens?" The name was somehow familiar to me.

"Molly, you remember. Samuel Clemens is the author Mark Twain. He came to one of our parties once."

"So he did." A picture came into my head of the white hair and bushy eyebrows, and a surprising endorsement of women's suffrage.

"So tell us about your adventures today while I go and make another pitcher of sangria," Sid said. "Only talk loudly enough so that I don't miss anything."

"Well," I began, enjoying the shock I was about to give them. "You'll never guess where I have been today—" I looked around. "Chinatown. My employer is a Chinese man of great wealth."

"Mercy me," someone muttered, but the others merely looked interested. Nobody swooned or reached for smelling salts as proper young ladies should have done.

"And what can you possibly be doing for a Chinese man of great wealth?" Gus asked, pretending to be shocked when I knew that little could shock her, in spite of her delicate appearance.

"Ah, well, I don't think I can share the details of my assignment," I said. "I assured the gentleman that I would keep our dealings confidential. He is most insistent that I not discuss it with Daniel."

"Phooey," Sid said. "As if we'd breathe a word to Daniel. And now that you have tantalized us with the mention of Chinatown, you can't leave us in suspense."

"We simply must know, Molly," Gus said. "Is it something awfully sordid? Will we blanch and swoon at the mere mention of it?"

They chuckled.

"Well, I suppose there is no harm in telling you, as it seems such a prosaic task," I said. "I've been asked to recover a piece of jade jewelry that has been stolen."

"What a letdown," Sid said. "A stolen piece of jewelry. That sounds more like a straightforward job for the police."

"That's what I said, but he claimed that the police would do nothing to help a Chinese person. He sees them as the enemy."

"And how does he expect you to recover this stolen jewel?" Sid demanded, leaning back from her route to the kitchen. "Does he think you're in touch with fences and crooks?"

"I've already tried all the pawnshops in the area," I said, "and most of the jewelers within a mile or so. Frankly I don't know what else he expects me to do or even why he hired me. Tomorrow I'll have to go and admit to failure, I'm afraid. And lose a fat fee."

"It's strange that he was so insistent about seeking you out in particular," Gus said. "Surely anyone could pay a call on the pawnshops and jewelers."

"I agree," I said. "I have to believe there is more to this than he's telling me. Maybe I'll find out tomorrow."

"Weren't you worried about going through Chinatown?" one of the women asked. "One hears such fearful stories."

"Oh, balderdash," Sarah said before I could answer. "It's no more dangerous than any other part of the city. Even less, as the Chinese don't get drunk and accost women."

I looked at her with amazement. "How do you know so much about it?"

She laughed. "I work just a stone's throw from Chinatown."

This seemed to me the most unlikely statement possible. Sarah did not look like a girl who had done a day's work in her life. She was about to marry an English peer. And the area around Chinatown was one of the most squalid in the city. "You work there?" I spluttered out. "Doing what?"

"Sarah is our champion do-gooder," one of the women

said before Sarah could answer. "She is resolved to save the poor, single-handedly."

Sarah flushed. "I volunteer at a settlement house, on Elizabeth Street just up from Canal."

"A settlement house? What exactly is that?"

"An experiment, actually, in which educated, upper-class young people live and work among the poor, thus improving the standard of their living. We work mainly with destitute girls and women, some of whom we've saved from prostitution."

"There are certainly plenty of brothels on Elizabeth Street," I said, and did get surprised looks this time.

"I worked on a case there once," I explained. "So does your family approve of your work?"

"Not really, but they tolerate it, knowing my temperament," Sarah said. "Most of my fellow workers actually live at the house, but my mother was so upset at the idea that I just help out by day. And so now she puts up with it, knowing that I'll be safely and suitably married soon and living far away from slums."

"I'll wager that your future husband doesn't look kindly upon it," one of the other young women commented wryly.

Sarah was still smiling. "Well, no, Monty is trying to force me to give it up immediately. He worries about my walking alone through those streets. In fact he insists on escorting me to and from Elizabeth Street even though I keep telling him that I am perfectly safe, but I believe he has visions of my being carried off as a white slave."

This brought much merriment from the other women.

"Anyway, his wish will soon be granted," Sarah continued, "as there is a lot of preparation to be done for the wedding. Gown fittings, seating charts—don't you find it an absolute bore, Molly?"

"I do, rather," I agreed. "In fact I've just fled from my future mother-in-law's house, where I was told that my sewing skills were sadly lacking and my future children would be walking around in rags. She nearly died when I pointed out that there were department stores in New York with ready-made clothes for my children."

They laughed again.

"And does your future husband approve of the work that you do, Molly?" Carrie Chapman Catt asked.

"Not at all," I said. "He's a captain in the police department and he doesn't think that being an investigator is a suitable job for a woman—especially as it treads on his toes."

"But you'll give it up when you marry, surely?" Sarah said.

"I suppose I'll have to. I've more or less promised him that I will, but I can't see myself sitting at home getting bored either."

"We can find plenty for you to do for the cause," Carrie said.

I grinned. "I don't think he'd be thrilled about that either."

"Aren't young men a bore," the sharp-faced girl said. "The world would be a much better place without them."

"It would rather limit the future population, Mildred," Carrie Chapman Catt said mildly.

"I wish humans could just split apart like amoebas," Mildred said.

"Don't you mean amoebae?" one of them teased.

I began to feel as I always did in such educated company, that my own education was sadly unfinished. I'd had to stop my lessons with the girls at the big house when my mother died. Sid returned with the sangria and glasses were refilled. I must say it was delightfully refreshing. I forgot that it was mainly red wine until a pleasant feeling of ease came over me. The other women seemed similarly affected.

"I suppose I should be getting home," one of them said at last.

"There's no hurry," Gus replied. "Stay for dinner if you like."

"I'm afraid that Monty will be coming for me any moment," Sarah said. "We are to have a late supper with his friends at the Waldorf, and he insisted on coming here to fetch me. You know how he likes to escort me everywhere. In a way it's sweet, but it can be so annoying."

As if on cue there was a thunderous knocking from the front of the house.

"The bridegroom cometh," Sid said as she disappeared inside. We heard the sound of a male voice and a few seconds later Sid reappeared.

"The bridegroom cometh, but it's the wrong bridegroom," she said with a wry look on her face.

Striding down the hall with a face like thunder was Daniel.

CHAPTER SIX

I got to my feet a little unsteadily, as the alcohol in my two large glasses of sangria was now making itself felt.

"Daniel!" I exclaimed.

"What on earth are you doing here, Molly?" he asked, then remembered his manners and tipped his hat. "Good evening, ladies. Miss Goldfarb. Miss Walcott."

"Captain Sullivan." Gus returned the compliment. "We persuaded Molly to leave darkest Westchester County so that we could give a small party in her honor."

"Ah, I see. How kind of you, but you might have told me, Molly. If I'd known you were coming back to the city, I would have made time for us to select the last few items of furniture together."

"It was all rather spontaneous," I said. I was conscious of those interested faces watching us. "Please excuse me, ladies." I went over to Daniel before there could be any kind of scene. I wasn't sure if he'd be angry with me for leaving his mother, but I wasn't taking any chances. "It's good to see you, Daniel," I said when we were safely in the conservatory. "I've missed you."

"I've missed you too," he said, looking down at me fondly. "I'm itching to show you the improvements I've made across the street. You haven't seen them yet, have you?"

Now I was in a quandary. I didn't want to tell an outright lie to him, but I realized that he would probably have wanted to do the grand unveiling himself. "I just peeked inside," I said, "in case you were there."

"And what did you think?"

"From what I saw it looked wonderful, Daniel. Like a brand spanking new house. So elegant. You've worked a miracle."

He smiled and I saw the tension lines leave his face. "I'm rather satisfied with it myself. Shall I give you the grand tour now then?"

"Why not?" I beamed up at him. "I can't wait."

"What about your friends and the little gathering?"

"They can do without me for a while. I'd rather be with you," I said. I poked my head back out of the door. "Daniel is going to give me a tour of his improvements across the street." I gave Sid and Gus a long, knowing look. Luckily they were both quick on the uptake and said nothing.

I slipped my arm through Daniel's as we emerged onto Patchin Place.

"It was good of those ladies to give you a nice little party," he said. "Those women are presumably their friends. I don't recognize any of them."

I realized then that he thought that this small gathering was the party.

"Oh, no," I said. "This is just some of Sid and Gus's friends stopping by. I came down to help with the planning for the real event."

"A fancy affair then, is it?"

"Who knows, with Sid and Gus." I smiled at him. "You're welcome to come, of course, but it will be with their more bohemian friends—ones we couldn't invite to the wedding itself."

He sighed. "I have no time for parties at the moment in any case. I'm on the job day and night."

"A big case, is it?"

He nodded. "And one I'd rather not have taken on. But the order came from high up and I couldn't refuse."

"And I don't suppose you can tell me any more about it?"

"You know I can't, but it's probably one of the most difficult things I've been asked to do. So forgive me if I haven't been the most attentive bridegroom."

"So what brought you here tonight?" I asked. "You haven't taken to secretly visiting my friends, have you?"

He laughed. "Hardly. I wanted to know if there had been a delivery for the house today. I gave their address. It's the last of the curtains."

He fished for his key outside our front door, then opened it with a flourish. "I shouldn't carry you over the threshold this time. It would be bad luck," he said. "After you, ma'am."

I was proud of my acting ability. I was suitably awed and excited by everything he showed me, especially the bed. "That's some handsome bedroom we've got there, Daniel," I said.

He slipped his arms around my waist. "Are you as impatient as I am to be making use of it?"

"You know I am."

He kissed me. It felt wonderful, but as I melted into his arms I felt a shiver of guilt that I was deceiving him by taking on this case. Maybe it was a good thing that I hadn't succeeded completely. A couple can't start off life together with deception.

"So how are the preparations progressing at my mother's house?" he asked.

"She has everything under control," I said. "The invitations have been sent, the menu for the wedding breakfast planned, and she is sewing my wedding dress as we speak."

"Splendid. So you're getting along well, are you?"

"She's being kind," I said diplomatically, "and very patient. My sewing skills are sadly lacking and she's had to take over the brunt of the work."

"She won't mind that." His arm was still around my waist as we came down the stairs together. "She needs something to keep her occupied. She still misses my father terribly. Maybe one day we can find a bigger house and she can join us."

I tried not to let my alarm show. "One day," I said. "I

think it's important to start our marriage on our own, don't you?"

"Oh, absolutely," he said.

"And we will go and visit her regularly," I went on.

We reached the street. "So you'll be going back to her later this week?"

"After the party," I said. "I have to do a little shopping for my trousseau. My attempts at undergarments have turned out rather disastrously."

He actually laughed at this. "I can imagine. How fortunate that we live in a big city, isn't it?"

We came out onto the street. The dying twilight had streaked the western sky with pink and the houses stood as dark silhouettes.

"Take care of yourself, Daniel," I said, slipping my hand into his.

"Don't worry about me."

"You know I do," I said.

The door opposite opened at that moment and Sarah came out, accompanied by a tall, angular young man with light ash-blond hair. His face was fine-boned and his hollow cheeks made him look almost frail. However, I presumed this was a normal quality of aristocrats. In fact his face was so pale that in the semidarkness he looked like a ghost. Sarah smiled when she saw us.

"Oh, Molly, there you are. I didn't want to leave without saying good-bye to you. And now I can introduce you to my fiancé. Monty, this is my new friend, Molly Murphy. And Molly, this is my future bridegroom, Montague Warrington-Chase."

"How do you do, sir." I nodded politely. "And this is my future bridegroom, Captain Daniel Sullivan," I said.

The men shook hands.

"Dashed annoying, this wedding business, isn't it?" Monty said in drawling upper-class English tones. "I'm rather of the opinion that an elopement might have been the best idea."

"Oh, Monty." Sarah slapped his hand. "You know our

families would have been furious if we'd deprived them of a proper wedding with all the relatives and all the trimmings."

"Luckily our wedding will be a modest affair," Daniel said, "and my mother is organizing most of it. I have the excuse of being stuck in New York on a case."

"A case?" Monty's voice sounded sharp. "You're a lawyer, sir?"

"Daniel is a police captain," I said.

Monty gave a brittle laugh. "Silly of me. When we were introduced, I assumed you were a sea captain. But then you don't have the requisite beard, do you?" He tipped his hat to us. "Now if you'll excuse us, I have to take Sarah home to change. We are expected at the Waldorf. I wish you all the best for your future—Miss Murphy, Captain Sullivan."

We parted with additional pleasantries. Halfway down Patchin Place, Sarah looked back. "Come and visit me at work, Molly. I'd love to show you what we've accomplished."

"I will," I promised.

"Sarah, I thought I made it clear that I want you to stop working," came Monty's voice as they walked down the alley.

"Now does that sound familiar?" I looked up at Daniel with a grin. "Is that something that all bridegrooms say to their brides?"

"She works? Where does she work?" Daniel asked.

"She volunteers at a settlement house on Elizabeth Street."

Daniel gave a snort. "Then I can understand why he wants her to stop. I would too. That's a rough part of the city for such a delicate-looking little thing."

"I know, that's what I thought."

Daniel continued to stare after them. "You know, I've seen that English fellow somewhere before," he said. "Somewhere I wouldn't have expected. . . ."

"Where?"

He frowned, then shook his head. "Can't remember. No matter. I expect it will come to me. I should be getting back to work. No peace for the wicked."

"Oh, are you wicked? I didn't know I was marrying a wicked man. What fun."

He laughed and gave me a peck on the cheek. "Enjoy your party with your lady friends. I'll be in touch." Then he was gone.

CHAPTER SEVEN

The next morning I rose to the smell of fresh brewing coffee and came down to find that Gus had been to the French bakery on Greenwich Avenue and had returned with the morning papers, croissants, and brioches. If Sid hadn't insisted on making Turkish coffee so thick that the spoon stood up in it, the breakfast would have been perfect. As it was, sitting with my friends amid the exotic plants of their conservatory, I thought eating fresh pastries and reading the paper a fine way to start the day. I scoured the papers to see if there was any hint of this big case that Daniel was working on, but there were only the usual petty crimes.

"So you'll be going back to work for your Chinese gentleman, I take it, Molly?" Gus asked.

"I'll have to go back and report to him, but when he hears that I've scoured the pawnshops and jewelers, I think he'll have no further use of my services."

"Maybe that's for the best, now that you've seen Daniel's face yesterday when he learned you were staying with us," Sid said, tearing off a hunk of croissant and dipping it in her coffee.

"I know. That's what I was thinking," I said. "I've got to admit that my career as a lady detective is over and a life of domesticity looms ahead."

"You make it sound like banishment to a penal colony." Gus laughed.

"Not as long as the two of you are across the street," I said. "I'll enjoy having more time to spend with you."

"So will we," Sid said.

"By the way," I said, remembering what had been forgotten in the fluster of the previous evening, "you'll never guess who I ran into on the Lower East Side? Seamus and the children."

"They're back in New York? That should make you happy."

"Indeed it does not," I said, and related the full story.

"Panama—now that sounds like an adventure," Sid said. "I've always wanted to cut a path through the jungle and meet anacondas and jaguars."

"But not with a small boy in tow," I said.

"They're surely not taking the little girl with them?" Gus asked.

I shook my head. "They want me to find her a position in service—nanny's helper or the like. Poor little thing. I think she's far too young for that. I'd take her in myself only I don't think Daniel would approve and it's no way to start a marriage."

"We'll put on our thinking caps," Sid said. "Maybe Gus knows a family who would like a companion to an only child. But I'm afraid the thinking will just have to wait until after the party. We still haven't settled on our theme, have we?"

I left them heatedly discussing the theme for my party and made my way down to Mr. Frederick Lee's office. He had an expectant, worried look on his face as he admitted me.

"Any luck, Miss Murphy? Did you find the missing item?"

"I don't wish to be rude," I said, "but I wasn't sure your employer wished you to know the details of my assignment. You left the room while he spoke to me."

Frederick Lee nodded solemnly. "I only understood it concerned something that was precious to him. Something that he wanted recovered as quickly as possible."

"Then I'm afraid I have no good news for him yet, Mr. Lee. I have searched diligently in the immediate area with no success."

He sighed. "My employer will not be pleased." But he himself looked almost relieved. "Oh, well, we had better go and deliver the news to him."

"I can go on looking," I said. "I've only covered a fraction of the jewelers and pawnshops in New York City. But the thief could just as easily have gone across the bridge to Brooklyn or to any other outlying community. It's like looking for the proverbial needle in a haystack."

"It certainly seems hopeless, but I'm sure my employer will not want you to abandon the quest."

He took my elbow to steer me across the Bowery. At this hour it was full of women doing their morning shopping for the day's meals while a gaggle of children clung to their skirts or raced ahead. The moment we turned into Mott Street the contrast was absolute. Here was silence and emptiness. There were no women and no children. We passed a couple of young Chinese men wearing the dark blue baggy jackets and pants that seemed to be the uniform of the Chinese. Their hands were tucked into their sleeves. They avoided my gaze and hurried by, heads down. I felt a stab of pity for them, living amid so much hostility and knowing that they would never have the chance to truly belong here, to get married and live normal lives.

The pity was short-lived, however, as Frederick Lee grabbed my elbow again and shoved me forward at a quicker pace. "Those men," he whispered. "They are Hip Singers."

"What kind of singers?" I looked back with interest.

"Don't look at them," he hissed. "Pretend they are invisible."

"What's the matter with them?" I too found myself whispering.

"Hip Sing is the rival tong," he said. "Have you not heard about the tong wars? There has been terrible bloodshed between Hip Sing and On Leong, which is our tong. At the moment there is a truce, but it's very fragile and the least little thing can set sparks flying again."

"I see," I said, realizing now why the man yesterday had

looked up and down the street before he hurried away. "So are tongs like gangs?"

He looked shocked. "Oh, no, not at all. They are benevolent societies. They offer us protection and loans and even a place to stay. Like your American gentlemen's clubs."

"Our gentlemen's clubs don't often condone killing each other."

"We have to defend the honor of our tong if the Hip Sing mob kills one of our own," he said. "They are not to be trusted. We are a merchant's association made up of civilized men; they are a bunch of rabble who work in the laundries and the cigar factories."

He stopped talking as a door opened and two elderly men came out, each carrying a cage with a bird in it. They held the cages up as they walked solemnly down the street.

"What was that?" I asked.

"They are walking their birds. They do it every morning so that the caged birds get fresh air," he said. "Just as you Americans walk your babies in their buggies."

"You say 'we Americans,'" I said to him. "Actually I'm Irish. I've only been here two years and I don't think of myself as American yet. But you were born here. Don't you think of yourself as American?"

"I would if I felt that I belonged here," he said. "But as the child of a Chinese man, I can never become a citizen. So I will never truly belong."

"Never become a citizen, even if you were born here?"

"That's right. Thanks to the Exclusion Act. But I wouldn't belong in China either. I am neither fish nor fowl."

"That must be hard for you."

He shrugged. "It is my fate. There's not much I can do about it."

We reached the storefront of the Golden Dragon Emporium. I noticed that it was next door to a building that proclaimed itself as the On Leong headquarters. So my employer must be heavily involved with the tong to have set up shop beside them. Again I waited until Frederick Lee informed me that we could go up to Lee Sing Tai's apartment. It was a complete reenactment of the day before. Waiting until the boy admitted us. Waiting in front of the screen until we were told to enter and the man himself sitting as before, in the high-backed carved chair. The drapes were half drawn and shadows hovered in the far corners. I glanced back at that curtain from which someone had observed me yesterday. I wondered who that person had been and whether he was there again, but I decided it wouldn't be wise to ask questions. Instead I stood in the doorway until my employer waved an elegant hand, directing me to sit on the bench and at the same time dismissing Frederick Lee from his presence.

"Miss Murphy," he said, nodding civilly. "You will take tea with me?"

He clapped his hands and the tea tray appeared. He waited until the leaves had settled, then poured it with ceremony, handing me the cup with two hands. I noticed the length of his fingernails—they stuck out a good inch or so, like claws. Again the tea was too hot to drink immediately, but I'd learned to be silent until I was spoken to.

"Is it a fine day outside?" Lee Sing Tai asked at last.

"Very fine."

"Not too hot?"

"Not as yet."

"That is good. I may venture forth. My songbird needs more fresh air than he receives on the balcony."

He lifted his teacup to his lips and took a sip. I followed suit, almost bursting with impatience to get this interview over. There was a strange feeling of unreality and foreboding that hovered over me in the half-light of the room. At last he put down his teacup. "You had a successful day yesterday?" he asked.

"If you mean did I find your missing jade piece, the answer is no, I'm afraid," I said. "I did my best, I can assure you. I visited every pawnshop, every jeweler within a mile or so of here. The pawnshop owners all told me that they never saw Chinese jewelry and they would have remembered if a Chinese person had come into their stores. The jewelers told me that jade was not worth much and they would only buy gold or silver." I paused, taking a deep breath. "So I'm sorry I couldn't be of more help to you. I could go on looking further afield, of course. There are hundreds more pawnshops and jewelers in the rest of Manhattan, and hundreds more across the bridge in Brooklyn and up in the Bronx and on Staten Island—but I can't see that it would be worth paying me for what would surely be several days' work after which I could well come up empty."

He sat there, staring across the room as if I didn't exist. The silence was overpowering and I began to feel uneasy. If he came from a country where men were beheaded for not wearing their hair a certain way, was he about to punish me for my failure? I decided to take the initiative.

"Mr. Lee," I said, "something about this doesn't make sense to me. You could have employed anybody to ask questions in pawnshops. If the piece has been stolen, isn't it likely that it's gone to an underworld fence? I'd have no way of knowing how to contact such people. I'm a private investigator, not a police detective."

"It will not have gone to a fence," he said.

I wanted to tell him that we were wasting each other's time and walk out of there. But I hate to give up on anything. "You haven't made clear to me why this particular piece of jade is worth so much to you," I said. "It must have some special significance or you would merely have had a copy made to replace it."

"You are a shrewd young woman," he said. "I knew this when I hired you."

"So why did you hire me?"

"To find a missing prized possession, I told you."

"Of course it's possible that the person who stole it intends to keep it, in which case I can be of no further use to you."

"I did not say it was stolen," he said. "It was taken. That is not the same thing."

"You have an idea who took it?"

He nodded.

"By a member of your household?"

It was a stab in the dark but I saw a flash of reaction. Then his eyes narrowed. "The situation is delicate."

"Mr. Lee. I don't see how I can help you unless you tell me all the facts. I think you have hired the wrong person. Surely one of your employees could go after a member of your household. He wouldn't have gone far from Chinatown, would he?"

There was a long pause. "I wish you to continue your search, Miss Murphy," he said at last. "I told you that a precious possession was missing. I had little hope that you'd find the jade but I wanted to see how diligently you pursued this and I wanted to observe your powers of deduction. I should now tell you that another of my possessions is missing."

"Stolen, you mean? At the same time?"

"Stolen—of this I am not sure. But missing. Definitely missing."

"More valuable than the jade?"

"More valuable."

Now we were finally getting somewhere. "Could I have a description of this object?"

He reached across to a side table and handed me a leather folder. "A picture of the missing possession," he said. "Open it."

I opened the folder. It was a photo frame in red leather. And inside was a portrait of a young Chinese girl. She was dressed in what looked like a padded silk jacket with bone buttons and a little round collar. Her hair was pulled back into a thick braid that was draped over one shoulder. I looked for any kind of jewel or adornment she might be wearing but could see none.

"I'm afraid I don't see the article you are referring to."

He jabbed the glass of the photo frame with his long fingernail. "Bo Kei. My new bride," he said. "My bride is missing."

"A person? The valuable possession you're referring to is a person?" He must have picked up the shock in my voice.

"A most valuable possession, Miss Murphy. She cost me

a lot of money. I had her brought over from China only a month ago. As you know, your government makes it impossible for Chinamen to bring their women into this country, so I paid a high price to have her brought here by devious routes. I paid her father a high bride price too."

"You bought a woman?" I was still staring at the young fresh face looking shyly at the camera.

"That is the way in my country. We have no foolish notions of falling in love, as you people in America do. Marriage is a business proposition. Each side must benefit. I am no longer young, Miss Murphy. I need a son before I die—so I bring in strong new blood from my own part of China. And now she is gone."

"So what do you think has happened to her?" I was still shocked and fighting to keep my composure.

"I wish I knew," he said. "I am most worried. Maybe an enemy has kidnapped her, or she has run away. In either case I want her returned to me immediately, together with the jade bride-piece that was given to her."

"You say an enemy may have kidnapped her. Do you know that you have enemies who might do something as bad as this?"

"Any rich and powerful man has enemies, Miss Murphy. And in my case I am closely aligned with the On Leong tong. Maybe you have not heard of this, but we have been at war with Hip Sing."

"Frederick Lee told me about this," I said.

He pursed his lips. "There has been a truce in recent times, but this peace is fragile and who knows if it will last forever."

"Would stealing your bride break this truce?"

"Naturally. If someone wants to hurt me, to embarrass me, to make me lose face, what better way than to steal my bride? We of the On Leong would want justice and revenge and so the bloodshed would start again." He paused. I couldn't think what to say next, but he added. "On the other hand, she could have run away."

"Do you have any idea why she might have run away?" I

asked, thinking that it would have taken something really horrible to make being alone in a strange city like New York seem preferable to remaining in a pampered life amid such rich surroundings.

He frowned as if he considered this question impudent. "Of course I have no idea," he snapped. "She would have a good life here. She was treated well. She had clothes. Good food. Any sensible young woman would be proud to become wife of a rich and powerful man."

But old, I thought. And she looked so young in that picture. Maybe having intimate relations with an old man like him was too big a shock for her. Maybe he demanded too much of her too soon.

"Mr. Lee," I began cautiously, "I have visited you twice now. It is not very easy to get into your residence. How and when do you think she was kidnapped or escaped?"

"This is what I ask myself. As you see, I keep my door locked at all times. It is a long way down from my balcony. I have a houseboy. I have a cook. I have employees working in my emporium next door. Nobody could enter or leave this place without being seen."

"She didn't go out and not come back?"

"Of course not. Chinese woman does not go out unescorted. In China she would travel in closed litter. Here in New York she does not leave her dwelling. It is not correct and it is not safe."

I took another deep breath, realizing how easy it would be to offend him. "And would it have been possible for her to escape at night? What I mean is, did she share a bed with you?"

He looked indignant and pursed his lips. "When I want her, she is brought to my bed. When I am done, she is dismissed. But houseboy, he sleeps on mat in front of screen. Like guard dog for house. Who could get past him?"

But somehow she had either managed to escape or been taken by a clever kidnapper. I thought about the latter.

"If she was indeed kidnapped by your rival tong, then this isn't a task I could undertake. As an outsider in your community, there is no way I'd want to stick my nose into a Chinese tong's affairs. And I'd have no way of finding out anything, not speaking your language."

"Of course," he said, dismissing this with a wave of his hand. "I have taken this fact into consideration. Already my spies have looked into the possibility most carefully, but so far they have learned nothing. If she has been kidnapped, then she is either well hidden or has been spirited far away."

"When exactly did she go missing?"

"Five days ago now."

"That's a long time. She could be anywhere."

He shook his head. "How far could she get on her own, huh? She would have no money—nothing but the jade, and no Western clothes. A woman in Chinese dress would soon be noticed if she ventured outside our community. And she knows nothing of New York. Where would she run?"

"I don't suppose she speaks much English, does she?"

"As a matter of fact her English is good. She was educated by Western missionaries. It was for this very reason that I selected her—I thought that it would be good that she has some knowledge of Western ways if she is to be useful to me here in the future. Now I fear that she has run looking for church people and is being hidden by them."

"Ah." I nodded. We were finally getting to the point. "You want me to visit the missions for you."

"Exactly. This is a job for a white woman, a Christian woman. You will know the right questions to ask. You will bring my bride back to me. You will tell her that she now belongs to me and obeys me. Her behavior disgraces her family in China."

"Which denomination were these missionaries?"

"I do not know one type of Christian from another. They are all equally annoying—and interfering with our people, trying to convert them from our religions to yours. But you will find no shortage of mission houses near Chinatown. They try hard, these Christians."

"And if your bride won't come with me?"

"Then you will come to me and I will have her brought

back. But it must be done discreetly. Word of this must not reach fellow Chinese. I should lose face in their eyes. They would say Lee Sing Tai cannot even control his woman— how can he control powerful tong? This must not happen, you understand. It is important beyond anything."

I wanted to say that the happiness of his bride should be important above everything, but he obviously didn't see it that way. To him a woman was the same as a piece of jade.

"Find her and I will make it well worth your while," he said. "It is for her own happiness as well as mine. If she does not return to me, then there is no hope for her. She cannot stay at mission forever. She cannot return home to China, even if she had the money to do so. Her family would not take her back after this disgrace. So where would she go? Only the houses of low women would welcome her. Tell her this. Make sure she understands that she is being foolish and childish. If she returns to me and behaves as a good wife should, then no more will be said and she will lead a happy life."

I had been feeling no enthusiasm for this assignment, but I did see his point. Much as I disliked his calling her his possession, she was his wife, and as such he had legal rights over her. And how would she survive? I had tried to survive alone in New York City when I first arrived and had nearly starved and frozen to death. How much harder would it be for a Chinese girl? It was all too likely that she'd be lured or snatched into prostitution.

I got to my feet. "Very well, Mr. Lee. I will do my very best to find your bride and bring her home to you."

He almost smiled. At least his face twitched in what could be interpreted as a smile. "I am pleased to hear this, Miss Murphy. I look forward to your returning to me soon with good news."

He was about to clap his hands when I picked up the photograph in its leather case. "May I take this with me? It might help jog people's memories."

"Take care with it, and return it to me safely," he said.

"I will."

He clapped his hands. The houseboy and Frederick Lee

appeared and I was escorted from the room. I couldn't help looking across at the red silk drapes as I waited for them to appear. I thought I saw a hand holding those drapes. A hand with long fingernails.

CHAPTER EIGHT

Frederick Lee said nothing as he escorted me down the stairs and out into the street. The street was still empty, but I could hear the distant clatter of commerce from Mulberry and the Bowery.

As Frederick took my elbow to steer me down the steep outside steps, a young man came flying up the steps, nearly colliding with us and butting me in the middle. At the last minute he checked himself, realizing that he was almost touching a white woman's skirt, and looked up into my face with astonishment.

"Why this person visit my father?" he demanded, not apologizing but glaring at me angrily for being in his way. And his very choice of the words, "this person," made my hackles rise. I wondered for a moment whether he believed I was a prostitute until he added, "If she is missionary lady, then too bad. She won't make my father change to her religion or make him change his ways." He gave a scornful laugh, still looking at me as if I wasn't a person at all.

I fought back my desire to tell him exactly what I thought of him, knowing I couldn't reveal the reason for my visit. Also I was puzzled by his calling Lee Sing Tai his father.

"Your esteemed father requested to speak with this young woman," Frederick Lee answered for me. He spoke with cold and measured formality.

"For what reason?" This young man spat out the words in

clipped syllables like the man he had called his father but not with the latter's command of English.

"As to that, it was personal business between Miss Murphy and your esteemed father," Frederick said. "Even I was sent away while they were in discussion."

"Even you? You are only secretary. I am his son."

"A paper son. Very different," Frederick said.

"In the eyes of the American law I am his son. That's all that matters." And with that he pushed past us and continued up the stairs.

"I must apologize for this man's rude behavior," Frederick said as we continued down the street.

"That was Mr. Lee's son?" I asked. "But I thought he had no sons. I thought the reason for bringing . . ." I bit off the words at the last second. It was probable that Frederick Lee did not know his employer had brought in a young bride from China, or that she was now missing. That was why he had been dismissed from the room while we spoke.

"He is only a paper son," Frederick said scornfully. "Bobby Lee."

"A paper son? I'm afraid I'm not familiar with the term."

He looked surprised. "Perhaps the practice is not well known outside of Chinatown," he said. "The Exclusion Act prevents Chinese men from bringing in their wives, but merchants are allowed to send for their sons. So one of the only ways for a Chinese man to come into this country is to pretend that he is the son of a merchant already here. This is simple to do. Your authorities do not read Chinese to understand our birth certificates. So if a young man in China is also from the Lee clan, who can prove he is not a true son? So he pays money, sometimes a lot of money. Mr. Lee accepts him as a son and he is allowed to enter. There are many paper sons in Chinatown."

"And he becomes a true son in the eyes of the law over here? He will inherit if Mr. Lee dies?"

"This is clearly what Bobby Lee hopes. But my employer is a clever and cautious man. I am sure he has drawn up legal documents that state that Bobby Lee is not a son of his body.

At the moment Bobby Lee is useful to him in his business. However, if he were to have a true son, as he so fervently hopes, then you can be certain that Bobby would be pushed aside or even sent back to China."

"He doesn't seem a very pleasant young man," I said.

"He is not, and he has let the idea of being Lee Sing Tai's son go to his head. He behaves as if he owns half of Chinatown. Such a man makes enemies, but unfortunately he is well positioned in On Leong, so we can say or do nothing."

"Does he live with his father?" I asked, wondering how much he knew about the missing girl.

"He does not. He runs his father's cigar factory in Brooklyn and he lives in rooms above the factory."

We continued down Mott Street. "May I ask if Mr. Lee wants you to continue your search for this—jade?" he asked. "I know it's not my business, but I just wondered . . ."

I glanced at him. "If Mr. Lee had wanted you to know, I suspect he'd have included you in the meeting," I said. "I don't mean to sound rude, but . . ."

"I quite understand," he said. "It's only that I—"

At that moment a voice called out after us. We turned to see Bobby Lee standing on the steps, beckoning. He barked out something in Chinese.

Frederick Lee flushed. "Please excuse me, Miss Murphy, but my employer wishes to have another word with me. If you would kindly wait here in the shade . . ."

"That's all right," I said. "I'm sure I can find my own way without anyone to escort me."

"If you're quite sure?"

"Don't worry about me," I said. "You'd better get back to your employer. I rather suspect he doesn't like to be kept waiting."

He nodded gratefully and hurried back down the street. I was about to go on my way when I realized that I should find out from Frederick where all the various church missions were located around Chinatown. There must be several of them if missionary ladies were seen as a problem. So I stepped under the shade of a balcony and waited. I studied the red

silk lanterns hanging from the balconies, the scrolls of
Chinese characters pasted to walls and windows, and then I
noticed something that I had overlooked before. Across the
street, presenting a hostile brick face to the world, was a
Catholic church. A small board announced: CHURCH OF THE
TRANSFIGURATION, FATHER BARRY, and mass times. There
were no messages in Chinese here and the studded oak door
was firmly shut. It appeared that the Catholics did not want
to welcome their Chinese neighbors.

The street remained eerily empty until the two old men
appeared again, bringing their caged birds back from their
morning outing. I was busy observing them and jumped a
mile when a door behind me suddenly opened. I half expected to be grabbed and dragged inside, but instead I turned
around and found myself looking at the most unexpected
person. She was a big-boned Irishwoman of middle age with
a round, fresh-scrubbed face and faded red hair twisted up on
top of her head. She was wearing a white apron over her summer dress, and she held a bucket in one hand and a scrubbing
brush in the other.

"I didn't mean to startle you, dearie," she said, in an Irish
accent even broader than my own. "Just coming out to do the
step. I do like a nice clean front step, don't you?" And she
gave me a warm, friendly smile. "I saw you passing by yesterday. And I notice you're wearing a ring on your left hand. So
I thought I'd be bold enough to find out whether you've joined
our ranks yet."

"Ranks?"

"Are you marrying that nice Chinese boy I saw you with?
Frederick Lee, isn't it?"

"No! What gave you that idea?" I suppose I sounded
shocked.

"Well, you don't look like one of those earnest missionary
ladies, so I couldn't think of any other reason an Irish girl
would be walking through Chinatown on the arm of a Chinaman. There's quite a few of us, you know."

"Married to Chinese men?"

"Exactly. Mrs. Chiu's the name. Aileen Chiu." She held out her hand to me. I shook it. It felt as rough as old leather.

"Molly Murphy," I said.

"A fellow Irishwoman. I knew it." She beamed at me. "What part of the old country are you from?"

"County Mayo. Near Westport."

"Are you now? I'm from Limerick myself. I couldn't wait to get away, but now I long for those green hills and that soft rain, don't you?"

"Sometimes," I said. "Especially when the weather is as hot as it's been lately."

"Isn't that the truth," she said. "Like most of the neighborhood, we've taken to sleeping on the roof this summer, it's been so unbearable in the house." She hesitated then said, "Look, this may seem forward, but would you like to come in for a spot of tea, Miss Murphy? The kettle's always on and I don't get much company from the outside."

"Thank you," I said. "I'd like that very much." It had occurred to me how useful she might be, watching the street from behind her lace curtains. And besides, I liked the look of her face. I followed her into the darkness of a small entry hall. Only a couple of steps inside we came upon a screen, similar to the one in Mr. Lee's apartment, with a large painted dragon on it.

"Watch yourself," Aileen warned as she steered me around it. "My man insisted on it. He's a Christian, you know, but he can't do away with all the old Chinese superstitions. 'We have to have a screen, Aileen,' he says to me when we are furnishing the place. To keep out the demons. And he still has an altar to the ancestors. Aren't they funny, bless them?"

She led me around the screen and into a fine living room that looked out onto the street. It was well-furnished in American style with a comfortable plush sofa and armchairs, marble side tables, and lace curtains at the window.

"Sit down, my dear," she said, gesturing to the sofa. "Kitty!" she called. "Kitty, where are you—we've got company."

A girl of about ten came running into the room. She had

light hair and skin like her mother, but her eyes were almond-shaped like those of her Chinese father. It was an extremely attractive combination. She gave me an inquisitive stare.

"My daughter Kitty," Aileen Chiu said. "My youngest. I've three older girls and a boy. Our boy goes to college—Princeton, no less, but he's home for the summer." She turned to the girl who was lingering in the doorway, still staring at me with interest. "Kitty, tell Ah Fong that we want tea and see if he made any of his soda bread this morning." She nodded to me. "We've a marvelous cook—he can cook anything, you know. Not just Chinese. Makes better soda bread than me."

The girl went running off and I heard her calling out something in Chinese in a high little voice.

"You seem to have a good life here," I said, looking around the room.

"I came to this country with nothing and I don't think I could have done better," Aileen Chiu said. "Certainly not if I'd married some drunken lout of a lazy Irishman. My man owns four laundries—two in Brooklyn and two here in Manhattan. He provides well for us and he's a good father too." She smiled, then the smile faded as she stared out at the net curtains. "Of course, it's a trifle lonely at times. We're neither one thing nor the other, you see. The Irish will have nothing to do with me; neither will the Chinese."

"That must be hard," I agreed.

"We survive. There are the other Irish wives to take tea with and sometimes we go to a theater and out to a picnic on Staten Island on Sundays, so I can't complain. But how about you, my dear? I don't often see a white woman coming up Mott Street, unless it's on one of these slumming tours."

"Slumming tours—what are they?"

She laughed. "Oh, it's the latest craze, so they tell me. This man called Chuck Connors—he gives guided tours of China-town, as if we're exhibits in a zoo, you know. He plays up all the vices—gambling and opium dens, houses of ill repute, and the tourists are suitably shocked and titillated. The young women pretend to swoon at the horror and degradation of it."

She was still chuckling as her daughter brought in a tray

of tea things and put it on the table in front of her mother. "Should I pour?" she asked.

"No, you go and get on with your schoolwork. I can do my own pouring," Aileen said.

"But Ma—it's the summer vacation," the girl protested. "Nobody else has to do schoolwork."

"You know how keen your father is that you get on," Aileen said. "Look how well your brother and your sisters have done. You don't want to let us down, do you?"

The girl sighed and stomped upstairs.

"My Albert is very keen on education," she confided. "He was quite a scholar back in China. Of course I had no schooling myself, but I can see the value of it. If you've enough education you can move where you want in society, can't you?"

"That's very true," I said. I watched her pour the tea and then hand me a slice of soda bread, liberally dotted with raisins. I ate with relish before I paused to ask, "Is there really that much degradation going on in Chinatown?"

"Of course there's plenty of gambling. One thing about the Chinese—they are all gamblers. They'll gamble on how many buttons the next man to come into the room has on his jacket or whether it will be fine the next day. Some of them will bet their clothing when they've spent their last cent and have to be given a sack to wear home. My man is more sober in that department than most, but I have to keep an eye on him."

"And opium? Are there really opium dens?"

"Oh, yes. They're here, all right. That stupid Connors fellow has concocted a fake opium den that he shows to his tourists—he hires actors to play the part of addicts. The real ones are hidden away, but they're here, all right. And it's not just the Chinese that visit them either. There are plenty of white men sneaking in at night."

As we talked I noticed that she kept a steady eye on the street beyond. I tried to phrase my question tactfully. "Mrs. Chiu—you have a good view of the street here and you obviously see a lot of what goes on—you didn't notice a young Chinese woman going past, about a week ago, did you?"

Her eyes opened wide in surprise. "A young Chinese woman? Out alone on the street? My dear, there are no young Chinese women. Why do you think the men marry us? And if there were, they wouldn't be allowed out on the street. There are a couple of small-foot wives—you know, the poor creatures with the deformed, bound feet?"

"I thought Chinese wives weren't allowed to come into the country?"

"These ones are older women who came here before the Exclusion Act. I feel sorry for them, personally. They're virtually prisoners in their own homes. At least I can walk down the street to visit my neighbors, but they can't even walk that far. You should see them hobbling. It's something pitiful. If they ever go out it's only in a closed carriage, door to door, even if they're only visiting a couple of houses down."

I returned to my original question. "So if a young Chinese girl had come down the street, you would have noticed?"

She tilted her head on one side with a puzzled look. "What's this all about? Why these questions about a Chinese girl? You're not from the authorities, are you? On the trail of a prostitute?"

"So there really are Chinese prostitutes here?"

"Of course there are. Not that they're ever allowed out either, but one hears rumors of what goes on."

"I assure you I'm not from the authorities." I took a sip of my tea while I tried to come up with a good reason for my question without giving away why I had been hired.

We ate in silence until suddenly she looked up. "Wait a minute. If you were with Frederick Lee, then it's true—old Mr. Lee Sing Tai did bring in another bride from China. Don't tell me she's gone?"

"How did you hear about this?"

"Their cook is friendly with Ah Fong. There's not much that Chinese servants don't know about. He's brought in a bride from China before, you know."

"And what happened to her?"

"From what I hear she couldn't produce a son so he got

rid of her. Sent her back to China as likely as not. So this one's run away, has she?"

"I really can't talk about it," I said. "Mr. Lee would be furious if he found out that anyone else knows his business."

Aileen Chiu laughed. "Listen, my dear, when you live in a narrow society like this, it's hard to keep secrets, and servants love to talk. So he's hired you to find her, has he?"

I nodded. It seemed pointless to deny it at this stage and I had now made a useful ally.

"Surely she can't have gone far." Aileen Chiu was frowning in a puzzled way. "The police would have picked her up if she'd strayed beyond Chinatown. They seem to think that all Chinese women are prostitutes."

"So she could be in jail, do you think?"

"It's possible. And if not, where else could she go? She won't have had money of her own. What did she hope to achieve by it? If he wants her found, he'll find her. He's a big noise around here with fingers in every sort of pie. And he's got the police in his pocket too."

"Really? He spoke of the police as his enemies."

"Don't you believe it. He's well in with the Sixth Precinct. He pays them good bribe money to keep out of his business interests—and out of On Leong interests too."

"So presumably he could have found out from the local police if his bride had been picked up and arrested?"

"Although maybe he wouldn't want to admit something like that to white men. It's all a question of losing face. They're very big on losing face, these Chinamen. He wouldn't have hired an outsider like you—and a woman at that—unless he wanted to try and keep the affair secret from the local community. So where does Lee Sing Tai think she might have gone?"

"She was educated by missionaries, so he thinks that maybe they have taken her in and are hiding her. I gather that there must be quite a few missionaries operating around here?"

"There certainly are. All the denominations out there competing to save poor Chinese souls. It's pitiful really. They lure the young men in with the offer of English language lessons and then they start preaching at them." She chuckled. "Of course the Chinese aren't stupid. They take the language classes and slip out before the sermon starts."

"You presumably know the various missions around here. Can you suggest where I should start?"

"You can't do much better than start with Miss Helen Clark. If any girl's been wandering the streets, Miss Clark will have snapped her up—interfering, do-gooding busybody that she is. Always poking her nose where it's not wanted."

I had to smile at her sudden outburst of anger.

"It may be unchristian of me to speak like that of someone who thinks she's doing the Lord's work, but she's caused a lot of trouble. If she spots a child out on the street, she assumes it's a slave and she kidnaps it, making it go to her classes. And if she hears of a white woman marrying a Chinaman, she'll try to break up the union."

She paused to take a gulp of tea and I nodded with understanding before she put the cup down firmly and added, "And she tries to come into Chinese homes to instruct their occupants on Christian living—the nerve of it. She tried to get in here once. I'm a good Catholic, I said, and so is my man and my children have been baptized at the Church of the Transfiguration across the street, so we need none of your help to get to heaven, thank you."

"And where would I find this Miss Clark?" I asked.

"If she's not out prowling the streets, she's got her school at 21 Mott, just down the street. Of course it's still summer vacation, so she may not be giving classes. If she's not there, you can always try the Morning Star Mission on Doyers, or there's the Evangelical Band at 4 Mott—but that's mainly just a Sunday school."

"Do you think any of these might have taken in a Chinese woman if she'd come to them?"

She frowned. "I've never heard of them having beds to offer. It's just the hall and a little room for making tea. But you could try the Rescue Mission also on Doyers. They try to rescue fallen white women, but I don't suppose they'd say no to a Chinese girl if they thought she was some kind of slave."

"Rescue Mission on Doyers," I muttered. "Thank you. You've given me plenty to start with. And if I wanted to check with the police, would it be at headquarters on Mulberry?"

"No, dearie. We're in the Sixth Precinct here. The police station's on Elizabeth, just up from Canal."

"Then I should be going," I said. "Thank you for the tea and the chat."

"Come back anytime," she said, eyeing me wistfully. "I'd love to talk more about the old country, although it was a hard life, wasn't it? Never enough to eat."

"It was," I agreed.

"So all in all we're better off here." She said it as if she was trying to convince herself, not me.

CHAPTER NINE

I took my leave, promising to return and having extracted a promise from her not to say anything about my commission in case it got back to the ears of Lee Sing Tai. Noting the ease with which she liked to gossip, I couldn't be sure that she'd keep to it. There was no sign of Frederick Lee when I came out into Mott Street, but a vendor's cart was standing at the curb nearby selling vegetables to a line of Chinese men and a couple of half-caste children. Even the vegetables in the basket looked strange—beans as long as my forearm, huge hairy cannonballs (God knows what they were), and tiny little white sprouts. The vendor was a fellow Chinese and was certainly doing a lively trade.

I picked my way past the fresh horse manure and looked for 21 Mott and Miss Clark. I found her in a bare upstairs room, lined with rows of benches, supervising a couple of little half-Chinese girls as they put out hymn books. She was quite the opposite of what I had expected—although no longer young, she was beautiful and elegantly dressed. No wonder she could lure those poor woman-starved Chinese men into services on Sundays. She looked at me with surprise and suspicion until I explained the reason for my visit. Then a smile spread across that lovely face. "So you're doing the Lord's work too—trying to save poor girls from a life of degradation. God bless you, my dear."

I didn't like to say that my employer wasn't the Lord but

a rich Chinese gentleman. "So you haven't seen a young woman like this? She didn't come to you?" I held out the picture.

She shook her head. "And it's a great pity that she didn't. I would have given her sanctuary. If she spoke English I might even have managed to find her a position as a servant safely far from the city. I've done that for girls before, you know—if they have not descended too far into a life of vice. I have to be careful whom I send to wholesome Christian families. One can't risk a corrupting influence."

"So if she didn't come to you, where do you think she might have gone?" I asked.

"I rather fear the worst, my dear. One has only to walk a few yards from here to the Bowery where every second establishment is a house of ill repute." She looked up as one of the little half-caste girls called out, "All done, Missie Clark."

"Nicely done, Elsie. We'll make a fine Christian of you yet," Miss Clark said, patting the child on her shining black hair.

She turned back to me. "You see how much we can do if we catch them early enough. Of course these girls do have the benefit of Irish mothers who have been raised as Christians so it is not such an uphill battle to claim them for the Lord and keep them from the sins of the flesh. Sometimes I despair for the full-blooded Chinese, though. It's a struggle to make them turn from their heathen ways. Even those who profess to be Christians still worship idols in secret. But one does what one can." She patted the child again. "Run along now and wash your hands and then we'll work on your letters some more. You too, Alice."

"Thank you for your time," I said and went to take my leave.

"If you'll write down your address for me, Miss Murphy, I will keep my eyes open. I try to rescue girls from degradation whenever I can, so who knows? Maybe I will hear of your girl."

I considered Miss Clark and her evangelizing as I made my way down the stairs to the street. Having witnessed the sordid establishments on the Bowery, I found it hard to believe that the Chinese were more prone to vice than their Western neighbors. But one of Miss Clark's sentences stuck in my mind: "If they have not descended too far into a life of vice." Those words immediately conjured up what I had witnessed on the Bowery—those girls lounging in provocative poses on stoops while nattily dressed men lurked nearby. It was all too possible that if little Bo Kei had not been picked up by the police, she might have been nabbed by a pimp. I saw how easily she could have been incited into one of those brothels—a young girl who knew nothing of the city and of Western ways. "Don't worry, my dear, we'll take good care of you and hide you from that Chinese monster." And then she'd be trapped.

I can tell you I wasn't anxious to make the rounds of the brothels, asking questions. I was all too likely to wind up kidnapped and trapped inside one myself, if the stories one heard were true. That's when I remembered that I might have an ally who could help me. My friend Mrs. Goodwin was a police matron who had now been turned into a female detective like myself. Only she was working officially on undercover assignments for the police. So in order to find her or leave a message for her I'd either have to go all the way back to Tompkins Square where she lived, or to police headquarters on Mulberry. Since the latter was also where Daniel worked, I wasn't in a hurry to do that. So I decided to try all other avenues first, and if I came up with no leads, then I'd visit Mrs. Goodwin's house on my way home.

I went back to my first plan, which was visiting all the missions around Chinatown. This proved to be fruitless. Some were only open on Sundays. The ones that were open were little more than church halls that ran Sunday worship, nightly language classes, Bible study, and sometimes Saturday socials. No places for a fugitive girl to stay or be hidden. So I now considered the options: if she had been kidnapped by an enemy, as Lee Sing Tai had hinted, then I had no hope of finding her. If he was a big noise, as Mrs. Chiu had described him and Frederick Lee had indicated, then presumably he knew how to send out spies to put pressure on those enemies to get her back. The fact that he hadn't succeeded already indicated to me that it wasn't an enemy who had taken her. Unless—a new disturbing thought came to me—unless that enemy had killed her and disposed of the body. But this again was out of my scope.

The other possibilities were that she was being hidden within Chinatown by someone like Mrs. Chiu—someone who took pity on a frightened young girl. But then how would she ever have met a person like Mrs. Chiu if she wasn't allowed out? How would she have known where to run and which door to knock on? Which left the third possibility: she had left Chinatown.

The next obvious thing to do was to pay a visit to the closest police station—the Sixth Precinct on Elizabeth Street—on the chance that she had been picked up for prostitution and was being held in jail. I was rather leery about going to the police, as my visit could possibly get back to Daniel, who would not be pleased. But I decided that I could take the risk. A constable at the desk there was not likely to recognize me and I could always give a false name if asked. I made my way up Mott to Bayard and then across to Elizabeth. It was remarkable how quickly the flavor of the neighborhood changed. The moment I was out of Mott I was back in a lively Italian scene—noisy streets, children everywhere, laundry hanging from balconies, street vendors calling out wares.

The Sixth Precinct police station was a short way up on the left. I paused outside, staring up at its severe brownstone facade, plucking up the courage to enter. On the way up the street I had worked out a plausible story, but I had to give myself a good talking-to before I went up the five steps to the front door and stepped inside to musty coolness. Police stations, in my experience, all had the same kind of smell—pipe smoke and disinfectant from the holding cells down below and a sort of dustiness as if they were never properly cleaned. A young man was sitting behind a tall oak counter that shut off a large room beyond. He jumped up when he saw me.

"Can I help you, miss?" He looked ridiculously young, with a fresh-scrubbed schoolboy face, and he gave me an eager smile. I wondered how long it would take in this profession before the enthusiasm wore off.

"Yes, you can help me," I said. "I've been sent from one of the missions in Chinatown." (Well, that wasn't an outright lie. Miss Clark had wished me luck in finding the girl.) "And I'm looking for a young Chinese woman, newly arrived in this country. Is it possible that such a woman has been brought in here by your officers during the past week?"

"A Chinese woman? We don't see many of those," he said. "In fact I don't think I've ever seen one, except an acrobat on the stage in the vaudeville once. You should see the contortions she could get her body into—"

He stopped abruptly as an older officer glanced up from his paperwork.

"So she hasn't been brought in here?"

"Maybe when I wasn't on duty. I could go and ask, if you like."

"Thank you. Most kind of you," I said.

He gave me that endearing smile again. I rather thought that the ladies of the trade would have him wrapped around their little fingers. He turned away from his desk and had only taken a few steps past the partition into the big room beyond when I heard voices coming down the stairs behind me.

"I don't like this any more than you do, Kear, but you have to understand my position. I'm getting my arm twisted to look into this."

I froze, not sure what to do next. I had recognized the voice as Daniel's. I had nowhere to run. I waited for doom, trying to make my brain come up with a good explanation of what I was doing in a police station in a bad part of the city. My brain refused to cooperate. I opened my handbag and pretended to be looking in it, just praying that they'd be so occupied with their conversation that I wouldn't be noticed.

"You've always been straight with me, Sullivan. I'll do my best," said the other voice. They were right behind me now. I hoped they'd go on past and out to the street. Instead

I heard feet on the tiled floor coming toward me. I heard the *click* as they opened the gate leading to the room beyond; then they passed me as if I were invisible.

I only had a second before Daniel turned around and saw me. I tiptoed to the front door and ran down those steps, dodging into the nearest shop. It was a baker's and I took my time, choosing some rolls, until the baker lost patience with me. "Do ya want to buy something or don'tcha?" he barked. "I've got a store full of busy people and you're keeping us all waiting." There was no sign of Daniel as I came out again and merged into the crowd.

One thing was certain, I wasn't going back into that police station. If the young constable knew nothing of a Chinese woman, then it was fairly certain that she not being held there, judging by the amount of interest she would have caused. The fact that a woman wearing Chinese dress would stand out as an oddity made me decide to try something else. Chinatown was essentially only three or four streets— Mott, Pell, Doyers, and Park. That made a limited number of ways out—five to be exact. Surely there were nosy or observant people at the entrance to each of those streets who would have noticed a young Chinese woman, in Chinese dress. Unless, of course, she had escaped in the middle of the night. Which didn't seem very likely, given the locked doors and the houseboy sleeping at the top of the stairs. I wondered if she could have lowered herself from the balcony. But then she would have left the rope, or whatever she had used hanging there as evidence of her escape.

A pretty puzzle. A young woman, vanished into thin air— unless . . . was I being set up? I had been used and duped before, being a little on the naïve side when it came to trusting humanity. What if the young bride had not proved satisfactory? What if he had killed her or had her killed and disposed of the body somewhere, then had hired me as his alibi? Judging by his attitude toward her, this was a good possibility. I should walk away now, I told myself. But I couldn't until I had tried every avenue. I never like to give up on anything—and I was becoming increasingly worried about that poor girl. Coming from a village in China to the middle of New York City must have been a terrible shock. If she had tried to run away, I rather thought that she would find she had jumped out of the frying pan and into the fire. I just hoped I wasn't too late and she was already in the claws of a Bowery pimp.

It occurred to me that I had once seen Mrs. Goodwin working on a case on Elizabeth Street. I looked up and down the street hopefully, but the only police presence was a stout constable with sweat running down his red face on this hot day. He was lingering near a fire hydrant, keeping a watchful eye on a group of young boys who were waiting their chance to set off that hydrant and play in the fountain it would cause.

I approached him, asking him if he'd seen Mrs. Goodwin recently. But he was a Sixth Precinct man and he didn't even know who she was. It seemed beyond his comprehension that the police were now using women as detectives. "And downright foolish," he added. "If they're using women on the force now, then that's the beginning of the end."

So I went back toward Mott Street, noticing any business that was in a good position to observe people coming and going from Chinatown. There were street vendors aplenty and they were in the best position to notice a fleeing Chinese woman, if she hadn't made her escape in the middle of the night. The aroma of roasting sweet potatoes and grilling corn from one of those carts reminded me that it was past lunchtime. I was luckily fortified with that soda bread, but buying a roasted sweet potato and an ear of corn was a good excuse to ask those vendors if they had seen a Chinese girl and showing her picture around.

"Those stinking Chinamen know better than to come out here," one of the vendors said in a heavy Italian accent. "We learn 'em good if they show their faces outside Mott Street."

"But if you saw a woman?"

"They don't have no women," he said. "And we keep our girls well away from them."

I moved on, munching on my corn with satisfaction, around

to the Bowery where I worked my way down toward Pell, asking questions along the way. One woman had seen a Chinese girl and my hopes rose until it transpired that she was one of the acrobats advertised at the vaudeville show at Miner's Bowery Theatre. I continued on, past Pell to Doyers and then to the other end of Mott, then up Mott again to Park Street. I had covered all the exits with no luck. Plenty of people had seen the half-Chinese offspring of people like Aileen Chiu as they went to school outside the neighborhood or went to play in the park at Mulberry Bend. But nobody had seen a Chinese girl, in Chinese pantaloons and a brocade blouse from the old country.

"Don't tell me they're letting them bring in women now," was a phrase I heard more than once. "Enough is enough. They keep themselves to themselves and that's all right, but bring in women and they'll start breeding like rabbits."

The depressing thing was that I didn't find one person with a good thing to say about their Chinese neighbors, even though, according to Aileen Chiu, they were good husbands and fathers, didn't get drunk or get into fights—if you didn't count the bullets that flew when the tongs were at war.

CHAPTER TEN

I was just trudging back up the Bowery, wondering what to do next, when I spotted a face I recognized. Monty Warrington-Chase was crossing the street toward me. He was striding out with a determined look on his face as if he was on his way to urgent business. I was about to greet him, but he passed right by me without noticing. He's just escorted Sarah to her job at the settlement house, I thought, and he's anxious to get out of this part of the city as soon as possible. I thought of Sarah and how warm and funny and generous she seemed to be, and then of cold, superior Monty and wondered how happy that marriage would be. At least I knew that Daniel and I were compatible and would make each other laugh. Was Sarah and Monty's marriage as much of an arranged affair as little Bo Kei's to Mr. Lee?

Of course the moment I thought of Sarah, I had a brilliant idea. If my girl had ventured a block or two beyond China-town, she might have found one of the settlement houses, and they did have beds for destitute women. They would have certainly taken her in. I decided that I would go and enlist Sarah's help right away. So I headed back up Elizabeth, across Canal, and located the settlement house. It was a tenement building like the others on that street, and the only things that distinguished it were the bright yellow painted front door and bright curtains in the windows. The front door opened and I went inside. It didn't smell like the usual tenement either, but more like a hospital with plenty of disinfectant. A bell jangled as I opened the front door and immediately a young woman appeared.

She appraised me, then smiled. "How can I help you?"

She was simply dressed, but the cut and quality of the cloth were evident, as was the smooth, educated tone of her voice.

"I was wondering if I could speak with Sarah Lindley."

"I'm afraid Sarah's not here today," she said. "And I don't know when she'll be in again. She sent word that she is so occupied with wedding preparations that she can't promise if or when she can return. She is to be married soon, you know."

"Yes, I know," I said. "I just saw her fiancé so I assumed he had escorted her here as usual."

"Not today. I'm sorry. Is there anything I can help you with?"

"Maybe," I said.

"Then please come through into the parlor. I believe it's unoccupied at the moment." She led me through to the room on the right. A young man was sitting on a sofa reading a newspaper, which he folded hastily when he saw us.

"I thought you were on kitchen duty this morning, Teddy," she said. "Don't tell me you've already finished?"

Teddy flushed and got to his feet. "Well, no, but the girls seemed to have it all under control so I thought—well, dash it all, Hermione, a fellow isn't exactly cut out for peeling potatoes."

"This fellow had better learn if he's going to stay here," the girl said. "Go on. Off with you. We need privacy. And don't take the paper with you."

She shook her head, smiling as he left. "That one's not going to last long. It's too much of a shock for some of them who have been pampered all their lives. Sarah was one of our best, unfortunately. It's too bad we're losing her. Do sit down, Miss . . . ?"

"Murphy. Molly Murphy," I said. "I've come to you with a strange request. I'm looking for a missing Chinese girl. I wondered if you've ever come across one at the house?"

"Actually we have a girl here at the moment," she said. "Frankly we're not sure what to do with her next."

"You do? How long has she been with you?"

"Only a few days."

"Then this sounds like the girl I am looking for. Could I possibly see her?"

"May I ask why?" Her face took on a guarded look again.

"I've been asked to find her by her family."

"Her family?" The expression changed to one of incredulity. "Her family is looking for her? We had no idea she had a family. They usually don't. Well, that can only be good, can't it? We were wondering what would become of her. She's not at all well, you see. I should warn you that we think it's possible she has tuberculosis—consumption, you know. So she could be infectious, but I'll bring you to her if you want to take that risk."

"Yes, I do." My heart was thumping with excitement. She wasn't well. Was that the reason she ran away?

Hermione led me up well-worn linoleum stairs, one flight and then two. The third flight was plain wood, narrow, and steep. "It's quite a climb," she said, "but awfully good for the figure, all this running up and down."

As we came onto the landing a door opened and another young woman came out, this one wearing a large white apron and a white cap over her hair.

"How is the patient, Marigold?"

"A little better. She's eating well, but she still has that terrible cough."

"She has a visitor, and maybe some good news," Hermione said, and ushered me into the room.

The frail Chinese girl lay propped on her pillows looking like a porcelain doll. The girl in my photograph had looked healthy and robust. This one looked as if she was wasting away, but she sat up as we came into the room.

"Hello," I said, smiling at her. "Do you speak English?"

"Little bit," she said. She was eyeing me warily.

"Are you Bo Kei?" I asked.

She frowned as if she didn't understand.

"Bo Kei? You came from China as a bride?"

She nodded, her eyes still darting as if she might be considering flight.

"Bride of Mr. Lee Sing Tai?"

Her expression changed. "Lee Sing Tai?" She spat out the words in staccato fashion; then she actually raised herself up and spat onto the floor.

"Annie, that's not nice," Hermione said. "No spitting. Not hygienic."

The girl lay back again as if exhausted.

From her outburst it was clear that she wouldn't be too keen on going back.

"He is looking for you," I said.

"No! Why he look for me? Not want me no more," she said, turning her gaze away. "Send me away. No son."

"Send you away? He sent you away?"

She nodded. "No give him son. No use, he say."

"I don't understand. You came from China a month ago, is that correct?" I asked her. "One month?"

Hermione touched my arm. "What's this about coming from China as a bride? We took Annie in when she was thrown out of a local brothel. Usually they turn them out with a very different sort of disease, but in this case they were worried she had consumption and would pass it to clients."

"A brothel?" I asked, completely confused now. "Then she's not the girl I'm looking for. And why do you call her Annie?"

"That's the name she gave us."

I sat on the bed beside her. "Annie? How long have you been in America?"

She wouldn't meet my gaze. "Five year," she said.

Something that had been said passed through my mind—something about Lee Sing Tai bringing in another bride before this, and then sending her back to China because she didn't produce a son.

"Did you come here as the bride of Lee Sing Tai?" I asked. "Did he have you brought here?"

She nodded, her face expressionless as if she was made of stone.

"And you didn't give him the son he wanted, so he sent you to a brothel?"

She nodded again. I looked up and met Hermione's concerned eyes.

"Annie, listen," I went on. "He's brought in another girl from China, but she has run away."

"She smart girl," Annie said. "He bad man. Bad man."

"I'm trying to find her," I said. "Do you have any idea where she might have gone?"

"Maybe she come place like this."

I looked up at Hermione again. "Are there other settlement houses around here? Other places where a girl might seek refuge?"

"There's the Henry Street Settlement and the University Settlement on Eldridge, but they are farther away from Chinatown and I don't know how she would have come across them," Hermione said. "There are a couple of Christian women's hostels, but I don't know if they'd take in a destitute Chinese girl."

"You're right," I said. "I stayed in one near the Battery myself when I first arrived in New York. They were extremely strict—and devout."

Hermione smiled. "That's why we make a point of being completely open and impartial. No hint of religion here, only humanitarianism."

Annie touched my hand. "This girl—she come from same nuns like me?"

Nuns! Why hadn't I considered that the missionaries might be nuns?

"Yes," I said. "I believe she came from the nuns."

Annie gave the ghost of a tired smile. "We call them white ghost ladies. They dress all white, like ghost."

I stood up. "Is there a convent of any kind around here?"

Hermione shrugged. "I don't know of a convent. I've seen nuns in the streets occasionally, so they may be attached to local churches."

I took a business card out of my purse. "I'm going on the hunt again, but if the girl should turn up here, please keep her and send someone to find me." I gave Annie a reassuring smile. "Nice meeting you, Annie. You're in good hands now. You'll get well soon."

"Okay, miss," she said flatly.

We started the long descent, our footsteps echoing on the bare boards of the stairs.

"She won't get well, you know," Hermione said when we were safely out of earshot. "Frankly we're in a pickle here. We don't know what to do with her. We shouldn't really keep her or she might infect the other women who come here, but there's nowhere to send her." She paused, sighing. "Poor little thing. So she came over here as a bride, did she?"

"It appears so. And she didn't give him a son, so he got rid of her."

"Sent her to work in a brothel. That's disgusting."

"From what I've learned of this Chinese gentleman, his people look upon women as objects to be traded and disposed of."

"Horrible." Hermione shuddered. "I wish you luck. I hope you find this girl before her lord and master does."

"So do I," I said. "Please give my best to Sarah when you see her."

And so I left the settlement house with my head in turmoil. From what I had now learned from Annie, did I really want to find Bo Kei? And if I found her, how could I possibly deliver her back into the hands of Lee Sing Tai?

CHAPTER ELEVEN

I visited the other settlement houses but, as I suspected, they hadn't seen my Chinese bride. So I began to look for Catholic churches and more specifically, for nuns. It was midafternoon and I was growing rather hot and weary. But I was now filled with a sense of urgency that I must find the girl before anyone else did.

I began to wish I had been a better Catholic. If I'd made a point of going to mass in New York, I'd have known where to find the churches here in the Lower East Side. But I'd too many sins to confess now to make me want to go back to church—and my few encounters with judgmental priests hadn't convinced me otherwise. So I wandered aimlessly around, trying first the Old St. Patrick's Cathedral on Mulberry. Here I moved warily again, as we were close to police headquarters. But nobody at St. Patrick's had seen a Chinese girl.

"They don't ever leave Chinatown," a young priest told me. "Not if they know what's good for them. And as for girls—well, I don't think I've ever seen a Chinese woman out in public."

I wasn't sure where to go next until an idea came to me. I had help on the spot, so to speak. So I made my way to Cherry Street, where Seamus and his children were now living with his sister Nuala and her brood. I can tell you that climbing the five flights to that tenement brought back painful memories of my arrival in New York. How far I'd come since then. Now I was safe and secure and about to be married to a wonderful man. I found renewed energy to bound up the last few of those stairs.

It was Nuala herself who opened the door. She looked me up and down, hands on hips. "Well, would you look what's turned up on our doorstep again," she said.

"That's a nice welcome, if ever I heard one, Nuala," I said. "I'm glad to see you looking well."

"So has your fancy man thrown you out?"

I laughed. "On the contrary. I'm about to be married. To a police captain."

Nuala looked back into the dark room beyond. "You hear that, boys!" she yelled. "You'd better mind yourselves when Miss High-and-Mighty is around these days, 'cos anything you say will be reported back to the police."

Several suspicious faces peered out of the darkness. I couldn't see much of them, but I didn't like what I saw. Nuala's boys were now looking like the typical Irish louts.

"I won't trouble you long, but I've a job for young Shamey, and your boys too, if they'd like to help."

Shamey was called to the door. I wasn't invited inside. When Bridie heard it was me, she rushed to me and flung her arms around me again. Shamey came with more of a swagger, to impress the cousins, I suspected.

I told him what I wanted. "All the churches in the area, where there might be nuns living. Your aunt Nuala probably knows where they are. Ask if any of them has taken in a Chinese girl. If they have, come and find me immediately."

"Are you paying him for doing this?" one of Nuala's boys demanded, pushing past Shamey to face me. He was now almost as tall as me, with a voice that hovered between boy and man.

"You too, if you'd like to help."

"How much?"

"Are you out of your mind?" His older brother grabbed

him by his shirtfront and thrust him aside. "She's obviously helping the police. Didn't you hear what she said? Monk'd kill you."

"So you've joined Monk Eastman's gang now, have you?" I asked.

"Junior Eastman." The boy stuck his chest out proudly. "Monk says I'm real useful to him."

"Then I think I'll leave the nuns to Shamey," I said. "You'll do your best for me, won't you, boy?"

Shamey nodded, but with a half glance back at his cousins to see their reaction. "Come and report to me as soon as you hear anything. You remember where I live, don't you? And at the moment I'm across the street with the two ladies. You can leave a message with them if I'm not there." I ruffled Bridie's hair. "I'll see you soon then. And you'll come to my wedding. I need a flower girl. We'll make you a pretty dress."

As I bent to hug her she whispered in my ear, "Let me come with you now. I don't like it here. Those boys, they're bad. They drink and they fight."

"Darling, I can't take you right now," I said softly, "because I'm sleeping in someone else's house. But I promise you I'll take care of you and we'll find a grand place for you. You just need to stick it out for a few more days—be brave for me—all right?"

She nodded. But after I left, I had terrible second thoughts. Was she actually safe there? I thought about asking Sid and Gus if I could bring her to share my room, but then I resolved to take her with me when I returned to Daniel's mother's house.

I started back in the direction of Chinatown. Churches. Where would a Chinese newcomer go, looking for nuns? Then, of course, I remembered the blank brick wall that was the face of the Church of the Transfiguration on Mott itself. It had never crossed my mind that she might be there, still in the neighborhood. Surely she wouldn't have stayed so close, within easy reach of Mr. Lee, would she? But she might have gone there for help. Perhaps she had found nuns there who had spirited her away to their convent. It was worth a try, anyway. I went back to Mott, which had become quite lively at this time of day. There were men going into restaurants, returning home with bags of provisions, standing together talking, sitting drinking tea. A few half-Irish children kicked a ball around, but there was not a woman in sight. I tried the heavy oak door of the church and it opened to my touch, leading me into a different world. The quiet peace and muted light through the stained glass windows was in contrast to the gaudy colors and loud, staccato speech outside. I stood, breathing in the tranquility, trying to collect my thoughts, and as usual wondering what on earth I was doing getting involved again in something so complicated. A piece of stolen jewelry was one thing, but now I had no idea how I should proceed if I found the girl. I was being paid to carry out a commission. Was it up to me to make a judgment on the moral validity of my assignment? Maybe that's why I wasn't a good detective like Daniel, who had learned to prevent himself from becoming personally involved in his cases.

The church was silent and empty apart from an old Italian woman, dressed all in black, praying at a statue of St. Anthony. I went up to her and asked where I might find the priest. She pointed at the confessional where a red light was on. I went and sat beside it, waiting patiently, and eventually he came out.

"Were you still waiting for confession?" he asked, in a voice that still betrayed a hint of the Irish.

"No, thank you, Father. I was wondering if a young Chinese woman had come here, seeking sanctuary."

"She did indeed." His lip curled with distaste. "Wanted my help in getting her away from some man. Probably her pimp, since the only women here are prostitutes. I told her there was nothing I could do for her." He folded his arms expressively over his cassock. "This used to be a good Italian and Irish neighborhood, you know, before those Chinese came and took over. And the last thing we want is Chinese women here—then the men won't ever want to go home again if their womenfolk are allowed to come here, and there will be no getting rid of them."

"So a young Chinese woman did come to you—about five or six days ago?"

"My housekeeper found her hiding in the church after the last mass of the day, when she went in to tidy up the hymnbooks. Brought her to me. I told her I was sorry but I wasn't going to get involved in Chinese business. They're a violent people, you know. You should see the killings that went on when the tongs were at war. Men shot and stabbed in broad daylight as they walked down the street or sat in the restaurants. I have to make sure I stay out of it."

"So you sent her away—where did you send her?"

"I've no idea. I told my housekeeper to feed her and then get rid of her."

"May I speak to your housekeeper then?" I asked

"I suppose so. What is your reason for seeking out this girl?"

I was about to say that I had been hired by her husband to find her, but instead I heard myself saying, "I want to help her."

"Come along then," he said. "Herself should have some tea on the table about this time. No doubt she can tell you in great detail what she told the girl—she loves the sound of her own voice." As he talked he made his way through the church, through a back room, and opened a door that led into the rectory.

"Mrs. McNamara," he called. "We've got company for tea."

A woman came scurrying down the hall toward us, wiping her hands on her apron as she came. For a moment I thought I was seeing a ghost, as she looked just like the woman who ran the shop at home in Ballykillin.

"Tea's all ready, Father," she said and gave me a broad smile. "And there's plenty for visitors too."

We went together into a rather shabby dining room where a table was laid with teacups, scones, and fruitcake.

"Sit yourself down, my dear," the priest said. "What was your name?"

"Molly Murphy, Father."

"That's as good an Irish name as you can get, isn't it?" He nodded to Mrs. McNamara. "We don't get too many Irish at the church anymore. It's all Italians these days. And Polish. Not like the old days, is it, Mrs. McNamara?"

"Indeed it's not, Father. Most of them don't even speak English and I hardly ever get a good chat, except with the father here."

"Never stops," he muttered to me.

Tea was poured and I ate heartily of the scones and cake.

"Miss Murphy's here asking about that Chinese girl you found. Any idea where she went?"

"No, Father," Mrs. McNamara said. "You told me to get rid of her, didn't you? So I had to send her on her way."

Then she did a strange thing. I looked up and caught her eye, and she winked at me.

"I'd best be going then," I said. "I really don't know where to look now. Maybe she's hiding out in one of the local parks, but that would be dangerous for a young woman alone."

"I'll see her out, Father," Mrs. McNamara said. "You put your feet up for a while."

She led me through the rectory to a door at the other end. As soon as we were out of earshot she whispered to me, "She's upstairs now, the poor thing. And I'm that glad you've come for her because I hadn't a clue what I was going to do with her."

"She's here? In the rectory?" I asked, my voice echoing louder than I intended through that high hallway.

She put her fingers to her lips. "Shh. We don't want himself to hear. Well, I couldn't just turn her out with nowhere to go, could I? So I put her in one of the rooms on the top floor. His reverence never goes up there—can't climb all those stairs any longer. So I've been feeding her and trying to find what to do with her next. I've always been too impulsive, you know. Let my heart rule my head. I'd never have

married that drunken lout McNamara if I'd stopped to think
about it. But, my, he was handsome when he was a lad. How
I suffered for it afterward. Knocked me around something
terrible, he did."

"Is he still alive?"

"He is not, God rest his poor soul. Killed in a street brawl,
five years after we came to America. I came to the good Father
here as housekeeper twenty years ago."

I was trying not to show my impatience.

"So do you think you could take me up to see the girl
now? I've come to take her off your hands."

"Thank the Blessed Virgin for that," she said. "I mean,
what could I do with the poor thing? She couldn't stay up in
our attic forever." She glanced back down the hall. "Come
on then. Tread quietly or you'll have himself snooping after
us. He'll have nodded off in a minute and then we'll be all
right."

She started up the stairs. I followed. My heart had been
beating fast ever since I had found out that Bo Kei was hidden here, but as we climbed flight after flight of stairs, it was
positively pounding in my chest. Mrs. McNamara was breathing heavily in front of me and paused on the landing to say,
"My old legs are not cut out for this sort of thing any longer.
Five flights. It's too much for a body."

As she put her hand on the door handle there was the
sound of scurrying beyond. The door opened to reveal a white
figure, trying to duck down behind the bed.

"It's all right, my dear," Mrs. McNamara said. "You can
come out. This young lady has come to help you."

The white figure stood up and I saw that she was wearing
a white nightgown. Her black hair hung in a heavy braid over
one shoulder and she was looking at me with terrified eyes. I
recognized her from her portrait.

"Bo Kei?" I asked gently.

She nodded.

"I've been looking all over for you," I said.

"Who are you?" She said the words carefully. "Why you
want me?"

"My name is Molly." I paused. What did I say next? *I've come to deliver you back to your husband?* I wished I knew how the law stood in New York. Could she legally be forced back to her husband? Was she officially his possession? Was I going against the law by hiding her? I didn't think Daniel would take kindly to finding his own bride fined or in jail for aiding and abetting a fugitive. But neither did I want to send her back to a man like Lee Sing Tai. I needed time to think. If I could get her to Sarah's settlement house, then she'd be safe for the moment and I could buy myself some time. "I've come to help you get away from here," I said.

"Where go?" she asked.

"I'm not sure yet."

"You can't take her out onto the street around here. She'd be seen," Mrs. McNamara said. "That man's spies are everywhere and you can't let her go back to him, the monster."

"Did he treat you badly?" I asked.

She nodded. "He make me do bad things. He say I belong to him now. He pay my father plenty money. He want I give him son pretty damned quick."

"So you definitely don't want to go back to him?"

"I no go back. I kill myself first."

"I'm sorry," I said. "We must think how to get you away from here, and then we can plan your future."

"She'll need some clothes first," Mrs. McNamara said. "She came here in her nightgown."

"How did you escape?" I asked.

She gave me a shy smile. "I hear church bell and look down on street. I see there is church, so close. So I wait see which day is Sunday. When it's hot night, master sleep on roof. He have boy bring me to him, and when he don't want me no more, he send me away again. So this night he think boy take me downstairs. But I come back up again. I hide on roof. When master sleeps I go on roof as far as I can, and when I can't go no more, I jump to next roof."

"Goodness," I said. "How far was it?"

"Far," she said.

"Weren't you scared?"

"I think if I die, is better than to stay with him."

"How did you get down from the next roof?"

"Down iron stair outside," she said.

"Fire escape," Mrs. McNamara corrected. "She came down the fire escape—can you believe the nerve of it?"

"Fire escape," she agreed. "And then down pipe to ground."

"Wearing your nightdress? Didn't people see you?"

"Middle of night. Nobody in street. I wait in alleyway and hide in garbage. When people go church, I go too."

"In your nightdress? Or did you have clothes with you?"

A sly smile crossed her face. "I steal sheet from laundry hanging on next roof. Throw down to street. I put it over head like this." She demonstrated. "Make me look like nun. People not look at nun. I go in church and I wait. I think where there is church, there will be nuns. They will help me. They will not want me to live in sin."

"Live in sin?"

"The brute never intended to marry her. He brought her over here as his concubine," Mrs. McNamara said, hands on hips.

"I go to hell if I am with a man and not married to him. That is what nuns say."

I put my hand on her arm. "That's not true. If you were forced to do things you didn't want to, then it's not your fault. You won't go to hell, I promise you."

She gave me a sad smile. "When man come to mission and say that rich Chinaman in America want me for bride I am happy. Nuns say Western life very civilized, say it's good I live in Christian country where women are respected. And I be bride of rich man. Never go hungry. But I come here and I find he already has one wife. He call me wife number two, but that is not true. Jesus say only one wife."

"So he already has one wife?"

She nodded. "She old woman. Very mean. Not want me there. She call me concubine. Tell me terrible things."

So those had been the fingers I had seen of the person behind the drapes. The old woman who did not welcome a new young bride.

"She tell me I no better than slave. I have to do what master want. Do what she want. And if I no give master a son pretty quick, he put me away, send me to house of fallen women."

That was no idle threat, as I had witnessed.

"I'll do what I can to help you," I said. "Where would you like to go?"

She gave a helpless shrug. "I know no one in America. I can't go home. No money and family not want to feed me. That's why they sent me to nuns when I was small. Too many daughters. Not want to feed me. But then when man come to village, my father happy to get money for daughter he didn't want."

It sounded as if she'd had a rotten life all around so far.

"Were the nuns kind to you?"

"Nuns okay. Very strict," she said. "Punish with stick. But I learn reading, writing. I like learning. I good student, so not punish much."

At the very least she could be a nursemaid or companion, I was thinking.

"So what I do now?" she asked.

I was trying to think. What on earth could she do? "I tell you what," I said. "You stay here until it's dark. Then I'll come back with clothes for you and we'll find a way to get you out of Chinatown without anyone seeing you."

"Okay!" Her face lit up. "You kind lady, come save Bo Kei."

I'm a lady who is about to get herself in a lot of trouble, I thought to myself.

CHAPTER TWELVE

I left Bo Kei and followed Mrs. McNamara down the stairs and out of a side entrance onto Park Street. This was still part of Chinatown, but at least I wasn't directly opposite Mr. Lee's Golden Dragon Emporium and his front balcony. It might be possible to spirit away Bo Kei from here, as halfway down Park Street the flavor turned from Chinese to Italian. Since I couldn't do anything until it was dark, I decided to go home. I had been on my feet since early morning. One big advantage a male detective has over a female one (and there are many) is that they wear much more comfortable shoes. Female shoes are not designed for walking miles, and my toes were throbbing in the heat.

I boarded the Third Avenue El at Chatham Square and endured being packed like a sardine until I was finally back in home territory. Sid and Gus's front door was rarely locked, so I let myself in, not wanting to disturb them if they were involved in their creative pursuits. Instead I heard the sound of laughter from the back garden. I went through and found my hosts sitting in the shade with a third woman. I went to back away, but I was too late. Sid looked up.

"Molly! The wanderer returneth. Or is it the conquering hero?"

I laughed uneasily. "I don't know about that."

"Have you located your missing piece of jade?" The third person turned to face me. It was Sarah.

I pulled up a wicker chair beside them and nodded my greeting to Sarah. "The answer is yes, in a way." I paused, looking from one expectant face to the next.

"And you've recovered it and your employer is overjoyed?" Gus added.

I took a deep breath. "I'm really not sure I should be telling you any of this. In fact my employer would probably be furious, but I do need to discuss this with someone, and you're the wisest women I know."

"We shall remain silent as the grave." Sid gave Gus a grin.

"Well, this is how things stand," I said. "It turns out that the missing prized possession was not jewelry after all. It was a woman whom he had imported from China to be his concubine." Then I related the whole story, ending with her daring escape across the rooftops. They were suitably horrified and angry.

"We must rescue her instantly," Gus said as she handed me a glass of lemonade.

"But what are you going to do with her?" Sarah asked. "If this man is powerful among the Chinese community, is it wise to incur his wrath? They are ruthless people, you know, and he may well seek vengeance."

"What, come as far as Greenwich Village to gun us down?" Sid didn't seem overly concerned.

"Probably send an emissary to do so," Sarah said. "We've had dealings with the Chinese at the settlement house and we've received awful threats when a prostitute manages to flee from one of their brothels and comes to us. In fact we've a young woman with us now. She escaped from a Chinese brothel."

"Actually she was thrown out, because she has developed consumption," I said.

Sarah looked astonished.

"I met her," I said. "I was at your house today."

"You were?"

"I thought that maybe the Chinese girl might have fled there. And I expected to find you there."

"Ah," Sarah said, and she sighed. "I'm afraid I won't be going there again."

"Too busy before the wedding?"

"Not exactly. Monty has forbidden me to work there anymore. He doesn't want me running the risk of being in such a dangerous neighborhood, he says, although I keep telling him I'm in no danger."

"And you will obey because he has forbidden you?" I asked.

She flushed. "I don't have much choice, do I? In a month's time he'll be my husband and then I must obey him. I'm sure he's only doing it for my own good, and I don't want him to have to worry about me and to give up his precious time to escort me to and from the house."

"I saw him this afternoon."

"At the settlement house?" Her eyebrows shot up.

"In that general area, coming from the direction of Elizabeth Street. He looked as if he was in a hurry and he walked straight past me. I assumed he'd just dropped you off at the house."

"How strange," she said. "What was he doing there? He told me he had to visit his tailor, and he's up on Thirty-ninth Street." She put her hand up to her mouth suddenly. "Oh, my. You don't think he went there to tell them that he's forbidden me to come anymore? He can be so overbearing and arrogant at times."

"So what are you going to do about it?" Sid demanded. "You can't start off married life under his thumb, you know. Look at Molly. She doesn't let Daniel browbeat her."

"I don't want to upset Monty at the moment." Sarah stared down at her hands, twiddling the diamond ring on her finger. "He hasn't been at all well recently, and add to that the strain of the wedding."

"I thought he looked not very well yesterday," Gus said. "Rather frail in fact."

"I know. I'm worried. He used to be so robust, you know.

A keen mountain climber and all-around sportsman. And he did wonderfully brave things when he was in the army in India."

"Do they know what's wrong with him?" I asked.

She bit her lip. "His doctor thinks it's nothing serious, but . . . I'm hoping his health will improve when we're back on his estate in England and he can get out in the fresh air every day."

"I'm sure it will," I said, remembering how much I had worried about Daniel when he had been so sick in jail. "So, Sarah, I was wondering if your settlement house might take in my Chinese girl. What do you think?"

"For the short term, maybe," Sarah said.

"In spite of the threats from vengeful Chinamen?" Gus asked.

"We've done it before. I think they know that the offspring of important Americans work at that house—children of congressmen, senators, and bankers. I like to think that protects us a little."

"I thought that perhaps we could take her there in disguise and after dark," I said. "Then nobody in Chinatown would ever know."

"Molly, how would you disguise a Chinese person so that she wasn't recognized?" Gus asked. "They do have a rather distinctive look, don't they?"

"I've been thinking. She sneaked into the church with a sheet draped over her head, to make herself look like a nun. You two have so many costumes up in your attic. You must have a nun's habit or two."

"As a matter of fact we do." Sid jumped up. "We gave a wonderful nuns-and-priests party once. Such fun, wasn't it, Gus. We had confession booths set up and you should have seen the wicked penances we handed out."

"Too bad we've already sent out the invitations for Molly's party on Sunday. It would have been fun to do that again," Gus said. "Especially since the happy couple are of that persuasion and know all about priests and nuns."

"You're not taking this seriously," I said, as they were

both laughing merrily now. "It's a girl's life that's at stake here."

"Of course it is, and we will do whatever you want us to," Gus said, her face becoming sober again.

"I'd like to borrow any nun costumes you might have. The girl was right. It's rude to stare at nuns. If two or three nuns come out of a Catholic church, it's going to look perfectly natural and nobody's going to see past the habit."

"I wonder how many we have, Sid," Gus said. "I hope there are enough for all of us. Wouldn't that be ripping fun? A gaggle of nuns."

I'm afraid I rather thought that those two would spoil the whole thing by giggling or doing something awful at the wrong moment, and was glad when we found only two nun's habits in the costume box.

"I had better go ahead and talk to the workers at the settlement house," I said, not relishing yet another expedition into the Lower East Side. "I can't just land her on their doorstep. They might even say no."

"Why don't I go and speak to them?" Sarah said.

"I thought you were forbidden to go there again?" Gus pointed out.

Sarah flushed. "Monty can't stop me from saying goodbye to my coworkers, can he? Besides, I'd like to set things straight with them, in case he's been rude to them. And I have some personal items to collect there anyway."

"That would be most helpful for me. Thank you," I said.

"I wish I could be there when you bring in the girl, but Monty is coming to dine with my parents tonight."

"Don't worry. If they can just take her in until I come up with a plan for her, I would be most grateful. Tell them I'll be bringing her under cover of darkness."

" 'Under cover of darkness'—doesn't that sound deliciously exciting," Sid said. "Gus and I want to join in the game, you know. Are you sure you can't come along—as fallen women, perhaps?"

"Holy Mother," I muttered. "The whole object is not to attract attention to ourselves. And if you two masquerading as fallen women doesn't attract attention, then I don't know what would."

This set them off laughing again.

"Spoilsport, Molly," Gus said. "We have always been dying to be partners in your cases and soon it will be too late and you'll be home having tea parties instead."

I smiled at her fondly. "My dear friend, if it weren't so serious, I'd be glad to let you come along. But if anyone spots my girl, then it's all over for her. Either Mr. Lee will take her back as a virtual slave or he'll have her killed. You do see that I can't risk it, don't you?"

"Of course," Sid said before Gus could answer, "but I'm concerned about you, Molly. Aren't you running a terrible risk yourself by crossing such a powerful man? If he finds out you were the one who spirited her away . . ."

"I know," I said, "but I have to listen to my conscience. How would you like to live at the mercy of a man who has made it clear to you that if you don't produce a son quickly, you're headed for one of his brothels? You wouldn't want me to return her into those circumstances, would you?"

"Of course not," Sid said.

"You and Gus could help out by asking your friends if any of them would take in the girl as a nursemaid or companion. She's been educated by Western nuns and she told me she was a good student, so I'm sure she'd be a quick learner."

"We can do that, can't we, Sid?" Gus said.

And so it was agreed. Sarah was to go and pave the way, and I would follow as soon as it got dark. Sid and Gus helped me into the nun's costume. It wasn't exactly authentic, but it gave a good enough impression and it helped to hide the face under an impressive white starched coif that curved forward then out like miniature sails on either side. I feared that I would be struck down by the Almighty as I stepped out into the balmy night air. I was also sure that I looked like a complete fake until the police constable on the corner saluted me and said, "God bless you, Sister."

Then, of course, I grinned to myself for the next four blocks.

A man jumped up to offer me a seat on the El. People stepped aside for me on the stairs and others murmured, "God bless you, Sister." I could see this was a disguise that would prove useful in the future—until I remembered there wasn't going to be a future in this profession.

Mott Street was more lively than I had seen it during the day. The restaurants were doing a roaring trade and interesting odors wafted out into the street—frying oil and sweet spices, not at all unappetizing. From an open door came the sounds of strange music—a voice singing in a high, tuneless manner against a background of screeching strings. Not what we'd call musical, but it appeared that the place was packed. I could see men standing just inside the doorway. I also noticed figures slinking into the alleyways between buildings and wondered if they were going to the famous gambling parlors and opium dens. I was interested to note that not all the evening revelers on Mott Street were Chinese; a young American couple was waiting in line for a table at one of the restaurants—the Port Arthur, it was called, and I wondered about the origin of the name. Then I saw a distinctly Western form slinking into one of those alleyways, heading for the opium den, I presumed.

The crowd on Mott Street streamed past me, giving me a wide berth. My hopes rose for accomplishing this successfully. I reached the back door of the rectory and tapped lightly. Mrs. McNamara opened it. "Can I help you, Sister?" she asked. "Father Barry is occupied at the moment."

"Mrs. McNamara, it's me, Molly Murphy," I said.

"Jesus, Mary, and Joseph," she exclaimed and crossed herself. "Whatever next? Well, I certainly wouldn't have recognized you. Come on in. Himself is just having his supper," she said. "He won't notice a thing while he's eating."

Up the stairs we went. Bo Kei looked amazed and delighted when a nun came into the room, then even more excited when she realized it was I. I showed her I had brought her a similar costume. I helped her into it and a few minutes later two nuns came out of the church rectory and melted into the Italian crowd on Park Street. Then it was an easy walk through the noisy Italian streets to the house on Elizabeth.

Hermione was still on duty. "Well, I never," she said when she saw us, and burst out laughing. "Come in, do." She whisked us inside and shut the door behind us. "Come on through to the kitchen and I'll make us some tea."

"I presume that Sarah came by and warned you about this," I said.

"She did indeed. Welcome." She held out her hand to the frightened girl. "You'll be safe here. And I expect you'd like to get out of that nun's habit. If you take a look in that closet you'll find some clothing that will fit you. Help yourself. And I'll go and make us some tea."

I followed Hermione down the hall.

"I hope you don't mind keeping Bo Kei here at least for a few days?" I asked.

"We're not about to turn her out onto the streets," Hermione said, then lowered her voice, "but let's just hope that nobody finds out she's here. I don't particularly want to find our house firebombed or our staff with their throats cut."

"I know I'm asking you to take a big risk," I said. "I'd take her in myself but my future bridegroom is putting the finishing touches to my house, and he must not find out that I'm doing this."

"I quite understand," she said. "Sarah Lindley is having the same problems with a bossy bridegroom."

"She is. I gather he came here today. Sarah was most embarrassed."

Hermione shook her head. "No, we haven't seen him today. Sarah thought he'd come here for some reason, but he hadn't."

"But I saw him on Bayard Street, just around the corner, so I assumed he'd come to escort Sarah. She was worried he'd come to tell you in person that he'd forbidden her to come here anymore."

"I don't know why he'd need to come in person after he already wrote us a letter," Hermione said. "I hope he wasn't spying on her to make sure she hadn't come here."

"A letter?"

She went across to a bureau and opened a drawer. "Read this. It will make your toes curl."

The letter was written in a tall, elegant script with extravagantly flourishing curls on the capital letters.

> *To whom it may concern. Please be advised that at my request Miss Sarah Lindley will no longer be working as a volunteer at your establishment. She needs to devote her full energy and attention to the preparations for our wedding.*
>
> *Yours faithfully, M. P. G. Warrington-Chase (The Honorable)*

"What a nerve," I said. "Did you show this to Sarah?"

"I thought it wiser not to. She told me that Monty was adamant that she give up coming here and she didn't want to upset him. I expect she'd have been livid if she found that he'd written to us." She looked up at me. "I hope Sarah is doing the right thing marrying him."

"But she loves him, doesn't she?"

"I think she likes the idea of being a grand English lady and living in a castle," Hermione said, "and of course he's in love with her money. Who wouldn't be?"

"But surely he doesn't need her money—he's from an aristocratic family with large estates."

"And has squandered his inheritance in riotous living, to paraphrase the Bible. Believe me, Mr. Monty Warrington-Chase can't wait to marry and settle his debts."

"How do you know this?"

"My brother is a member of the same club. Monty spilled out his problems one night while in his cups," she said. "Naturally I've said nothing to Sarah. If she really does love him, then all is well."

"I think she does," I said. "She was most concerned about his health."

"His health? I put that down to aristocratic pallor." She

laughed. "Then I wish them every happiness. Here, take this tray into the living room and I'll follow with the teapot."

A few minutes later Bo Kei reappeared in a Western skirt and shirtwaist. "Now I am proper American lady," she said, laughing with relief.

"Tell this lady your story," I suggested, but Hermione shook her head. "Let's not put her through that again. Sarah has already given me a most riveting account. I gather you leaped between rooftops and shimmied down drainpipes."

Bo Kei nodded, her hand shielding her mouth as she giggled. "Nuns always call me tomboy."

We took tea together and then Hermione suggested that she meet Annie. "We have another Chinese girl here you might know," she said.

We proceeded up the stairs. Annie was lying as if asleep, but she opened her eyes as we came in.

"A visitor, Annie. A Chinese girl like you."

Bo Kei gave a squeal and rushed toward Annie's bed, letting out a stream of Chinese. Annie recoiled for a moment, then threw her arms around Bo Kei. We watched them as they sat together, holding hands, looking incredulously at each other's faces. Then Bo Kei looked up at us.

"This girl my cousin. She went away from my village and nobody knew where she has gone. We think she is dead."

CHAPTER THIRTEEN

Job well done, I said to myself as Sister Molly of the Unholy Order made her way back to Sid and Gus. They were waiting anxiously and were delighted that the story had ended so happily.

"But what are you going to tell this Chinaman who hired you?" Sid gave me a worried stare.

"That's a problem, isn't it. I'm not quite sure," I said. "From what I hear he's a powerful and ruthless man. I don't like to think what he'd do if he found out I'd helped the girl escape from him."

"Molly, you can't risk putting yourself in that kind of danger," Gus said. "This girl isn't anything to you and I'm sure this kind of marriage arrangement is usual in their culture. Would this life be so much worse than a marriage to someone in her village at home?"

I sighed. She had made a valid point. If women could be bought and sold in China, could she have expected any better for herself? And at least here she would have enough to eat and nice clothes. And if she produced that son, she'd be treated well. But she clearly did not want to be treated as chattel. She had taken a terrible risk to run away. I knew how she felt. I had fled from Ireland when the odds had seemed against me. I had received help when I least expected it. How could I deny it to Bo Kei?

"Maybe I'll tell him that I've looked diligently but that

the girl is nowhere to be found at any of the missions—which is true of course."

"Are you sure that nobody at the settlement house will betray the presence of Chinese girls there?"

"No, I'm not at all sure. If they stay hidden upstairs, then maybe they are safe, but if they come down to communal meals, then anyone could inadvertently give them away. The house is too close to Chinatown. Our only chance is to spirit her far away as soon as possible. So if you two could get to work trying to find a position for her—"

"Molly, we're planning your party, remember?" Gus said. "We've a host of people coming who will need to be fed and entertained. We've decorations to design, food to make, drinks to order. Can't you put off reporting in to your Chinaman for a day or so? He can't expect you to work miracles in a single day, surely?"

"I suppose you're right," I said. "I'm sure he'll want to hear from me immediately, and I don't think I could face him in person, but I could write a letter to let him know that I am still working hard on the case, and then hand-deliver it to his secretary."

This decision made me feel better. At least I had bought myself some time and the girl would be safe, unless Mr. Lee had his own spies out looking as well. I went to my room and composed the letter carefully, trying not to tell an outright lie in it. It must have been that Catholic upbringing and the beatings from my mother that made it so hard for me to tell an untruth. So I simply stated that she had not been at any of the missions around Chinatown—which was true—and that I was now expanding my search further afield and hoped to have news for him soon.

And I hoped to come up with a brilliant solution before I had to see him again. Maybe if Sid and Gus could find someone to take Bo Kei in as a servant, I could truthfully claim that she had left the city and I had no means of tracing her. Or maybe a convent somewhere would take her in. I could look into convents suitably far from the city.

I was feeling considerably more hopeful by the time I

alighted from the El at Chatham Square the next morning.
One way or another this would sort itself out. I made my
way through the bustling Saturday morning crowd to Frederick Lee's office on the Bowery. I went up the stairs and
found the outer door shut. I knocked on it, gently at first and
then louder. Nobody came. I waited, then had to admit that
Frederick Lee was not there. Was his employer enlightened
enough to give him Saturdays off, I wondered.

I wasn't sure what to do now. I could just post the letter
through the mail slot, but then tomorrow was Sunday and
the next day was the Labor Day holiday so Mr. Lee would not
receive it until Tuesday. This might mean that he'd send
someone looking for me long before then. I supposed my only
course of action was to take the letter to the Golden Dragon
Emporium and ask one of the employees there to deliver it to
Mr. Lee. Of course there was a risk that I might encounter
Mr. Lee himself on the street or in the shop, but I decided that
was preferable to Mr. Lee sending someone to find me where
I was living. I didn't want to put Sid and Gus in any kind of
jeopardy. So I took a deep breath and crossed the Bowery to
Mott Street.

Again there was the instant contrast between the chaos of
the Bowery and the relative tranquility of the Chinese street.
I spotted Kitty Chiu playing jump rope with some friends
and a couple of old Italian women in black veils, huddled
together and clutching each other's arms for protection as
they went into the Catholic church. Then I heard the sound
of footsteps and a loud American voice booming, "This way
if you please, ladies and gentlemen." And around the corner
from Park Street came an unlikely procession. It was led by
a large, florid man with that typically Irish face. He was wearing a bowler hat perched jauntily on top of an impressive head
of hair, and a jacket adorned with a row of pearl buttons, in
spite of the warm day. He was carrying a megaphone. Behind
him came a group of well-dressed and respectable-looking
American men and women—mostly women, it must be noted,
and mostly women of my own age.

"What you are about to see will shock you to the very

core," the Irishman boomed through the megaphone to his wide-eyed charges, his voice echoing back from the tall buildings on either side. "Please, ladies, do not faint. Deese streets here are particularly dirty underfoot and you would spoil dose pretty dresses." In spite of the Irish appearance, he spoke with the strong accent of the New York gutter. He paused outside an open door with steps leading down to a basement. "Down these steps you will see the ultimate in depravity. Deese poor people are slaves to the opium habit. They have spent the night in this sqalid den, smoking opium, not knowing if it's one day or the next. Why, they even do it on the Lord's day—think of that. The ultimate heathens."

One of the ladies gasped and had to fan herself. Her friend grasped her in case she fainted. I tried not to smile because I had realized that this was the slumming tour that Mrs. Chiu had told me about and the so-called opium den they were about to see was a fake one. The Irishman looked at me with interest as he passed me.

"And can you imagine this," I heard him saying, not through the megaphone this time, "there are Irishwomen of such depravity that they actually enter into so-called marriage with Chinamen."

Another gasp from the crowd and I suspected that he was probably pointing at me. I reached the Golden Dragon Emporium and stood outside, hoping that someone would come out and thus make this task easier for me. Nobody did. The Irishman and his slumming tour had descended into the fake opium den and the only sound on the street was the rhythmic chanting of the girls as they turned the rope. I peered into the store. The interior was so dark that I could detect no sign of movement. I took a deep breath and stepped inside. As my eyes accustomed themselves to the darkness I could see that the walls and ceiling were richly carved, like the screen at the front of Mr. Lee's apartment. There were displays of bolts of silk and stacks of porcelain on one side, and open boxes of teas and spices on the other, producing heady and exotic scents. I waited, expecting someone to come forward, but nobody did.

From a backroom beyond I heard a clattering sound and then a sudden shout. I plucked up my courage and went through beaded curtains, down a narrow hallway. The room beyond was dark and full of smoke, but I could make out the long braids of men sitting around a table. As I watched they slapped down tiles, yelling out excitedly. By this point I had realized I was looking at a gambling den, and the moment I had taken this in, I knew that I shouldn't be here. I tried to retreat quietly. I crept back down the hallway, past the bead curtains, but they made a tinkling sound as they fell back into place.

A voice called out behind me. There was no point in trying to run or hide. I turned to see Bobby Lee coming after me.

"You—what you doing? What you want here?" he demanded, pointing an accusing finger at me.

I decided that attack was the best form of defense. "Such a gracious welcome," I said. "Your father greets me most politely. Don't you think he'd expect you to do the same?"

He frowned. "What business you have with my father? You not missionary lady?"

"I told you before that I am not a missionary lady," I said. "And I understand that Mr. Lee is only your paper father, not a blood relation at all. What's more, I'm afraid I can't tell you the nature of my business with Mr. Lee if he hasn't chosen to share it with you."

His frown deepened; in fact he was positively scowling now. "What you want here?" he demanded again.

"I was hoping to see Frederick Lee," I said. "I went to his office but it was shut."

"Frederick Lee no work there no more," he said, and there was a note of triumph in his voice.

"Oh, has he been transferred?"

"Not work for my father. Gone."

"He's left Mr. Lee's employment?"

"My father dismiss him. He not trustworthy," Bobby Lee said.

"I see." I had a strong feeling that Bobby Lee had something to do with this sacking. I had witnessed his intense dislike of Frederick yesterday. And the feeling was reciprocated. But whatever the reason for their dispute, Bobby Lee was the paper son. He had won.

"So why you need to see Frederick Lee?" he demanded. "You his sweetheart?"

"Certainly not," I said. "I came to see him as your father's secretary. I had a letter I wished to give to your father."

"My father not here today," he said. "You give me letter. I give to him."

There was no way I was going to hand over a letter to Bobby Lee, who would undoubtedly open it and read it. I couldn't remember whether I had said anything specific in it about looking for the girl, but I couldn't take the chance. Bobby Lee obviously hadn't been informed of the reason for my visits, or he would know why I was here today and would ask if I had been successful in my search. That meant that Mr. Lee didn't want him to know.

"I'm sorry, but the information in my letter is for Mr. Lee alone," I said. "I will return on another occasion when he is at home. Good day to you."

I gave him a curt nod and walked out. When I was safely down Mott Street I let out a sigh of relief. Maybe it was the exaggerated rumors that one heard about Chinatown, but I had definitely not felt safe in that room with Bobby Lee.

I arrived back at Patchin Place to find a hive of activity. Sid was up on a stepladder, stringing paper lanterns across the garden. Gus was in the kitchen loading the contents of her basket into the pantry. "I hope none of this spoils before tomorrow," she said, looking up as I came in, "but the market doesn't operate on Sundays so I had to get the fruit and vegetables now. Luckily Mr. Klein has promised to deliver the smoked salmon and cheeses tomorrow, so I don't have to worry about them. So—have you safely delivered your letter?"

"I couldn't do so," I said. "It appears the secretary has been sacked and Mr. Lee's obnoxious paper son was only too anxious to get his hands on my letter, so I'll have to go back at another time. I was told that Mr. Lee wasn't there today anyway."

"No matter," Gus said. "You can put your worries aside for the rest of the day and have fun with us decorating the house."

"Did you finally decide on your theme?" I asked, peering out at Sid on her stepladder.

"We toyed with another nuns and priests, or priests and prostitutes, but we thought they were not suitable as a celebration of marriage, so we've simply invited people to come in costume if they feel like it, and we will create a festive environment. We have strolling musicians and a fortune-teller. Sid really wanted fireworks, but it's hard to set them off in our backyard without offending the neighbors, so we'll limit those to sparklers."

I was rather relieved that my wedding party was not to be turned into a Greenwich Village spectacle.

"You must go up to our costume box and choose yourself something to wear." Gus straightened up as she put a box of peaches onto the pantry floor.

"Not the nun's habit," I said. "It was hot and uncomfortable."

"Quite right. We've a lovely French maid or there's Cleopatra or a milkmaid. I'm sure you'll find something."

I couldn't tell her I'd rather just be myself and I was finding it hard to concentrate on the party, so I offered to help with the preparations. I needed to be busy to take my mind off things. I was in the middle of draping paper streamers across the living room ceiling when the doorbell rang. I looked out of the window to see Frederick Lee standing there.

"Miss Murphy," he said, his face showing relief when I opened the door. "I am so glad to find you here."

"I went to find you this morning," I said, "but instead I met Bobby Lee, who told me that you had been sacked. Is that true?"

"I'm afraid so. A bad business."

I remembered my manners. "Please, won't you come inside? Can I fetch you a glass of water?"

"No, nothing, thank you," he said. He perched nervously on the edge of the nearest chair as I sat opposite him.

"I should not bother you with my problems," he said.

"I take it that Bobby Lee had something to do with your being sacked? He seemed very happy that you were gone."

"He is a bad person," Frederick said. "He is jealous that Mr. Lee relies on me and asks my advice. Also I know a bit about his underhanded schemes, so he wants me out of the way. He told Mr. Lee a horrible untruth about me, and Mr. Lee believed him. . . ." He paused, opening and closing his mouth nervously, like a dying fish. "Miss Murphy, I came to ask you—have you been successful in your search?"

"Not yet," I said.

"But you are still searching? You haven't given up?"

"No, I haven't given up."

I tried to read his face. He was staring at me in a worried way.

"Mr. Lee," I said, "if you no longer work for Lee Sing Tai, why should you be interested in my looking for a possession he has lost?"

"I know," he said. "I know what this possession is, and it is dear to me."

"A piece of jade?" I asked.

"Not a piece of jade. I overheard your whole conversation—in fact I have to confess that I was listening deliberately. I know that his bride is missing and he is trying to find her. So I ask—have you found any trace of her yet?"

I didn't know what to say. I was all too aware that this could be a trap. He went on, "You see, he sent me to Vancouver to bring Bo Kei to him. On the way back to New York Bo Kei and I were together on the train for several days. I have to confess that I developed—feelings for her. I could never reveal these feelings, as it would be disloyal to my employer. It broke my heart to deliver her to this cruel and sadistic old man, but what can I do? I had no choice. To betray my employer would be to betray my tong and my clan. Besides, I have no idea whether she returned those feelings or not. I believe that she did, so I wondered if she had run away and was looking for me."

"I have no way of knowing whether she was looking for you, Frederick," I said.

"So I wondered if you had any idea where she might be. If she's hiding somewhere she'll need my help. I'll do anything for her. And now that I no longer work for Mr. Lee, my first duty is to her. I'm prepared to risk all for her happiness."

I tried not to let my face betray me. I had heard Lee Sing Tai described as wily. Perhaps he had never quite trusted me and somehow knew by now that I was not going to return the girl to him. Why not pretend to sack Frederick, then have him worm Bo Kei's hiding place out of me?

"I beg of you, Miss Murphy, if you find Bo Kei, please come to me before you tell my employer. Please don't deliver her back to him. I know this will cost you a large amount of money and it may even put you in danger, but I care about Bo Kei's happiness and she would face a life of misery with that old man."

He was looking at me expectantly, but I had learned patience the hard way during my time as an investigator, and I had learned that people are not always what they seem.

"I understand that you are worried," I said cautiously, "but I can't tell you anything at the moment. If you would like to give me your address, I will send word if I succeed in my quest."

He shook his head. "No, I will come back here tomorrow. My rooms may be watched. Mr. Lee has his spies everywhere."

"Very well," I said. "I'll see you here tomorrow. I hope to have news for you by then."

His whole face lit up. "That would be wonderful."

I was so tempted to tell him where she was and even to lend them money to take the next train out of New York, but I had to see Bo Kei herself first and hear from her mouth that she wanted to be with Frederick Lee. And I had to weigh the risk that he might betray her to his former employer.

"You understand that this whole thing is impossible, Miss Murphy," Frederick said with a heavy sigh. "Lee Sing Tai is a powerful man. He has connections in every Chinese community. Even if Bo Kei chose to be with me, we could never find a place where we would be safe. If we tried to run off together he would find us and have us killed, or at least have me killed. He'd want her returned to him. She is his possession."

I nodded. This was all too true and I had no words of encouragement.

"I just pray that she can still be found," Frederick said. "It must be almost a week now that she has been away. Where can she be hiding? I wonder if she is still alive. I wonder if that rat Bobby Lee might not have killed her."

"Why would he do that?" I asked.

"Clearly he lusted after her himself," he said. "I could see this. He is a man who does not like to be crossed. If she refused his advances—who knows how he might have punished her? And I believe he must have seen me as a rival. He told his father that I had tried to meddle with her on my way across Canada. I treated her with the greatest respect. I never touched her in any way."

"Let us hope that she is alive and well, Frederick," I said. "And I am sure that Bobby Lee could not have killed her."

"How can you be sure?"

I smiled at his worried face. "Are you not half Irish? We Irish are known for our sixth sense. I sense that she is still alive."

"You give me hope, Miss Murphy," he said. "God bless you."

He rose to his feet. "I will go now. But Miss Murphy, once more I beg you—if you find her, please tell me before you go to Mr. Lee. If we run away together, if we have already vanished, then it will not be your fault that she doesn't return to him and he will not try to harm you."

"Very well," I said. "Come to see me tomorrow."

"I will do so. I will be extra careful and make sure I am not followed. If you find her, I will forever be in your debt."

I let him out and watched him walk down Patchin Place and out into Greenwich Avenue. I wanted to believe him. I trusted his earnest, open expression, but I couldn't put aside the thought of old Mr. Lee waiting like a vulture in the semi-darkness of that ornate room for Frederick to report back. "Well? Did she tell you the girl's hiding place? Has she found her, do you think?"

CHAPTER FOURTEEN

I finished my task with the paper streamers before I decided to pay a call on Bo Kei. I was itching with impatience to go and see her, but I realized I had to behave with a great deal of caution—hard for someone as impatient as I. I half expected that Frederick or one of Lee Sing Tai's henchmen might be lurking in the shadows, watching me to see where I went, so I started by fulfilling the shopping commissions given me by Gus—things she had forgotten to buy this morning. I hoped that seeing me with a bag of bread rolls or a jar of pickles might convince whoever was watching me that I was only on normal housewifely errands.

I looked around as I came out of the grocer's and saw no sign of Frederick nor of anybody who looked in any way Chinese. Of course I didn't know if Mr. Lee employed Westerners as well, but I decided not to put Bo Kei at risk and hailed a passing hansom cab. This was extravagant, considering that I wouldn't be paid anything for this case, but some things are worth more than money.

The commerce of the Lower East Side forced the cab to come to a halt halfway down Elizabeth Street. "Are you sure this is where you want to be?" the cabby asked me as pushcarts and half-naked children spilled around us. "Not a safe place for young ladies around here, you know. Do you want me to wait?"

I hadn't anticipated a cab fare back, but it did seem like a good idea. I had less likelihood of being spotted by one of Mr. Lee's henchmen.

"I won't be long," I said and went into the house.

Hermione came out of the kitchen to greet me, wiping her hands on an oversized apron. "Well, if it isn't the miracle worker," she said. "Your bringing the Chinese girl has done wonders for poor Annie. Until now she's just lain in bed and hardly eaten a thing. Frankly I thought we'd lose her soon, but today she's as sprightly as anything and ate a good breakfast with Bo Kei. And you should hear them laughing—like two naughty schoolgirls up there."

"I am glad," I said. "So nobody has come here looking for Bo Kei?"

She shook her head. "Although I've had to warn them that it might not be the smartest thing to betray their presence by talking to each other so loudly in their language. Sound does carry through open windows and we're not far from China-town."

"I hope she won't be here too long," I said. "May I go up and see her?"

"Of course. You know the way, don't you? I'd escort you but I'm facing a mountain of washing-up." She gave me a wry smile. "Sometimes I wonder why I thought this would be preferable to making a good match and living a life of ease."

"Maybe because you are free to choose to do the washing-up," I said.

"Exactly." She nodded as she went back to the kitchen, while I made my way up the stairs. Bo Kei and Annie had been sitting on one of the beds together, but they jumped up as I came in. Bo Kei gave me a relieved smile. She looked like a young girl again and I realized that she probably wasn't more than fifteen or sixteen.

"How are you today, Bo Kei?" I said. "Hermione said you sounded very happy."

"Bo Kei happy to be safe and free," she said.

"You're not out of the woods yet," I said.

"Please? Which wood is this?" She looked puzzled.

"An expression," I said. "It means that we still have to decide what to do with you. You can't stay here very long."

"Missie Molly," she said slowly. "I not ask you yet—who send you to find me?"

How was I going to answer this one? Do I make up some story about the good people at the house hearing of a runaway Chinese bride? I couldn't bring myself to come out with a lie.

"Who do you think might be looking for you?" I asked.

She dropped her voice to a whisper. "My master. Lee Sing Tai."

"That's right," I said. "He hired me to find you."

She shrank against Annie, clutching her as if she was drowning. "Why you bring me here and say you want to help me then? Why not take me straight back to him?"

"Because I do want to help you," I said. "When he hired me I had no idea it was a person he was looking for. He asked me originally to look for a piece of jade."

"My bride-piece. This belong to me," she said, patting at her chest to indicate it was hidden under her clothing. "I have a right to take it with me."

"And you still have it?"

"Of course. I no sell my bride-piece. It was present. Given to me."

"It was only when I couldn't find it in pawnshops that Mr. Lee told me he was really looking for a woman. The way he spoke frightened me. I won't help anybody to keep another person as a slave."

Annie looked up at me with dark, expressionless eyes. "You foolish woman. Lee Sing Tai not forgive you. He find you and punish you, just like he find Bo Kei and punish her. I tell her, she not be free from him ever."

Bo Kei shivered and grasped even harder at Annie.

"Bo Kei?" I asked. "Was there someone else you hoped was looking for you? Someone you wanted to find you?"

Her eyes gave her away before she shook her head and said, "No. Nobody."

"I just thought . . ." I said. "Frederick Lee came to see me today."

Again her face betrayed her before she spoke. "You saw Frederick? He is well?"

"He wants to find you," I said. "He wants to rescue you and take you away."

"Lee Sing Tai not allow him," she said flatly.

"He no longer works for Mr. Lee," I said. "Mr. Lee fired him because Bobby Lee told him lies about you. He said that Frederick made advances to you on the train coming here."

"Not true," she said vehemently. "He treat me with respect, he behave like gentleman, always like gentleman. He never say or do anything wrong, but I know that he likes me. I can tell."

"Yes, he likes you lot. And now that he no longer works for Mr. Lee and no longer has to show loyalty to his employer, he wants to take you away somewhere."

"No use!" Annie spat the words. "You think you can hide from Lee Sing Tai? Where you think you go, huh?"

"I have rich friends," I said. "Maybe they can find you both jobs working in a white person's household far from here. I don't think Mr. Lee is likely to find you if you live in an American community miles away."

"You think this is possible?" She was staring at me with hopeful eyes, exactly as Frederick had looked at me.

"I'll do my best for you," I said. "Tomorrow Frederick will come to see me again and I will arrange for the two of you to meet somewhere safer than this. Before that time, please stay quiet and hidden."

"And what you tell Lee Sing Tai?" Annie demanded.

"I will tell him that by the time I picked up their trail they were already far away."

"*Wah*," she said in scornful tones. "He not let you get away with that. Lee Sing Tai one smart man."

"Would you rather I just delivered her back to Mr. Lee?" I asked.

"No," she said hesitantly. "But I know. I have seen. This is a bad man. He kills a person like snapping the neck of a chicken."

I swallowed hard, physically feeling a hand grasping my

own neck. "My future husband is a policeman," I said. "If Lee Sing Tai knows this, he won't dare come near me."

Annie actually laughed out loud at this. "You think police not do what Lee Sing Tai wants? He pays them plenty money and they shut their eyes. He has houses of women, gambling places, opium too, and the police walk right by."

"There has to be an answer," I said. "You are living in a free country now. Men are not allowed to treat women as slaves here. One way or another we are going to make sure that Bo Kei and Frederick get away from here safely, I promise you."

I left then, hurrying back to the waiting cab. But I have to confess that my heart was beating rather rapidly. I had taken some risks in my life as an investigator, but I certainly didn't want to go up against a man who snapped the neck of a man as if he was a chicken and who had the police in his back pocket.

CHAPTER FIFTEEN

id and Gus were already in a party mood that evening and wanted me to try out various silly costumes as well as experiments in rum punches that Sid was concocting. At one point Sarah Lindley stopped by and joined in the festivities. Monty was out with English friends, so she was enjoying a rare evening of freedom with her women friends. "One of my last ever, I suppose," she said wistfully.

"You make it sound like a long prison sentence," Sid commented drily.

"Not really, but it seems strange that I will be with one person, all the time, from now on," she said. "Especially if we are on his estate in England. I know he'll want to entertain, but most of the time it will be just us. I wonder what we'll talk about. Don't you feel the same, Molly?"

It had never entered my head that Daniel and I would not know what to talk about. "I don't think that will be my complaint," I said. "I'm only afraid I won't see enough of him. When he's on a case he'll be working twenty-four hours a day and be too tired to talk when he comes home."

"You are so lucky that you'll still have your friends living across the street," Sarah said. "I'll know nobody. I don't even know how the English behave. I expect I'll be considered the crass American."

"It sounds to me as if you're getting cold feet," Gus said, looking at Sarah with an affectionate smile.

Sarah grinned. "I expect that's normal, isn't it?"

As she said this I realized something that made me sit up with a jolt: I no longer had doubts about marrying Daniel. He was a good man and I wanted to be with him. I suppose it was seeing Bo Kei and how bad life could be for other women that had finally driven home to me how lucky I was to have a man who loved me and wanted to protect me. And perhaps I had finally had enough of a life of danger and uncertainty.

The conversation turned to Bo Kei and we discussed what we could do for her. The others were not too keen on my idea of finding them domestic employment.

"She needs to be with her own kind," Sid said.

I was surprised. "I shouldn't have thought you'd be prejudiced," I said.

"Quite the opposite," Sid replied. "I know how hated and despised the Chinese are. How would you like to be treated with suspicion and prejudice every time you set foot outside your door?"

"Then what do you suggest?" I ask.

"Perhaps we should give them money to go far away—back to Canada, maybe?"

"Monty says there is a flourishing Chinese settlement in the East End of London," Sarah added. "Surely this horrible Mr. Lee couldn't trace them there."

I obviously didn't have the money for such an expense and I realized that the others were interested in helping in theory but not so keen in practice. It was my problem, not theirs, and they were impatient to get back to party planning. Having never had to work a day in their lives, they didn't understand that I couldn't just work when I felt like it or drop a case if it no longer appealed to me.

They also couldn't come up with a solution for me as to what I could tell Mr. Lee. So I went to bed troubled and my sleep was full of disturbing dreams—in one of which I was standing at the altar with Daniel, but when I turned to kiss him it was a strange, withered old man. "Now you will be my slave," he said, "or I'll snap your neck like a chicken."

I woke to a humid dawn. Clouds were heavy with the promise of rain. This was depressing enough until I remembered what day it was. The day of my party, a day that I should have been looking forward to. Surely it wasn't going to rain after Sid had put so much effort into decorating the garden? It seemed like a bad omen. I tried to feel happy and excited, but I couldn't get Bo Kei out of my mind. Why had I ever taken on this stupid case? I knew I was going against Daniel's wishes and nothing good ever seemed to come when I was being underhanded. It was probably my mother up in heaven making sure I was duly punished.

As I washed I looked at my worried face in the mirror and I came to a decision. I was not going to let an old Chinaman spoil my day. I had a perfectly simple answer. I had told my friends that I couldn't just drop a case once I had taken it on. But why couldn't I? I was my own master, after all. I would write Mr. Lee a letter telling him that I no longer wished to handle this case since the buying and selling of human beings went against my conscience. I would not charge him a fee for the time I had already put in on his behalf and I considered the matter closed. I was going to simply drop the letter into the mailbox, but then I realized that the next day was a public holiday and he might well send someone to find me before that. And I still had the photograph of Bo Kei he had lent me. I had to return that to him. So I wrapped it up well, placed the letter on top of the package and decided to hand it to the first person I met at his emporium.

I dressed and let myself out quietly without waking Sid and Gus. The city was unnaturally quiet and peaceful on this Sabbath morning. Distant church bells rang out and families passed me, clutching prayer books and dressed in their Sunday best. A flight of pigeons made a flapping sound that echoed in the still air as they wheeled around Washington Square. I wished I could enjoy this rare moment of tranquility, but I was wound tight as a watch spring.

"In an hour's time it will all be over and you can start to enjoy being a bride," I told myself. But I knew I couldn't re-

ally start to enjoy myself until Bo Kei was safely far away and
I had no idea how I was going to manage that. It wasn't really
my problem, was it? It was up to Frederick and Bo Kei to decide where they wanted to go and what they wanted to do. I
should just leave well enough alone. But I've never been good
at doing that.

Nothing stirred on Mott Street. The door of the Church
of the Transfiguration was open and from inside came the
sound of a voice intoning. Snatches of Latin floated toward
me and with them that customary jolt of guilt that I had
skipped mass yet again and was destined for hellfire. Then
I detected a movement out of the corner of my eye. I spun
around and my heart lurched as I saw a ghostly figure coming toward me from an arched entrance to some kind of tunnel or arcade between buildings. He was deathly white, pale,
almost luminous. Then he came out into Mott Street, pausing
to steady himself against the corner of the building and I
saw it was a white man, but in a sorry state. He was in his
shirt sleeves. His hair was plastered across his forehead. His
eyes were staring vacantly, he was breathing hard, and he
didn't seem to know where he was. I thought for a moment he
might be drunk, but I've seen plenty of drunks in my life,
including my own father, and they didn't look like this. Then
it came to me that he was emerging from an opium den. Mrs.
Chiu had told me that it wasn't only the Chinese who fre-
quented these places. The man looked around as if he was just
coming to his senses and started at the sight of me, as if I too
might be a ghost. He gave a little moan, then turned and staggered down Mott Street in the opposite direction.

I went on my way toward the Golden Dragon Emporium.
The sight of that man had unsettled me even further and I
wanted to get this over with. I reached the store and saw that
shutters covered the windows and the front door was firmly
locked. I hadn't expected the Chinese to follow the laws of
the Sabbath, and it now occurred to me that perhaps it would
stay shut on the coming holiday. I just hoped that the mail
slot on the front door to Mr. Lee's residence would be big

enough to take my package, because I wasn't going to risk coming back here a third time.

I went up the steps slowly. Before I reached the top several Chinamen ran past, shouting to each other in animated fashion. My thoughts turned to tong wars and I shrank into the shadow of the building, half expecting shots to ring out. But they didn't seem to notice me and disappeared into the On Leong headquarters next door. When I reached the top of the steps I was surprised to find the front door was open. I was just leaning inside to put the package on one of the stairs when I heard the most extraordinary sound—it was the wailing of a soul in torment, the sound of a wounded animal, unearthly and frightening. And it was coming from the top of those stairs.

I looked up and saw that the upper door was open, which was also strange, considering that it had been locked on the other occasions I had been here. Telling myself I was being a fool I crept up the stairs toward the sound. There was no houseboy in the hallway and the sound came from just behind the screen into the living room, so loud that it now echoed through the high ceiling of the hallway. My thoughts went to the Chinese demons that screen was supposed to keep out, but I had to find out what it was. I crept toward the screen and peeked around it—and reeled in surprise: a tiny old Chinese woman sat on the sofa, rocking back and forth. What drew my attention immediately were her feet. Her little legs stuck out like a china doll's, too short to reach the floor, and peeping through from the hem of her shiny black trousers were tiny little stumps instead of normal feet. Each stump had a red brocade shoe on it, no bigger than a baby's slipper. I recoiled, thinking she had had both feet amputated until I remembered what had been said about small-foot wives. I was actually looking at a small-foot wife.

All this passed through my head in an instant until the intensity of the sound obliterated any rational thought. Her mouth was open and from it came a continuous wave of horrific wailing. Her eyes were wide open and staring and I wondered if she was having some kind of fit, and should I perhaps go to help her. I also wondered where Lee Sing Tai and the servants were that they didn't hear her and let her carry on like this.

At that moment I was conscious of another sound over the wailing—heavy footsteps. Someone was coming down the flight of stairs from the floor above. I tried to dart back into the stairwell, but I was too late. I saw big boots, dark blue trouser legs.

"For pete's sake stop that row, woman," a deep voice boomed in English. "It gives me the willies." Then a burly New York police officer came into view. I had nowhere to hide. He saw me and reacted with surprise.

"Who are you? What the devil are you doing here?" he barked. He took in what I was wearing, my neat straw hat and gloves. "Don't tell me you're on one of these slumming tours, poking your nose into other people's business?"

If I'd been smart I would have said yes. But I didn't want to be seen as a nosy parker with no right to be in the house. "I'm delivering this package to Mr. Lee," I said.

"What kind of package?"

"A photograph that he lent me."

Without warning he took it from me and ripped it open.

"Hey," I said angrily. "That is private business between Mr. Lee and me."

"Is that so?" He glanced at the photograph, put it on the hall table, then proceeded to open the letter.

"You have no right to do that," I said indignantly. "It's personal correspondence. What do you think you're doing?" I tried to snatch it back from him, but he fended me off.

"Oh, I have every right," he said, something akin to a smirk crossing his face. His eyes scanned down the letter. "He hired you? What for exactly?"

"If you really must know, he'd lost a piece of jade and he wanted me to find it for him."

"That's not what it says here." He was staring hard at me with cold blue eyes. "You no longer wish to handle this case since the buying and selling of humans goes against your conscience?" he read, raised an eyebrow, and then waved the letter at me.

"This is not what you might think," I said hastily. "He arranged to have a young bride shipped over from China and—somehow she has gone missing. Naturally Mr. Lee is most worried and hired me to find her. Nothing criminal and therefore nothing of interest to the police."

"Really?" He was still staring hard at me. "A bride shipped over from China?"

"That's how the Chinese arrange marriages, apparently."

"Then who's the old broad on the sofa if he's just marrying a young bride?"

"I gather she's his first wife. They can take more than one in China."

"But not here in the States. It's called bigamy."

I lowered my voice. "Look, Officer, between you and me, I don't think he actually intended to go through a proper marriage ceremony over here with the new one. She'd be called wife number two, but really just a concubine."

"And now she's run away, has she?"

I could feel my cheeks getting hotter. When I am being backed into a corner I start to defend myself. "Look, I just told you—this has nothing to do with the police," I said. "I don't know why you are grilling me. It's a missing persons case, not a crime. And besides, if you're trying to pin some kind of criminal activity on Mr. Lee, I thought he had an understanding with the police and they left him alone."

"I don't know who told you that!" the policeman snapped. "But perhaps it would have been better for him if we hadn't left him alone."

"What do you mean?"

"Which way did you come down Mott Street this morning?"

"From Chatham Square. Why?"

"Because had you come from the other direction, you might have noticed a commotion around the corner on Pell Street—you'd have spotted a crowd, including some of my men. It appears that Mr. Lee Sing Tai fell off the roof of his building during the night." He paused to watch my expression, a rather satisfied one on his own face.

"Fell off the roof? You mean he's dead?"

I have to confess that the wave of emotion that shot through me was not of horror but of relief. Now I would never have to face him. Now Bo Kei would be free of him.

The satisfied expression turned into a smirk. "There aren't many people who survive a fall from that height unless they have wings," he said. "Of course he's dead. Smashed as flat as a pancake."

"I'm sorry to hear that," I said, because it was expected of me. Actually I wasn't sorry at all.

"So the only question in my mind," the officer said, still not taking his eyes from my face, "is whether he fell by accident or whether he was pushed."

CHAPTER SIXTEEN

I stood there in the dark hallway, trying not to let my face register any emotion. I recognized the policeman now. He was the officer who had accompanied Daniel at the Elizabeth Street station.

"When did this happen?" I asked.

"Sometime during the night, I suppose. The old guy is wearing his nightshirt and I gather he'd been sleeping on the roof."

"That's right," I said. "I was told that he liked to sleep on the roof during hot weather."

"That will certainly make it easier for us," he said. "He walked in his sleep and tripped over the low parapet."

"And if he didn't?" I asked.

He eyed me critically. "Then somebody pushed him, and if I don't find out conclusively who that person was, then the rumor will go around that it was a member of Hip Sing. In case you don't know about such things, it's—"

"The rival tong," I said. "I do know."

His eyes narrowed. "You seem to be remarkably well versed in Chinatown politics," he said. "What exactly are you—one of the Irish wives from around here?"

Again I should have kept my mouth shut and just claimed to be a friend. But I don't always stop to think through consequences. "Not at all," I said. "I'm a private investigator. That's why Mr. Lee hired me."

"Really?" He was looking at me with interest tinged with amusement now. "A female dick. That's a novel one."

He glanced down at my letter he was still holding. "Murphy, is that the name? Molly Murphy? I've heard of you before somewhere."

I wasn't going to say that my name had probably been mentioned as Daniel's future wife. "I have worked on cases in this part of the city," I said.

"Have you, by george? What kind of cases?"

I tried to think of harmless things I might have done in the Lower East Side—certainly not dealing with Monk Eastman and his gang. "Another missing person case once. A girl who had come over from Ireland. Her family wanted to trace her."

I hoped he'd be satisfied with that, but he was still frowning. "And why exactly did old Lee hire you particularly to find this bride?"

"I suppose he thought that a young woman like myself could move among other young women in the world outside of Chinatown, without arousing suspicion."

"I see." He paused. "And what made him think that his bride had run away and not been kidnapped by Hip Sing, for example?"

"I asked him the same question," I said. "He indicated that his spies had looked into that aspect thoroughly before he thought of hiring me." I hesitated, then went on. "From what I understand of the Chinese, I don't think Mr. Lee would have resorted to hiring an outsider and a female unless he'd done everything he could himself to recover the young woman."

"That's true enough," he agreed, then he stood looking at me, head cocked to one side, like a bird's. "You know what I find interesting? That Mr. Lee smuggles in a new bride from China—which I might point out to you is breaking the law to start with, Chinese women not being allowed to enter the United States. Then this bride does a flit, he hires you to find her, and immediately afterward he plunges to his death. Odd chain of events, don't you think? And in my twenty years of experience in the New York Police Department, I've always found that when strange things happen, one after the other, there's always a connection."

He was staring at me, long and hard, as if he expected me to crack and confess all. "Now look here," I said, my hackles rising. "I don't know if you're hinting that I might have had anything to do with his death. If so, I've no idea why you'd think that. For one thing, he hasn't yet paid me my fee—and now he's not going to, so I'm left out of pocket. Besides, I'd never met the man before and I have no interest in Chinatown or its inhabitants."

As I said this, unwanted thoughts were racing through my brain. I could think of several people who might want Lee Sing Tai dead, and first on the list was his runaway bride. The officer's mind must have been working along the same lines because he said, "So you haven't located this runaway bride yet?"

Now what do I say? Lying to the police was a serious matter, but I also realized that she'd make a perfect scapegoat for them, so that the case could be solved neatly and a new tong war would not erupt. "I did start to look for her. I went around the local missions. But as you can see from the letter, I decided to withdraw from the case," I said. "I realized that I didn't wish to be any part of this sordid business. I don't approve."

Suddenly his expression changed. He was no longer looking at me as if I was his prime suspect. I could see an idea had just come to him. "Look, Miss Murphy, I'm Captain Kear of the Sixth Precinct," he said. "Can I ask you to do something for me? Nobody has officially verified the identification of the body for us yet. The old woman in there couldn't make it down the stairs on those feet, even if we could get her to shut up."

"What about the servants?" I asked.

"They must have run off when they heard the police were on their way," he said. "There was nobody in the house when we got here and the door was wide open. Probably thought we were going to blame them. And the Chinamen in the crowd suddenly can't understand any English or claim to be complete strangers."

"Is Mr. Lee's son nowhere around?" I asked.

"He has a son?"

"Bobby Lee," I said.

"Oh, Bobby Lee, that's right. Old Lee's paper son, isn't he? I haven't seen him for a while. I heard old Lee shipped him out to the cigar factory in Brooklyn after the last dustup with Hip Sing."

"He was around here yesterday," I said.

"Was he? I'll send someone to look for him. But in the meantime I wondered if you'd take a look at the body yourself. If you're not too squeamish, that is? I need him officially identified before we move him. These Chinese would lie to their grandmother if it suited them. They all claim they've never seen him before."

"All right." I swallowed hard. Frankly I was not at all keen to view a body described as flatter than a pancake, but I had my image as a cool-headed detective to uphold, and I was rather flattered that Captain Kear was treating me as an equal and not as a helpless woman who might swoon at any second.

He ushered me down the stairs ahead of him. The street was still deserted and the church was now silent. I thought that probably any sensible Chinese had shut himself in his rooms, just in case he found himself grabbed as a suspect or new tong violence erupted. There was still a crowd around the body. Hardly any of them were Chinese, but there were curious Italians, Jews, and Irish, being held back by constables. I heard one of them saying, "Here's the captain now," as Captain Kear elbowed his way ungraciously through the crowd.

"Is the morgue wagon on its way?" he asked one of the constables holding back the crowd.

"Yes, sir. Should be here any moment."

"And the doctor?"

"Been summoned, sir," the same constable replied. "Might have a problem locating him. It's a holiday." His tone implied that it should have been a holiday for him too, if he hadn't been summoned to this scene.

"And has somebody been to HQ on Mulberry to request a photographer? I want a photograph of him before he's moved."

"I'd say he's not looking at his best for a photograph," one of the constables quipped and got a general laugh.

"Get going then, Mafini." The captain barked the order.

One of the constables forced his way through the crowd and took off, running.

"I've brought this young lady to identify him," Captain Kear said. "If you don't mind taking a look, Miss Murphy."

I sensed the curious stares of the crowd as they parted for me to step closer. I took a deep breath, then looked. He was lying on his back, spread-eagled like a starfish, limbs sticking out at unnatural angles like a broken rag doll. His mouth was open in surprise, his eyes staring up at the sky. He was wearing a nightshirt that made him somehow look even more pathetic, like Scrooge in *A Christmas Carol*. The white nightshirt was now spattered with blood. There was a great pool of blood around his head, now black with a carpet of flies. I shut my eyes and looked away.

"Yes," I said, turning back to Captain Kear when I had composed myself. "That is definitely Lee Sing Tai."

"Thank you," he said. "Come away now. I'll just need a few particulars and then you can go."

I looked back at the corpse. "There is no way he'd have landed like this if he'd tripped and fallen," I said, as the thought came to me. "He'd have fallen forward and landed on his face. He had to have been pushed."

As I said the words I heard a murmur go through the crowd and a couple of Chinese at the back took off running. Captain Kear looked up and frowned. "It wasn't the smartest thing to say that out loud," he said. "They'll be reporting back to On Leong in seconds."

"I'm sorry," I said. "I didn't think. Besides, you said they didn't understand English."

"Only when it suits them. Most of them understand pretty well." He took my arm and dragged me away from the crowd.

"If what you say is true, then we'd better make it quite clear that we don't see this as a tong murder. For starters, I'd like to question your runaway bride. Why don't you come back with me and you can give me her particulars and tell us how far you've got on the search."

He'd phrased it as an invitation, but it really was a command.

"You'd better come along to take notes, O'Byrne," the captain added. "And I want the missing servants found. Houseboy and cook, wasn't it? And I gather there are usually bodyguards outside his place. Where the hell were they? They've run off too. Get to it, Hanratty, and spread the word that these men are our main suspects if they don't show up immediately. The rest of you keep the crowd away. Ask if anyone saw him fall, or saw anything at all. Not that I'm hopeful that anyone will come forward, but we can try. Oh, and make sure someone comes to get me the moment the doctor and photographer arrive."

He shoved his way back through the crowd, clearing a path for me. While he had been giving his orders, I had been taking a long look at the corpse and I'd noticed something else. I moved closer to Captain Kear. "He's got a wound on one side of his head," I said, this time in a low voice so that nobody else could overhear. "He couldn't have received that during the fall."

"He could have hit something on the way down," Kear said.

I looked up at the building. There was a succession of balconies, but they didn't project in any way; in fact his descent would have been smooth and swift.

"I think somebody killed him first," I said, "or at least knocked him out." Even as I said it I could hear a voice in my head yelling at me to shut up. If he was lying where he landed on the street, then there was the possibility that he tripped and fell, however strangely he had landed. If, on the other hand, he had a large dent in one side of his head, then it was obvious that somebody knocked him out before throwing him over the edge.

"I'd keep that to yourself if I were you," Captain Kear

muttered. "For the moment the official line on this is going to be accidental death. If I get word that On Leong is going to blame it on Hip Sing and we're about to be back in a full-flown tong war, then I'll have to come up with a suspect pretty damn quick."

I had observed that he was not toning down his language in the presence of a lady. This surprised me until I realized that he was not treating me like a lady. I was a detective, a professional. That made me feel a certain sense of satisfaction.

We turned the corner back into Mott Street with Constable O'Byrne leading the way.

"Is it possible that it was committed by Hip Sing?" I asked. "I understand that Mr. Lee was very thick with On Leong."

Captain Kear shook his head. "It doesn't seem like their method of operation at all. Gunning down someone in the street, a quick stab in the back—that would be normal tong tactics, not a death made to look like an accident. They actually want the other side to know when they are killing someone. Besides, it's in Hip Sing's interest to keep the peace right now. They suffered far worse in the last round of violence than On Leong did. They need to build up to full strength again before the next round begins."

"You think it will break out again?"

"Bound to. While you've got struggles for control of the Chinese community they'll keep on at it until one side wins."

"I understand that On Leong pays you to turn a blind eye to their activities," I said. "What about Hip Sing?"

"You mentioned that before," he said sharply. "Are you talking about bribes? Bribes are not allowed in the police department. Who told you that?"

"It was old Mr. Lee himself," I said, realizing that once again I'd let my mouth run away with me and this wasn't the wisest thing to say. "He said he had the police in his pocket."

Captain Kear's face was flushed. "Well, he might have made a donation to our benefit fund, in return for which we kept an eye on his businesses and saw that nobody robbed them or firebombed them, but that's another thing entirely."

So he'd just confirmed by his guilty bluster that Lee Sing Tai had been bribing the police—which might have given someone else a motive for killing him. What if Mr. Lee had threatened to spill the beans at police headquarters? It seemed to me that given the diverse nature of Lee Sing Tai's business ventures, any number of people might have wanted him dead.

"And another thing," Captain Kear said. "How the hell could Hip Sing gain entry to Lee Sing Tai's home? He always had bodyguards lurking on the street nearby. He kept servants around him. They'd never have admitted a Hip Singer. The tongs always meet on neutral turf at the Port Arthur restaurant."

I gave myself a facetious reminder never to go and eat there in case a gun battle broke out around me and I grinned. I suppose one has to make light in the middle of tension. But then I considered what he had just said.

"If Mr. Lee was sleeping on the roof, might it not have been possible to gain access from the roof of a nearby building?" As soon as I said the words I realized that once again I should probably have kept quiet. Now I was actually putting into his head a way to pin the crime on Bo Kei. And if he did, I couldn't save her without admitting that I knew that she was safely in the settlement house. I've always liked to appear clever, I suppose, or at least to prove I'm equal to any man. It's one of my failings.

He looked surprised. "You think that's possible? That never occurred to me. You might be right. You hear that, O'Byrne. The young lady suggests it might have been possible to access the roof from another building."

"Have to have been a darned good jumper," O'Byrne said.

I knew it could be done, but this time I said nothing.

"Let's take a look, anyway," the captain said. He paused outside the Golden Dragon Emporium and looked up and down the street, which still remained unnaturally empty. "Where is everybody, for God's sake?" he demanded. "O'Byrne, go and round up someone who can interpret for me. I want to question the old woman and also the servants when Hanratty brings them in. They'll sure as hell all claim that they can't speak English."

"I'll do my best, sir," the constable said, looking dubiously at all those closed and shuttered doors.

"Start with On Leong headquarters," the captain said. "There has to be someone inside and they'd lose face if they didn't come to the aid of a top man like Lee Sing Tai. Remind them of that."

O'Byrne sighed as if he suspected it wasn't going to be an easy task. Captain Kear turned and stomped up the steps to Lee's apartment. The wailing had stopped and the place was now eerily silent. The old woman was no longer on the sofa. Captain Kear started up the next flight of stairs and I followed, having not been told I couldn't. This flight opened onto a landing with several doors. One of them was open, revealing a large and ornate bed beyond.

"He definitely slept on the roof last night, did he?" I asked. "Not in his bedroom?"

"How would I know?" the captain said shortly. "When I got here the front door was open as you see it and there was only that hideous old crone making a racket on the sofa. There was no way of getting through to her."

So the wife was already wailing when Captain Kear got here. He wasn't the bringer of the bad news. That meant that the whole neighborhood had heard about Lee's death and everyone was lying low before the police arrived. And where did Bobby Lee fit into this? Had he been around and also quietly slipped away when he heard the news?

As Captain Kear started up the next flight of stairs, I nipped across the hall to take a look at that bedroom. It was as overfurnished and as ornate as the living room downstairs had been—the huge carved mahogany bed, cabinets, a vast wardrobe, and in one corner a shrine, containing a statue of a goddess with more arms than necessary. There were sticks of incense in holders around it and a strange, cloyingly sweet smell lingered in the room, making me want to sneeze. I backed out hastily and hurried to catch up with the captain.

CHAPTER SEVENTEEN

A strong breeze was blowing as I came out onto the roof, bringing in more ominous clouds from the south. It really did seem as if it was going to rain and spoil Sid's party decorations. There was a flat area of roof ahead of me, bordered to the right by a brick wall where it joined the much taller On Leong building. A brass bedstead was the only item of furniture on the flat part of the roof, and the bed-sheets flapped in the wind. Captain Kear was prowling the perimeter, moving distinctly warily and peering down at intervals.

"Couldn't access it from here," he was muttering. "Nor from here."

He made his way down the edge of the roof that over-looked Pell Street, where Lee had fallen to his death, then reached the back of the building where there was a gap be-tween this building and the next. He paused. "I suppose it would be possible for a fit person with plenty of guts to jump across here," he said, "or to have brought a plank to walk across. Okay, when O'Byrne gets here, I'll have him find out who owns that building and how easy it is to get up to their roof."

While he peered down and muttered to himself, I was noticing something quite different. The tar on the roof had become soft in the heat. There were distinct footprints near the edge of the roof—some of them small and dainty, but another set larger, and with deep indentations, like a work-ingman or laborer's hobnailed boots.

The small feet could be explained, of course, as Bo Kei had told me herself that she had fled this way. But I could detect that same print facing in both directions—coming and going, so to speak. Had she reached the edge, changed her mind about attempting that formidable leap, retreated, thought it over, then finally plucked up courage to do it? All possible, but for a policeman looking for clues it would spell out that she came, killed Lee, and then left by the same route. Of course I knew that she had a perfect alibi for the crime—she was safely locked away in the settlement house on Eliza-beth Street.

And as for the large hobnailed boots—who could they possibly belong to? Most of the Chinese I had seen wore soft cotton slippers, and they worked in laundries or restaurants or apparently cigar factories—no place where heavy boots would be needed. And the footprints were large too—when the Chinese men I had seen had been smaller than me. There was no way of knowing when the big prints had been made, but it would seem to be recently, judging by the lack of dust and grime over them, compared to other areas of the roof.

I joined Captain Kear and peered down over the edge. It was a long way down, but I'd developed a good head for heights, clambering on clifftops on the Irish coast as a child. I could see the fire escape on the next building. That was the way Bo Kei had escaped. She must have felt desperate to have attempted it. Even the climb from the end of the fire escape to the ground looked daunting to me.

"There doesn't seem to be a door opening onto that roof over there," Captain Kear said. "I don't see how anyone could get up there. And as for taking that leap across—well, those Chinese with their little short legs would have a hard time doing that. And I wouldn't want to try it myself. No, let's as-sume that our killer gained access by another means—maybe climbed in via one of the balconies. I expect they keep the windows open on hot nights, and if the bodyguards down be-low weren't completely vigilant or they don't work at night, then maybe a daring kind of guy could climb up the carving on the side of the building and in through the balcony."

"Then that would rule out the missing bride, wouldn't it?" I said. "A woman out alone on the street—especially a Chinese woman—would surely have been noticed."

"That's true enough." He paced around the roof, head down like Sherlock Holmes, hoping to find a clue of some sort. He straightened up and pointed excitedly. "Look at those small footprints. Your runaway bride, huh? She did come this way, after all."

"If she lived in this house, then she might have been up on the roof at any time," I pointed out. "She probably slept up here and she might have wandered around at times."

"Not near the edge like that. It's not natural."

"She might have been looking for a way to escape."

"Hey, would you look at that—I was right!" He pointed excitedly at the adjoining rooftop. "See that. It looks like a scrap of white fabric, caught on the brickwork. What's the betting she tore her dress when she jumped or climbed across."

"That could just as easily be a scrap of laundry that blew away in the breeze," I said. "Besides, this doesn't make sense. If the young woman fled and can't be found, do you really think she'd risk coming back to the place she fled from? And do you really think a delicate little Chinese girl would climb up there and make that leap? I know I wouldn't."

He sucked in a breath and nodded, grudgingly. "Yeah, you have a point there, Miss Murphy. I'd sure like to make her the one who killed the old guy. Perfect motive. Shipped from her homeland against her will. Doesn't want to marry him, so the only way out is to kill him. That would satisfy the tongs nicely."

"I'm sure there are other people with a good motive," I said.

He looked at me strangely. "You seem mighty keen to prove it's not a girl you've never even met."

"I'm just trying to think things through logically," I said, trying to keep my face from turning red and my expression suitably distant. "And logic tells me that a delicate young girl wouldn't want to come back here once she'd fled and certainly wouldn't have the strength to kill a man and hurl him down to the street."

He paused long enough to take this in; then he said, "We need to find her anyway. Maybe she can shed some light on this business."

"She's been gone a week now," I said. "She could be anywhere—miles away."

"When O'Byrne gets back, he can take down her particulars. And we have her photograph downstairs. We'll put out a bulletin for her. It should be easy enough to spot a Chinese woman. Not too many of them in New York, are there?"

"If she hasn't already left New York," I said.

"Then someone will have spotted her on a train. We'll find her, don't you worry. Ten to one she paid someone to do the dirty deed for her—those bigger footprints, maybe."

"Paid someone? She'd just arrived from China. How would she have gotten her hands on any money?" I demanded.

"Stole it from the old guy. Stole something and pawned it."

"I've already tried all the pawnshops," I said. "She hasn't pawned anything."

"You're a thorough little thing, I'll give you that," he said. "Too bad you're not a man. I could use you at the precinct."

"You already have some female detectives," I said. "Mrs. Goodwin is a friend of mine."

"They are just glorified matrons," he said. "They might be useful at times, but the last thing we want is women on the force."

I was wise enough not to pursue this subject. Captain Kear and I were not going to see eye to eye about women.

"Where the devil is O'Byrne with that interpreter?" he snapped. "Surely he can find one damned person who can translate for us?"

Again I was about to chide him for his offensive language in front of a woman, but thought better of it. I had been so used to Daniel, who always watched his language in front of me and apologized if he uttered a curse word by mistake.

Clearly this captain was not Daniel's equal in refinement or intellect. Standing on that windswept rooftop in this alien part of the city, a feeling of longing for Daniel swept through me. I was so glad this case was over and I wouldn't have to deceive him when I saw him again.

Captain Kear had gone ahead of me to the stairwell and began to descend. I hurried to catch up with him. As we went down into the darkness, we heard feet coming up from the floor below.

"Ah, that will be O'Byrne now," he said. "Up here, man," he called. "Have you got us an interpreter yet?"

Instead we heard loud commands barked in Chinese and Bobby Lee's face appeared, coming up the stairs toward us.

CHAPTER EIGHTEEN

Bobby Lee recoiled in surprise when he saw the policeman.

"*Wah!* What happening here? What you doing in my father's house? You got search warrant?"

"Hello, Bobby. Haven't seen you around for a while," Captain Kear said pleasantly. "I take it you haven't heard the news yet?"

"News? What news? I just came from Brooklyn. Is this a raid?"

"No raid, Bobby. I'm sorry to have to tell you that Mr. Lee is dead."

"What? How he die? Heart attack?"

"He fell from the roof."

I was watching his face. He seemed shocked enough, but the moment I saw him, it struck me that he, of anyone, had a good motive for killing Lee Sing Tai. He might well be able to convince an American court that he was the rightful son and heir. And if the bride was returned to Mr. Lee and had produced a real son, then he'd stand to lose everything. As Frederick had pointed out, he could even be sent back to China.

"He fell from roof?" He shook his head violently. "Not possible. He don't like heights. He would never go near the edge of roof. Never look down."

"His bed is up there," Captain Kear said. "Maybe he walked in his sleep and tripped over the edge."

Bobby Lee considered this, then shook his head again. "Walk in sleep? No! He not fall," he said. "Someone push him. Someone kill him. Hip Sing do this. They been waiting to get even."

"Let's not jump to conclusions, Bobby," Captain Kear said. "We don't want to start another tong war unnecessarily, do we? If there's out-and-out fighting, then your businesses suffer as much as theirs. And you'd be high on their list to be assassinated first."

Bobby was scowling. "You are supposed to look after us. How this man get to my father, huh? How come police no see? He have servants. He have bodyguards. And his wife— what about wife? Or new bride? What does this bride say, huh? Ah, so. I see now. Maybe she kill him."

"What makes you think that?"

"She don't like it here. She don't want to be his concubine. She want to go home."

"His new bride is missing and until a few minutes ago we couldn't get any sense out of the old wife," Captain Kear said with a note of superiority in his voice.

"New wife missing? When this happen?" Bobby asked.

I realized with some satisfaction that Lee Sing Tai had kept this news from his paper son. Maybe wives were supposed to keep to their own quarters, so Bobby hadn't noticed anything was wrong—which would make his motive even stronger. He thought the new wife was still around and might conceive a son at any moment.

"A few days ago, Bobby. This young lady has been looking for her."

He stood aside to reveal me, standing in the darkness a few steps above him.

Bobby gave me an incredulous look. "Her? That's what she tell you she's been doing—looking for my father's bride? She came to see my father. Then she comes to give him special message, but she won't give message to me. Maybe someone pay her to spy in our house, see how best to kill my father." His voice had risen angrily as he spoke. He tried to push past Kear to get at me. "Make her tell truth."

"Let's go down to the living room, shall we?" Captain Kear held him up and forcibly turned him around. "There is no point in jumping to any conclusions at the moment. And if you can find the number one wife and persuade her to come down to talk with us, then maybe we can hear what she has to say on the matter."

"Where houseboy go?" Bobby asked.

"You tell me. Ran off before we got here," Kear said as he took my elbow to escort me down the stairs. "How well do you know the servants, Bobby? Are they trustworthy? Been with Mr. Lee a while?"

"Cook been with my father many years," he said. "Houseboy just come last year, but he is son of On Leong man who work for my father in cigar factory. Good man, so must be good son."

"One doesn't always signify the other," Captain Kear said. I felt that this was being directed personally at Bobby Lee. The captain didn't think much of him. "And why did they run away if they are innocent of any crime?"

"Chinese always scared when police come," Bobby said. "They scared police will say they did it and not bother to find real killer. Police think one Chinese look like one another and what does it matter which one they throw in jail? That's what most men in Chinatown think."

We reached the living room. Captain Kear indicated I should sit on the sofa and took the big chair himself.

"Take a seat, Bobby," he said, waving graciously at an uncomfortable-looking upright wooden chair.

Bobby scowled as he perched on the chair.

"Okay, Bobby, now let's talk about what happened to your father," Captain Kear said. "Do you know anything that can shed some light on this? Can you think of anyone who would want to kill Lee Sing Tai?"

"Hip Sing, of course," Bobby said quickly. "They would be happy if no more Lee Sing Tai in On Leong. He control too much of Chinatown."

"Do you really think they'd be stupid enough to risk starting the war again right now?" the captain asked. "And if they were going to kill Lee, do you think this is the way they'd choose to do it?"

Bobby pursed his lips, thinking. "Okay. Maybe not. Push man off roof is coward's way. They would shoot him or stab him in his bed and leave him there to be found."

"Exactly my thoughts," Kear said. "So what about other rivals—rivals within On Leong, for example, or business rivals?"

"Members of On Leong know that Lee Sing Tai is good for them and good for Chinatown," he said. "They do what he say. Lee Sing Tai only one who does business with white people outside of Chinatown. He important man. Nobody to take his place."

"And business rivals?"

"Business rivals? Lee Sing Tai control business in Chinatown, except for Hip Sing properties."

"So you're saying he had no rivals who might want to kill him to get him out of the way?"

Suddenly Bobby Lee's face lit up. "Ah," he said, waving a knowing finger at Captain Kear. "I know who did this. Of course. It was Frederick Lee."

"Frederick Lee? Another paper son?"

"No, he not son. He was only Lee Sing Tai's employee. His secretary. My father dismiss him yesterday. So maybe Frederick angry that his job has been taken from him and he come back to kill. This would be easy. He knows my father's apartment well. I am sure he has access to keys."

I was now sitting on the edge of my seat. "I'm sure Frederick wouldn't do a thing like that," I said hotly. "He spoke of Mr. Lee with great respect. And he was a quiet, educated man too."

"How come you know Frederick Lee?" Captain Kear asked, looking at me with surprise.

"Lee Sing Tai sent him to find me. He escorted me to Chinatown and looked after me. I was impressed with him."

"Men who have lost their jobs have acted irrationally

before now," Captain Kear said. "Especially Chinamen. They care about losing face more than losing money. So do you know why Frederick Lee was fired by your father, Bobby?"

"I do. He try to touch my father's bride. My father send him to bring his bride to New York and he betray my father's trust."

"That's not what I heard," I said, really angry now. "I heard it was you who tried to force yourself on your father's bride."

Now they were both looking at me suspiciously.

"Who told you this?" Bobby Lee demanded.

I realized I had to tread cautiously here. "Frederick Lee," I said. "I asked him if he had any idea why Bo Kei had run away and he said that she was frightened when Bobby tried to attack her."

Bobby Lee pursed his lips in scorn again. "He lies! Of course he says this, to protect himself. I would not dare to touch bride of my esteemed father."

Captain Kear looked from me to Bobby Lee as if he was trying to decide whom to believe.

"Let's hear what this Frederick Lee has to say for himself, shall we?" he said. "I'll have him brought in right away."

I could read from his expression that he was feeling satisfied. He'd come up with a suspect who would suit everybody and not ruffle any tong feathers. My one thought now was to get back to Patchin Place as soon as possible, so that I could warn Frederick when he came to see me, expecting good news about Bo Kei. But even as this thought formed, another, more worrying idea crept into my head. *Was it possible that this crime had been carried out by Frederick?* A man will do much for a woman he loves, and clearly their lives would be in danger as long as Lee Sing Tai was alive. But his would not have been those large hobnailed footprints on the roof. He was of slender Chinese stature.

I had no chance to consider this further as there was the sound of voices from downstairs and Constable O'Byrne appeared, dragging an indignant Chinese man by the arm.

"I not do anything," the man was saying. "Let go of me."

"You can go home once you've helped out the captain," O'Byrne said. He shoved the man ahead of him into the room. "Here's your interpreter, sir. He's a scribe, so I know he can translate. And we've got On Leong men rounding up the servants. I put the fear of God into them—told them their police protection ends as of now if those men aren't found right away."

"Nice work, Constable." Captain Kear nodded with satisfaction. He pointed at the Chinaman, who stood almost quivering with fright. "You, sit. And you," he turned to Bobby, "go and find the wife and tell her to get down here, or we'll come and question her in her bedroom."

"I can't go up there," Bobby said. "It wouldn't be right."

"Just do it," the captain barked. "Or it's not Hip Sing you've got to worry about, it's Sing Sing. I've enough on you to put you away for years if I wanted, so I suggest you cooperate."

Bobby shot him a look of pure hatred and went upstairs. We heard raised voices, both male and female, and then Bobby returned. "She comes down, but she's not pleased."

"Well, she wouldn't be, would she?" the captain said. "Her old man's dead. What's going to happen to her now? How is she going to survive alone in a country where she can barely speak the language and she can't even go outside? She doesn't have a child to take her in—unless you're going to act the dutiful son, Bobby, and you come here and look after her."

"Of course I look after her," Bobby said. 'I know my duty as son. I will take over from my father and do what he expects of me."

I bet you will, I thought. The businesses and the power in the tong. It was probably just beginning to dawn on Bobby Lee that he was now a very rich man.

"So where would we find Frederick Lee, Bobby?" the captain asked.

Bobby got to his feet. "I do not know where he lives, but my father will have his address in his cabinet. He have particulars on all employees."

He crossed the room to the ornate ebony cabinet in the

corner. There was a little gold key in the lock, which he turned. He opened the carved doors to reveal a series of little drawers inside, each one inlaid with mother-of-pearl designs of animals and flowers. It was truly a wonderful piece of furniture, the likes of which I'd never seen before, and I gazed at it in admiration. Bobby Lee pulled open one of the drawers, then recoiled. "*Wah*. What happen here? Someone has been here. Someone has touched my father's papers."

CHAPTER NINETEEN

C aptain Kear went over to the cabinet. From where I was sitting I could see that the drawer was hastily stuffed with pieces of crumpled pieces of paper. Bobby opened another drawer, then another. All were in disarray.

"Hold it there, Bobby," Kear said. "Don't touch anything else. There might be useful fingerprints. So these drawers were normally neat and tidy, were they?"

"My father keep everything just so. He could find any record in seconds. All in order. He liked order. Someone was looking for something here."

"The question is whether he found it," the captain said. "And whether it was the reason old Lee was killed. When we've dusted for fingerprints, you and I will go through this cabinet."

"No use to you," Bobby said scathingly. "All in Chinese."

"That's why you're going to read it for me, and we'll bring along that interpreter fellow to make sure you're reading exactly what it says."

I opened my mouth to say something, then closed it again. Sticking out of one of those drawers I had seen a very Western scrawled signature. But then the captain would find it for himself later, wouldn't he?

"Knowing the way that your father did business, my guess is that he had quite a few items that someone might kill for," he said. "We know there was protection money, maybe even blackmail."

He took out a handkerchief and carefully closed the cabinet again. Then he removed the key, wrapped it in his handkerchief, and tucked it into his top pocket. "Perhaps he had something incriminating on Frederick Lee—something he wouldn't return when he fired Frederick. Well I want this Frederick brought in right now. O'Byrne. Go and find him."

"Find him, sir? How do I do that if I don't know where to start looking?"

"If he was employed by Lee Sing Tai, you can bet your boots he's an On Leong member and they'll have his address in their files. And his family details too. He might be hiding out with a clan member. They all band together when one's in trouble, don't they?" Captain Kear sat down again. "Go on, then. Jump to it."

"Very good, sir." O'Byrne stifled the sigh. He was a big red-faced Irishman and all this running around on a muggy morning was not to his liking.

"Oh, and on your way send someone to headquarters and tell them we need to have the cabinet dusted for fingerprints."

O'Byrne was clearly wishing that the captain had selected another constable to accompany him. He nodded, then we heard his big boots going down the stairs.

"Now where's the wife got to?" Captain Kear demanded. "Didn't you make it clear that I wanted to speak to her? Go up and tell her that if she doesn't come down, I'm coming up to her bedroom to get her."

Bobby stood up very reluctantly.

"And you can start giving me the details on the missing woman, Miss Murphy." He glanced up at me as he removed a small pad from his top pocket.

"As to that, I know little more than you do—her name is Bo Kei, and you've seen the photograph I was given."

"And where exactly have you been looking for her?" he asked. "If she's been gone for a week you haven't been too successful, have you?"

"I was only told about her the other day," I said. "And New York is a big place."

"You mentioned missions—was there any reason you started looking there?"

"I thought she wouldn't know where to go in a strange city and she would certainly be frightened to stray far from Chinatown. And you know that the missionaries are always prowling around, looking for converts, so they would definitely take in a young woman alone on the streets."

"So which of these missions did you visit?"

Fortunately at this moment we heard groans from the hallway and Lee Sing Tai's number one wife appeared, hobbling painfully on those little stumps. She was now wearing white, and appeared to have white powder on her face, making her look like a walking ghost. She made her way forward, using the furniture to support herself, while Bobby Lee stood in the doorway, not offering to help her. Captain Kear had risen and offered her the big chair. She shook her head. She wasn't going to sit in her husband's chair, even if he was dead. Instead she came toward me. I moved along the sofa and she sat beside me.

"Mrs. Lee," the captain said, "I am sorry about your husband. I know this is upsetting for you. I hope you can help us." He turned to the translator, who presumably repeated this in Chinese. I wondered if Mrs. Lee actually understood any English and was playing dumb. She had certainly eavesdropped on my conversations with her husband. The old woman looked at him suspiciously, then asked a sharp question.

"She says how can she help you? It is other people who should be helping her," the interpreter said.

"We want to know if you have any ideas who might have killed your husband?"

The interpreter repeated the words. Her eyes shot open and it was clear that until now she had considered his death an accident. She rattled off an angry string of Chinese.

"She says how can anyone have killed him? He was asleep in his own bed. His houseboy sleeps at the bottom of the stairs. The front door and the bottom door are always locked. There is no way into the house."

"Just supposing someone did find a way in—any ideas who that might have been?"

She listened, then considered this and replied. "That young woman," the interpreter translated. "She must have returned and done this awful deed."

"The new bride, you mean?" the captain asked gently.

She nodded. "She did not want to be here," she said through the interpreter. "When she finds that I am number one wife, she does not want to obey me. She is lazy. She does not want to work. I say to my husband—this one is no good. Send her away. But he wants a son very much. I tried to give him a son for many years, but I failed him." And she looked down at her hands as if embarrassed at what she had just said. I noticed that she had thin, wrinkled hands topped with long, claw-like nails, so the effect was hen's feet with rings on them. Then she looked up again, defiantly this time, and spat out more words with venom. "He has brought in other women before, but none of them can give him a son. I tell him he is being foolish to bring in these girls. Spend our money for nothing. He is an old man now. Too old to have a son anymore."

"If it really was this girl he brought in from China, how do you think she found a way into the house to kill your husband with nobody seeing her?" the captain asked.

"How did she find a way out when she vanished? The doors were locked. Our men were down below in the street, but she managed to run away." She looked up at him. "Maybe she is a demon—a being with supernatural powers. I wouldn't be surprised at this. I did not trust her from the moment I saw her face. It was an evil face. When I looked at how her eyes were formed, I knew that she was evil."

As she spoke, I realized one thing was very clear. Bo Kei was absolutely right when she had said that wife number one had not welcomed her into the house. And I found myself wondering if she was angry with her husband for bringing in a succession of young women, reminding her that she was old and barren, and spending their money needlessly, as she had pointed out. Had she finally decided that she'd had enough of living like this? After all, who had a better opportunity to push Lee Sing Tai off the roof than the woman who presumably shared his bed?

"Supposing it wasn't this young woman," Captain Kear insisted. "Can you think of anyone else who might want your husband dead?"

"Hip Sing," the interpreter translated for her with vehemence. "They have already made several attempts on his life. They will stop at nothing until they have killed him and destroyed On Leong. This is their sworn duty."

"Anyone else?" the captain insisted. "Has anyone been to visit your husband at the apartment recently? Anyone you didn't know?"

The interpreter looked at her expectantly. She shook her head. "I am not invited to be present when my husband does business. I know my place and stay away."

But you listen behind the drapes, I wanted to say.

Without warning she stood up. A great flood of Chinese preceded the translation. "Why do we sit here, discussing who might have killed my husband? Maybe it was an accident. Maybe nobody killed him. What does it matter? He is dead, isn't he? Nothing will bring him back. And I am left alone. What is to become of me, huh? Who will look after me? He promised he would make money in America and then take me back home to our village. Now I am stuck here and alone."

"You have young Bobby here," the captain said. "He's already volunteered to take care of you."

The interpreter dutifully translated.

"Him?" She looked at him, her lip curled like a dog's. "He is good for nothing. He bleeds us dry. It would not surprise me if he hadn't pushed my husband off the roof."

"How can you say that!" Bobby Lee demanded. "I treat him with the same respect I give to my real father. I obey him. I make his businesses prosper for him. I even do his dirty work for him. And I tell you that you do not need to worry. I will prove to you that I will take care of you as if you were my mother."

"Pipe down, everyone," Captain Kear said. "All this noise is giving me a headache. I'm not concerned with what's going to happen now. I want to know what happened on that rooftop, and believe me, I'll get to the bottom of it."

"You will see that Frederick Lee came back here for revenge," Bobby said. "Perhaps he and the girl have planned this together. Perhaps this woman here is also part of the plot." And he pointed at me.

"Don't be ridiculous," I said. "I am a well-respected private investigator. Mr. Lee hired me to find this runaway girl. It's as simple as that."

"Then why you not find her yet?" Bobby Lee demanded.

"I had only just begun to look," I said. "Why did your father not find her for five days before he hired me? I'm sure he had plenty of men at his disposal."

I shifted uneasily on the hard seat of the sofa. I was feeling increasingly uncomfortable about being here, not just physically but mentally too. I longed to be back in the security of Patchin Place. And I still wanted to meet Frederick Lee before Captain Kear's men caught up with him.

"Do you need me any longer?" I asked. "I've told you all I can about the missing girl and I'd like to go home."

"So I can't persuade you to go on looking for the girl?"

"The man who hired me is dead," I said. "As far as I'm concerned, she is free to go wherever she wants to."

"I'll need to know where to find you," the captain said.

I opened my purse. "I have a card in here somewhere," I said, reluctant to hand my card to a policeman, who would take it back to a precinct where Daniel had been observed only two days ago. I could just picture his sharp eyes picking out my name. "But at the moment I am not living at home. My house is being redecorated, so let me write down the address of my neighbors for you."

Loud noises from down below announced that someone was coming up the stairs. The houseboy and an older Chinese man in cotton blouse and baggy pants were muscled into the room by a couple of unsavory-looking characters, all of them complaining and yelling loudly.

"These men have brought you houseboy and cook," the interpreter said.

"Tell them 'Thank you,'" Captain Kear said.

He did so. They waited and muttered something to the interpreter.

"They expect their reward for finding these men," the interpreter said cautiously.

"Tell them they should consider themselves lucky I'm not questioning them as suspects in this," the captain replied. "And then tell them to beat it before I change my mind."

The interpreter translated, most unwillingly by the look of it, and the two men renewed their protestations while the houseboy started wailing.

"Quiet!" Captain Kear shouted. "Or I'll arrest the lot of you."

"What the devil's going on up there?" a voice boomed. "Are you up there, Kear?"

I recognized the voice instantly.

CHAPTER TWENTY

I looked around the room, like a trapped animal. I even wondered if I could run up the stairs and successfully make that jump across to the next building, if I hitched my skirts high enough. But even as thoughts of flight went through my head, Daniel came bounding up the stairs, around the screen, and into the room.

"What's going on in here, Kear?" he demanded. "Some idiot comes rushing into headquarters babbling about dead Chinamen and tong wars starting again, and then one of your men arrives to request the police doctor and photographer and fingerprint kit, so I thought I'd better come down and take a look for myself."

"It's okay, Sullivan. It's all under control," Captain Kear said.

"That's not what it sounded like from downstairs," Daniel said. "It sounded like chaos to me."

"It's just a routine Chinatown murder. Nothing unusual. Besides, it's Sixth Precinct business and I'm handling it." Captain Kear gave Daniel a long, hard stare.

"Then why were they babbling about tong wars starting up again?" Daniel asked. He looked around the room. "If this thing is going to get out of hand, we need to stop it right now and if you need extra men to do that—"

He stopped in midsentence. "What in God's name are you doing here?" he demanded.

"You know Miss Murphy?" Captain Kear asked.

"Know her? In two weeks' time she's going to be my wife."

"Well, I'm damned. You omitted to mention that little fact, Miss Murphy. A husband-and-wife detective team—how convenient." Captain Kear grinned. "So is she going to help you solve your cases, Sullivan?"

"Miss Murphy has told you she's an investigator?" Daniel asked.

"She has. In fact she was working for the man who has just been killed."

"Working for him?" Daniel was now glaring at me.

"Daniel, that's not how it sounds," I began, but he held up a warning hand. "We'll discuss this later, Molly. So who was this man?"

"Lee Sing Tai. I take it you've heard of him."

"Lee Sing Tai—oh, Mr. Lee and I are well acquainted. Protection racket, drugs, prostitution, and the On Leong tong. Not a very nice man, was he, our Mr. Lee? I'm just surprised he lived as long as he did. So someone finally put a bullet through him, did they?"

"Pushed him off his own roof, actually," Captain Kear said.

"And how did anyone manage to get into his house to throw him off the roof?" Daniel demanded. "Don't these On Leong types usually keep a pack of bodyguards around?"

"I've sent someone to find the bodyguards," Captain Kear said, "but these two are the servants that have just been brought in. They'd run off before I got here."

"Run off before their master was killed or after?" Daniel asked, looking at the still-trembling men.

"Well?" Captain Kear barked. "You heard the policeman. What have you two got to say for yourselves? Do you realize that by running off I'm going to think that you killed your master?"

This was duly translated and a great wail came from the houseboy.

"I no do this terrible thing," he said in English. "It must be demon who do it. How he get in master's house? I sleep on my mat in hallway, same as always. Nobody come past me. This I swear."

"And your master slept on the roof?" Captain Kear asked.

"On hot nights."

"Why didn't you sleep up there beside him?"

"He no like me beside him. He say he need me to guard hallway—like watchdog," the boy said. "I swear nobody got into master's house. All doors were locked, same as always."

"And what about you?" Daniel pointed at the cook. "Who are you?"

"This man is the cook," the interpreter said after the cook had given a long speech with much hand waving. "He says he sleeps in little space behind kitchen. Far from front of house. He does not hear anything all night. This morning he gets up and starts to make breakfast when houseboy comes and says that master is dead and policemen are coming. They are frightened that policemen will think they did this terrible thing, so they run off."

"Not very bright, was it?" Daniel said drily. "By that very act you make yourselves appear guilty. And who are these other people?"

"I Mr. Lee's son," Bobby said. "And this his number one wife."

"Paper son," Captain Kear corrected. "Bobby Lee. You may have come across that name too."

"Ah, yes, Bobby Lee. Familiar name from the last tong war. You've been out of the picture for a while, haven't you, Bobby?"

"I run Father's factory in Brooklyn," Bobby said. "I do what Father want, like good son."

"I'm sure you do." Daniel smirked, then pointed at the other men who had now moved off to one side, hoping to slip around the screen unnoticed. "And what about these two? Are they the bodyguards?"

"They are On Leong men. They found the cook and houseboy for us."

"Nice work, boys," Daniel said. "Did you tip them yet?"

When the captain frowned but didn't answer, Daniel reached into his pocket and handed them some coins, which the men accepted with cupped hands, bowing low.

"You can go now," Daniel said. If I hadn't felt so sick and scared, I would have been amused by the way that Daniel had simply taken over against Captain Kear's wishes. It was clear in police hierarchy that he was the superior officer.

One of the men muttered something in Chinese. Daniel looked at the interpreter.

"This man asks if Hip Sing did this terrible thing like everyone is saying."

"Definitely not," Captain Kear snapped the answer. "You can tell them this does not look like the work of Hip Sing and we are pretty sure who the culprit was. He will soon be arrested. You will see that American justice is fair and swift."

"So you've already figured this one out, have you?" Daniel asked.

"I think we're well on our way," Captain Kear said. "Old Lee had just had a new bride brought in from China."

"A new bride? For him? At his age?"

"It wouldn't be the first time," Captain Kear said. "They're vain, these old Chinamen, and money buys anything over there."

"So where is she?"

"She's run off and your young lady here, Miss Murphy, was hired to find her and bring her back. And then there's Lee's former secretary, Frederick Lee, who was fired yesterday for putting his hands on the new bride. Either one is a good suspect—not involved with the tongs in any way. In fact I'm inclined to think that they planned it together. They certainly had time to get very pally on their train trip across Canada together. And he's young and she's young and Lee was definitely past his prime."

"Have you spoken with Frederick Lee yet?"

"I've sent men to bring him in for questioning."

"And where's the body now?"

"Still lying in the street. I'm waiting for the doctor and

the morgue wagon to arrive. I thought I'd question the people in the household and get a jump on things while we're waiting."

Daniel nodded and I realized that the other man was seeking his approval. "What did you need the fingerprint powder for? You think there might be prints on his back from the man who pushed him?"

Captain Kear scowled and Daniel laughed. "I'm pulling your leg, man. Where's your sense of humor?"

Captain Kear's expression indicated that he didn't find it very funny. "That cabinet in the corner appears to have been tampered with," he said primly. "That's why I requested the fingerprint powder."

"Tampered with?"

"Papers rifled through and out of order as though someone was looking for something in a hurry."

"Have you been through it yet?"

"Give me a chance, I've only been here half an hour at the most. Besides, it's all in Chinese characters. I'll need someone to read it to me."

"Then let's leave it for later. I suggest we station your constable on duty to keep an eye on the place and go and take a look at the body. Where is it?"

"Around the corner on Pell Street. But let me remind you again that this is my precinct, Sullivan. My case. You're not just coming in to take over from me, even if you are officially my superior."

"Nobody wants to step on your toes, Kear," Daniel said easily. "I'm just doing what I can to help—throwing in a little expertise so that we don't find a full-fledged tong war on our hands again. You have to admit that you're still wet behind the ears when it comes to detective work, right?"

"But I do know all about the streets around here. I know how things operate."

"I'm well aware that you know how things operate, Kear," Daniel said. The two men stared at each other like dogs who have just encountered each other unexpectedly. There was a tension I didn't quite understand. "But we're wasting time.

We've got a body on a busy street and we don't want it lying around all day, do we? Where's your man to guard the room?"

"I sent him to find Frederick Lee."

"Don't you have more than one man working on this?"

"Of course, but I've a team of them keeping the crowd away from the body, and the others are rounding up suspects." Captain Kear got to his feet. The tension was now palpable.

"You understand?" he barked at the people in the room. "Mrs. Lee should go back to her bedroom. Bobby, I want you to leave the place, and nobody touches anything in here at all. Understand that, boy?" He gestured at the wide-eyed houseboy. "No cleaning, no dusting, nothing. You stay in kitchen with the cook and don't touch anything or I'll have you locked up."

The interpreter translated the instructions into Chinese. Mrs. Lee said something.

"She wants to know if she can have her breakfast," he said. "And she wants to know when she can see her husband's body."

"She can have her breakfast if she wants it and we'll let her know when the body can be released to the funeral parlor."

Mrs. Lee rattled off another string of Chinese.

"He has to go back to China," the interpreter said. "His bones have to be returned to the place of his ancestors."

Bobby Lee obviously said something reassuring to her and reached out to touch her, but she shrank away as if burned. He shrugged and went ahead of us down the stairs. As we came out into the street the wind had grown even stronger, sending papers and refuse swirling and making the lanterns hanging on the balconies swing. I hoped that Sid's paper lanterns were surviving.

"The heat's broken at last, thank God," Captain Kear said. Then he pointed down the street. "Ah, here's O'Byrne now. Did you find Frederick Lee?"

"Yes, sir." He was panting as if he'd been running hard. "We found him, about to leave his rooms, and you know what? It looks as if he was packing a suitcase. And there were train timetables lying on his table."

"Where is he now?"

"At his place. Twenty-seven Park Street. I took a couple of On Leong men with me and they are guarding him, sir. I thought you might want to examine his room as well as question him."

The captain nodded with satisfaction. "Good thinking, O'Byrne. I don't suppose you found he was hiding the girl, did you?"

"No sign of a young woman there, Captain. At least no obvious sign."

"It will be interesting to see if she's been there recently—a nice long hair or two, or did he wear the queue?"

"He is only half Chinese," Bobby Lee said. "He behaves like an American."

Captain Kear looked at him. "Off you go then, Bobby. I'll be able to get in touch with you through On Leong if I need you when we go through the cabinet or need to ask you more questions. But don't think of going back to the apartment before that. You won't be allowed in. Hear that, O'Byrne. I want you to stay here and keep an eye on this place. You might want to seal off the living room and the master's bedroom. Don't let the occupants touch anything and don't let this one back inside."

"Very good, sir." O'Byrne looked relieved that his next task didn't involve running around the city.

Daniel had pulled out his pocket watch from his waistcoat. "You'd better question Frederick Lee before he bribes the On Leong types to let him slip away. And if you want my advice, bring him to the precinct for questioning. Shut him up overnight. There's nothing like a night in the cells to get the truth out of a suspect. You can take him to the Tombs if you like. I'll let them know."

"Kind of you," Captain Kear said in a way that might have been sarcastic.

"And put out a city-wide bulletin to look for the girl. You have a description, do you?"

"Miss Murphy has just given me a photograph." Captain Kear held up the package.

"Excellent. She should be easy enough to find then, if she hasn't skipped town. In my experience nothing works better than playing one suspect against the other. If Frederick Lee thinks we've got her in the Tombs, I guarantee he'll talk."

"Very well." Captain Kear looked long and hard at Daniel, then said, "And I take it you'll know where to find Miss Murphy, if we need to ask her any further questions."

CHAPTER TWENTY-ONE

It was a good parting blow as Captain Kear walked away and I saw Daniel's mouth twitch. The moment we were out of earshot Daniel grabbed my arm and spun me to face him.

"What the devil do you think you were doing?" he demanded. "Do you realize what you've done? You've made me the butt of jokes in the police department for years to come, not to mention starting up the tong wars again single-handedly."

He was shouting loudly and his voice echoed back from the tall tenements and the empty street. He was glaring at me, his eyes blazing. "Did you or did you not promise me that you'd give up this ridiculous nonsense?"

I decided that this time fighting was not going to get me anywhere. "I did promise, Daniel, and I'm sorry. I never intended to get involved in something like this. Only the man who came to see me was so persistent and said his employer wouldn't take no for an answer and would pay me generously, so I went to see him, just out of curiosity, and to start with all he asked me to do was to locate a piece of jade jewelry that had gone missing. That seemed like a harmless enough commission, didn't it?" The words came flying out in a torrent. "It was only later I found out that he was really looking for a missing woman."

"And yet you continued to look for her." His eyes were still blazing.

"You're very attractive when you're angry, you know," I said, attempting to lighten the mood.

"Don't try to make light of this, Molly. It's a very serious matter," Daniel said. "You betrayed my trust. You broke a promise. What sort of start to a marriage is that?"

All right, I had tried being meek and it hadn't worked. My usual fighting spirit could not be suppressed any longer. "Maybe if you hadn't insisted that I stay at your mother's house, sewing undergarments all day and hearing over and over how I didn't measure up to any of your other lady friends, I wouldn't have been so anxious for a little excitement," I said, my own voice rising now.

"That's beside the point," he began, then stopped. "My mother actually told you that you didn't measure up to my other lady friends?"

"All the time. In a very subtle and genteel way, of course. 'Dear Miss So-and-so. Daniel was so fond of her when they were growing up and such a good family too. And the way you sew, your poor children are going to run around in rags.'"

"She said that?"

"I didn't mean to tell you," I said. "But you pushed me into a corner. That's why I couldn't wait to escape. But I'm sorry I took this stupid case. I'm sorry I deceived you. If you want to know the reason I was at Mr. Lee's house this morning, it was to hand him a letter tendering my resignation. Only I arrived to find Captain Kear in charge and Mr. Lee lying dead in the street."

"A tricky business, Molly," he said, speaking quietly now. "You know nothing of the way things work in Chinatown. This Lee was a wily old fox and a powerful figure in one of the tongs. Until a year ago there was the most awful bloodshed on a daily basis—men gunned down as they ate in restaurants, firebombs thrown into shops. We worked hard to bring about a peace that was beneficial to both sides. This death could start the whole thing off again. That's why I felt I had to step in."

He was frowning down at me, like an earnest schoolmaster giving a pupil a stern lecture. "And I really don't want to be known as the police officer whose fiancée started a new tong war."

"Daniel, that's absurd," I said angrily. "I was asked to look for a missing girl. How could that have had anything to do with Mr. Lee being killed?"

"We'll just have to see, won't we?" He started striding out around the corner into Pell Street. "I've always been suspicious of coincidences. Something happened to make a person choose last night to kill Lee Sing Tai, rather than any other night. So the immediate thought that comes to mind is whether the girl realized you were hot on her trail and took the ultimate step not to be returned to the old man."

"I don't believe that," I said.

"Oh. Why not?"

I hesitated, debating whether to tell him that I knew where the girl was. "If she was frightened enough to face being alone in a big city rather than staying where at least she got food and shelter, then I can't see she'd want to risk going back there," I said. "And for another thing, how would a young girl be strong enough to throw a man off the roof?"

"Then Kear was probably on the right track. She and Frederick Lee formed an attachment on their way to New York and he carried out the murder with her help. Let's hope that's how it turns out. At least it will satisfy the tongs."

We reached the corner of Pell. A crowd was still milling around. Daniel turned back to me. "I'm going to take a quick look at the body and then get it moved off the street. We don't want the whole world gawking at it and spreading rumors of tong killings. However, you don't need to come any farther. I will spare you having to look at an unpleasant sight."

"I've already seen the body," I said. "Captain Kear asked me to make a positive identification because none of the Chinese would do so. And when you look at it, take note of the wound to one side of the head. He was obviously struck before he was thrown off the roof. I didn't have a chance to examine the apartment carefully, but I'm sure if you go back there you'll find blood spatters—on the bedding would be my guess."

"Good God," Daniel muttered. He shook his head. "You never fail to astonish me, Molly. No wonder my mother thought you were different. Most other women I know would swoon at the very mention of blood spatters."

I chuckled. "You see, there will be some advantages to having a wife who understands your profession."

"I don't doubt it. Now if I can just persuade that wife to stay home and not go rushing out to solve my cases for me, I'll be happy." He reached out to touch my cheek in a playful half-slap. "Go on, off to home with you, and for mercy's sake, stay well away from any crime scene in the future. This is now in the capable hands of the police."

"Yes, Daniel," I said in my dutiful bride voice. "And don't forget that Sid and Gus are giving a party for me tonight. I'm sure you'll be too busy to attend and it's a costume affair, so I'm sure it wouldn't be your idea of fun, but it would be nice if my friends could at least meet my bridegroom."

"I can't promise anything," he said. "I have enough on my plate already, but given the potential for serious repercussions in this case, I have no alternative but to assign some of my men to assist Captain Kear."

"I take it you don't think much of him?"

"I have my reasons," he said. "I especially have reasons for not giving him carte blanche with a case involving the Chinese tongs." He looked up. "Ah, here's the morgue wagon now. Off you go and enjoy your party."

Then he hurried off, leaving me standing there. I knew I should do as he said and go straight home, but I couldn't. I had been too late to save Frederick Lee, but it would only be a matter of time before they found Bo Kei if every policeman in the city was looking for her. I had to go and warn her immediately. I made my way with all haste to Elizabeth Street. Hermione wasn't on duty and I was surprised to find Sarah coming down the stairs toward me.

"Molly!" she said. "How nice to see you."

"What are you doing here?" I asked. "I thought his lordship had forbidden you from coming here."

"He changed his mind," she said. "He said that he could see how much this work meant to me and it was wrong of him to deprive me of these last weeks of satisfaction, so he would not object as long as I allowed him to escort me. Wasn't that sweet of him?"

"Very understanding," I said, mentally reversing my opinion of Monty as a spoiled, arrogant, and stuck-up Englishman.

"I'll only be helping out occasionally, as there is so much to do for the wedding," she said. "Isn't it incredible how many fittings are needed for a wedding dress that one will only wear once in one's life."

"My mother-in-law is making mine," I said. "I was supposed to be helping but my sewing was so terrible that she banished me to undergarments. I am a hopeless failure, according to her."

Sarah laughed. "Oh, dear. In-laws are not all they should be, are they? Monty's mother looked through her lorgnette at me as if I was something that had crawled under the door. Have you come to see your Chinese girl?"

"Yes, I have."

"She's doing awfully well. In fact they both are. The other girl seems to have a new lease on life since Bo Kei arrived. We thought she wouldn't be long for this world and that the consumption was at a late stage, but now she seems so much brighter that we have hopes she may even recover."

"I'm glad," I said. "May I go up to see Bo Kei?"

"Of course," she said. "She's in the room facing the stairs on the third floor."

"Not with Annie?"

"We're keeping Annie in isolation as much as possible. It wouldn't be wise to have anyone sleeping in a room with her, considering how sick she is. I don't think consumption is horribly contagious, but one can't be sure."

I started up the stairs, hesitated, then made up my mind.

"Sarah, can I be frank with you?" I said, looking up and down the hallway to make sure we were not being overheard. "The police will be searching for Bo Kei. They think she might somehow be involved in a murder that took place last night."

"But that's absurd. She was here last night."

A wave of relief came over me. Of course she had a perfect alibi.

"Would you swear to that? The doors are locked, and nobody comes and goes?"

"Well, no," she said. "Our doors are never locked. We are known to be a haven for battered women and prostitutes escaping from brothels."

"So it would be possible for anyone to enter or leave during the night if they wanted to?"

"I'm afraid it would."

"Oh, dear," I said. "I'm sure she's innocent, but you know what some of the police are like, and she doesn't know anything about life in America. They can probably trick her into confessing anything. Would you be prepared to hide her?"

"Hide her?"

"If the police came to the door, I mean. Would you be prepared to lie and say that she wasn't here? Or hide her away in a cupboard if they wanted to search the place?"

Sarah looked worried. "If I was hiding someone in my own home it would be different," she said. "But I'm just one of many volunteers here. I can't risk the future of this house by lying to the police and harboring a fugitive. They'd shut us down, and then who would do the good work that we do here?"

I did see her point. "Then I've no choice," I said. "I must get her away as quickly as possible. Could you send someone to hail me a cab? I'll go upstairs and get Bo Kei ready. That way, if anyone asks you if she is with you, you can truthfully deny it."

Sarah sighed. "I really think that would be best. But where would you take her?"

"I'll see if Sid and Gus would be prepared to take her in," I said. "If not, then my own house is across the street and nobody's living in it at present. I could hide her there, at least until we decide what to do with her."

Sarah put a hand on my arm. "Is this wise, Molly? You're going to marry a policeman and yet you are deliberately and knowingly going against the law."

"But I don't think she killed anyone, Sarah, and I really don't think she'll get a fair trial. You should have heard that Captain Kear concocting the perfect case against Bo Kei and a young man."

"Captain Kear? Oh, we know all about him. As crooked as they come. He even suggested to us that we pay him protection money. As if we have any spare money."

"So what did he say?"

She smiled. "Luckily one of our workers at the time happened to be the son of the New York state attorney general. It was suggested that he leave us alone."

"It's good to have friends in high places," I said. "But I shouldn't stand around talking. I should remove Bo Kei before the police come looking for her."

"I hope you are not taking too great a risk, Molly. You'll be harboring a fugitive, won't you? You can go to jail for that. And think of the disgrace for your future bridegroom."

I hesitated. What she was saying was actually true. I had already incurred Daniel's wrath once today. Could I knowingly take this risk? But if I didn't, Captain Kear's men would drag her off in no time, and once they had her and Frederick in custody, they wouldn't bother to look any further for the real killer.

"I have to do this," I said. "Sid and Gus have a strong sense of justice. They'll understand and want to help me."

With that I went up the stairs. I tapped on the door and thought I heard scurrying as I entered. Bo Kei was perched warily on the edge of her bed, as if poised for flight, but her face broke into a smile when she saw me.

"Missie Molly?" Bo Kei said. "You have found Frederick for me? You will take us to safety?"

"I'm afraid it's not as easy as that, Bo Kei." I sat down beside her. "Something terrible happened last night. Lee Sing Tai was murdered—pushed off his roof."

"Oh!" She put her hand to her mouth in horror. "Last night? Somebody killed him last night?"

"That's right."

She sat there, hand over her mouth, just staring as if she was taking it in.

"But this is good news for me, isn't it?" she said shakily. "Now Lee Sing Tai is dead, I am free. I do not belong to anyone. I can go with Frederick."

"It's not good news, Bo Kei. The police think that you and Frederick may have had something to do with his death."

She looked horrified. "Me and Frederick? How do they even think that we know each other? We have not spoken since I was delivered to Lee Sing Tai's house. You did not say anything to them to make them think this, did you?"

"Of course not. It was Bobby Lee who suggested that Frederick might be the murderer, because his father had dismissed him from his position. And because he was attracted to you. He suggested you two had planned the crime together."

"Bobby Lee said this? He is a wicked man. He tried to force me to do a terrible thing, Miss Molly. He wanted my body for himself. He say his father is too old and he can give me the son instead. Make his father happy. Father will never know. Now he wants revenge because I pushed him away."

"I believe you," I said. "Bobby Lee is a most despicable man."

"Then I will go to your police and tell them that Frederick and I are innocent. The nuns say that American law is fair and just."

"I wouldn't do that, Bo Kei. Not all policemen are fair and just, in fact I am told that the policeman handling this case is known to be crooked. He would concoct a case against you, because it would satisfy everyone and look good for him." I looked at her terrified face with sympathy. "The fact that you ran away makes you a suspect in the eyes of the police,

Bo. There will be policemen all over the city looking for you."

"Then I am not safe here."

"No."

"And Frederick—are they looking for him?"

"They have already found Frederick and the police have gone to question him. I'm worried for him, Bo Kei."

"Then what must I do?"

"We must hide you somewhere for now. This is exactly the sort of place that the police will come hunting for you. I have friends who have connections outside of the city. Maybe they will find somewhere for you to hide. I wish I had been able to warn Frederick; then we could have spirited the two of you away."

"He will go to jail now? They will say he murdered Lee Sing Tai and they will execute him?"

"I hope it won't come to that," I said.

"But he didn't do it, I swear to this."

"You can't swear to it, Bo. You weren't with him last night. You can believe in his innocence based on his character, but that's not the same as swearing."

"I understand. But I know in my heart he is not the killer. They will find out who really killed Lee Sing Tai, won't they?"

"American policeman are smart and I'm sure they could find enough clues to point to the real killer if they want to. The problem is that they may not want to. They don't want to do anything that might start another tong war, you see."

"So it is like China here. Magistrates decide who they want to be guilty and nobody can say anything or they will be guilty too."

"I hope it's not quite as bad as that," I said. "I'll do my best, Bo Kei. My future husband is an important policeman and he is not crooked. I will try to make him find the real killer and to have Frederick set free."

"You are wonderful woman, Missie Molly." She reached out and shyly touched my hand.

I didn't feel like a wonderful person. I felt sick and scared.

I wasn't at all sure that I was doing the right thing. But I needed to buy time. "We must go now, Bo Kei."

"We can take Annie with us?" she asked. "She also will not be safe here."

"I don't think we can take Annie," I said. "She's sick, and I can't bring someone with consumption into my friends' home. Besides, she has nothing to worry about from the police. She's not involved in this at all and she's in good hands here."

"No, the police will see Chinese girl and make her answer their questions. Maybe they will hurt her."

"Don't worry. The ladies who run this place come from important families. They will tell the police that Annie is not the girl they look for. The police will listen to them. Annie will be quite safe, I promise."

I could see her thinking this through, wanting to say something, but not daring to. Finally she said, "I have to say goodbye to her."

"That may not be wise, Bo Kei," I said. "She should not know that you are going with me. The less she knows, the better. If she doesn't know where you have gone, then the police won't be able to get it out of her, will they?"

"You say police not harm her!" Bo Kei wailed. "You promise."

"They won't harm her, but they may ask her questions."

"Then we must take her too," Bo Kei insisted. "She can sleep in my bed. I don't mind. I am strong. I will not catch this disease. Please, Missie Molly. We can't leave her here."

"We have to. I'm sorry, Bo Kei, but she will be well looked after here and the police won't bother her."

"I don't know." Bo Kei still chewed at her fingertips, her face an agony of indecision.

"Are you worried that the police might mistake her for you? Or is it because of her previous connection with Lee Sing Tai? Don't worry. The police don't need to know about that, and the workers here will testify that she has been lying at death's door all week. So let's go quietly now, Bo Kei.

We'll ask Sarah to tell Annie that you've gone away. It really is much safer for us all."

She shook her head vehemently. "Then I not go either."

"Don't be silly. You're the one who is in danger, not Annie. Come on." But she shook herself loose from my hand.

"I must speak with her before I go. I promise I'll not tell her that I go with you. Just a few words. I must."

"Very well," I sighed. "But you realize you may be signing your own death warrant."

She shook her head. "No. Annie would never betray me. Never. She is my family, and family takes care of each other."

With that she marched defiantly to Annie's room.

CHAPTER TWENTY-TWO

The cab was waiting outside the front door. I bundled Bo Kei in, her face hidden behind a shawl, and we set off for Patchin Place. Gus greeted me with a worried face when I knocked at the front door. "Molly, where have you been? We were so worried when we arose this morning and found your bed empty. And then when you didn't return and didn't return we thought something must have happened to you." She broke off as she noticed Bo Kei, standing behind me.

"Something has happened," I said. "Let us inside and I'll explain everything."

We sat in the conservatory, where they always ate breakfast, while I told the whole story. Bo Kei sat beside me, looking at her hands, saying nothing.

"I know I'm taking a horrible risk," I said at last. "If you don't wish to be involved, then I'll hide Bo Kei away in my house across the street and you can pretend we never came here."

There was silence. I saw a look pass between Sid and Gus.

"Why don't you take Miss Bo up to your room so that we can discuss this," Sid said. I picked up the restrained civility in her voice.

"Very well." I got to my feet. "I'll show you my room, Bo."

She touched my arm. "Missie Molly, I don't want to cause trouble. You can take me back to the house. I'm sure police will believe that I had nothing to do with Mr. Lee's death."

"Don't worry, I'm sure it will be all right," I said. "My friends are naturally being cautious, but they are very good people and I know they will want to help."

I led her up to my bedroom on the third floor.

"You have pretty room," she said wistfully. "You are lucky to live here with friends."

"I don't actually live here," I said. "I am staying here until my wedding. Then I will move with my bridegroom into that house directly across the street."

"You get married?"

"In two weeks' time."

"He is good man? Did you choose him or does your family arrange this?"

"I chose him," I said. "And he is a good man. A little difficult sometimes, but good."

"I am very happy for you." Her face grew wistful again. "Frederick is a good man, I think. I am sure I could be happy with him, if only. . . ."

"It will all work out right, I'm sure." I touched her shoulder gently. "Now just wait here until I talk this through with my friends. They have been very good to me and I don't want to put them in any danger."

"I should never have run away," she said flatly. "I should have accepted my fate, as we are taught in the Chinese way. For us there is no question of happiness, only duty. This man paid my father a bride price for me. I should have accepted that I belonged to Lee Sing Tai."

"In America they say that everyone has the right to life, liberty, and the pursuit of happiness," I said. "Nobody here would expect you to face a life of misery with that old man, his wife, and his son making advances to you. And the knowledge that he'd send you to one of his brothels if you didn't give him a son, when he is clearly too old to have children . . . no, you definitely did the right thing, Bo Kei.

It's just a pity that somebody chose this moment to kill Mr. Lee."

As I came down the stairs Daniel's words did pass through my mind—what looks like a chain of coincidences usually turns out to be linked. Did her running away somehow lead to Mr. Lee's death? When I thought about it, I came to a sad conclusion. The only person who would have felt himself forced to act at that moment would indeed have been Frederick Lee.

As I arrived back in the kitchen, Sid and Gus were standing, heads together and talking quietly. I felt my stomach do an uneasy lurch. Had I really stretched our friendship too far this time?

"I'm sorry," I said. "I should never have brought her here, but I had to act quickly, before the police raided the settlement house. I'll go upstairs and fetch her and take her over to my place. You can claim no knowledge of her if the police ever question you."

"Oh, no, Molly, don't misunderstand us," Sid said. "Of course we want to help. It's just that—" She paused and looked across at Gus for reassurance again. "Molly, are you quite sure that she is innocent? This is a girl who has already proven that she is prepared to take tremendous risks and is remarkably agile. She leaped across rooftops once. What was there to stop her from repeating the action?"

"She was in the settlement house last night," I said.

"I've been to those places," Sid said. "People are always coming and going. She could certainly have slipped out if she'd wanted to."

"And she does have such a perfect motive," Gus added. "She could never be safe or free while the old Chinaman was alive. These people are so different from us and it is not easy to read their expressions. How can you tell if she is telling the truth? Even our own kind can sometimes lie and deceive us."

"This is all true," I said. "And the answer is that I don't know if she is innocent. But I don't see how she could have done it alone." As I said it I thought of those dainty footprints in the soft tar on the rooftop. "But you've seen how petite she is. How could she have the strength to hurl a grown man to his death?"

"Then perhaps her lover Frederick is not the nice, innocent boy he seemed to you," Sid said. "You're a kind person, Molly Murphy. You've let people use you before now."

"I know that too," I said. "But I also know that my Celtic sixth sense has often served me well, and my gut feeling is that Bo Kei is innocent. If another policeman was on the case—if my Daniel would only take it over—I'd be happy to leave the whole thing in the hands of the police. But you haven't seen this Captain Kear. He is brash and arrogant and I could see that he'd already made up his mind that Bo Kei and Frederick are the guilty parties. He won't even bother to go on looking for the true murderer."

Sid glanced across at Gus and sighed. "We want to help, Molly. We feel angry at the way this girl has been treated. Of course we can't condone the buying and selling of women."

"Sid even thought she was quite justified in killing him," Gus said with a grin, "but you know that Sid sometimes does get a little heated on the subject of women's rights."

I shook my head. "No. I've just realized that I can't leave her here. I know she hadn't exactly been charged with a crime yet, but I can't let you run the risk of harboring a fugitive. I'll take her over to my house. She can stay up in the attic and I'll take her food and drink until we can decide what to do with her."

"And if your bridegroom decides to make a sudden inspection or brings back the paper-hanger, what then? He'd be furious if he knew you were even working again."

I sighed. "I'm afraid he's already discovered that much. He burst into the room at Mr. Lee's house. And believe me, he was furious. I was tempted to tell him that I knew of the whereabouts of the Chinese girl, but while that Captain Kear is in charge of the case, I just couldn't risk it. They were already talking about throwing Frederick in the Tombs to soften him up. What if they did that to Bo Kei too?"

Gus slipped her arm around my shoulder. "Don't get upset, Molly. She can stay here. We don't want to do anything to cause friction between you and Daniel. I'll make up a bed for her in my studio. Then she'll be well hidden away when the guests come for the party tonight."

"Oh, the party." I started to laugh. "So much has happened today that I completely forgot. Did your lanterns survive the wind so far, Sid?"

Sid glanced out of the window. "So far, but the sky does not look too promising, does it? We must make alternative plans in case we have to move the whole thing inside."

"Candles," Gus said firmly. "We'll need hundreds of candles. Paper lanterns are just too dangerous, but we do need to set the mood. What a pity we took down that big chandelier in the dining room when we moved in here. Do you think we still have it in the attic, Sid? Maybe we could rig it up again."

"No time, dearest. We have so much to do as it is."

"Put me to work," I said. "I'll do anything I can."

"We could send Molly out to every candlemaker in the Village," Gus said.

"The bad weather may pass over," Sid said. "We may be able to hold it in the garden and use our paper lanterns after all. It's more important to make sure the ice is delivered or our tubs of ice cream will be a disaster."

And they were off, discussing party provisions and whether they should serve the fruit salads in individual rock melons. I found it hard to think of domestic details while a girl waited up in that room.

"I'll go and make up a bed in your studio then, Gus," I said. "And if I may, can I take up some food and drink to Bo Kei? I don't know what she's had to eat today."

Then, of course, they fussed around, suggesting all kinds of delicacies that might tempt a Chinese palate. Sid even wanted to get out her Chinese cookbook and see how to make bird's nest soup. I stopped them and took up a cheese sandwich and an orange. The way she devoured them made me think that she hadn't had breakfast. I then explained about the party, how busy we'd be, and how she must stay well hidden when the guests arrived. I found her some books, although I wasn't sure whether she had learned to read much English. She was more interested in the dolls that Gus had sitting on a corner shelf and I was reminded again that she was little more than a child herself.

Then I went down to join in the preparations. As with everything that Sid and Gus did, they threw themselves into it wholeheartedly. Some might say that they went overboard. By evening the tables in the conservatory were groaning under the weight of hams and cold chicken and salads and exotic cheeses. There was asparagus in aspic and oysters and potted shrimp, fresh fruits of all kinds, including pine-apples, which I had never seen before, cake stands of tiny French pastries, and tubs of ice cream keeping cool for the right moment. Then there were drinks of all descriptions—fruit punches and chilled white wines for the ladies, claret and stout for the men. They had even borrowed the young man who normally worked in their favorite tavern to act as barman. There were Japanese lanterns and banks of candles waiting to be lit, flowers on the tables, and greenery trailing from the picture rails.

As I stood and surveyed the scene and thought of the cost of it all, it dawned on me that this was all for me. The thought was so overwhelming that I felt tears springing into my eyes. They had been good friends since they took me under their wing at a difficult moment in my life and they had constantly rescued me and cheered me up ever since. And I—I had repaid them by constantly rushing around and making demands on them. I watched them standing there, admiring their handi-work, and I came to a sudden decision.

"I've changed my mind," I said. "I want you two to be my bridesmaids."

They looked around. "But I thought we'd been through this. Daniel doesn't approve of us. His mother wouldn't ap-prove of us."

"I approve of you," I said. "You are my dear friends, closer to me than family. If you are not at my side, then the wedding won't be perfect."

"Well, if you insist . . ." Gus looked pink and pleased.

"Only one stipulation," I said. "You are not to dress as French maids or nuns or anything else outlandish."

"Spoilsport." Sid laughed. "Don't worry, we shall not disgrace you. We were both brought up to behave properly in polite society and you shall help us select the most demure of dresses. And you'll find that Daniel's mother will be overwhelmed by having one of the Boston Walcotts in the bridal procession."

I laughed too. "You're right. She'll be thrilled."

CHAPTER TWENTY-THREE

At six o'clock the heavens suddenly opened and we rushed into the garden, frantically trying to carry in furniture and rescue the lanterns. We were soaked to the skin by the time we had finished.

"Look at us," Gus said, laughing as water trickled down her face. "Talk about orphans of the storm. Let us just pray that our guests don't arrive early."

You can see why these two women were so dear to me. Most young ladies would be mortified that their coiffure was ruined. Sid and Gus were simply amused.

"I think we should sample the punch to fortify ourselves, don't you?" Sid poured us each a generous glass.

I went up to change and visited Bo Kei on the way. We had been having such good fun that I had forgotten for a moment that she was virtually a prisoner up there in Gus's studio. She eyed me hopefully as I came in.

"You have news of Frederick?" she asked.

Then I felt guilty that I hadn't done more. But in all honesty, there was nothing I could do at this moment, other than keep Bo Kei safe and out of Captain Kear's clutches. I could hardly go to the Sixth Precinct and petition on Frederick's behalf without revealing my own involvement. And Daniel had made it quite clear that I was to stay away.

"I'm sorry," I said. "I've heard nothing yet. They will probably keep him in a cell overnight. They do that sometimes, hoping that a prisoner will break down and confess. But Frederick is innocent. We know that and I'm sure the police will realize it too."

"Poor Frederick. That he should suffer for me," she said. "Surely the American police are smart and they will soon discover who really killed Lee Sing Tai."

"I hope so," I said, not wanting to tell her that Captain Kear was probably not going to investigate when he had a bird in hand, so to speak.

"Who could have killed my master, I wonder?" she said, staring out of the window at the rain.

"Do you have any ideas on the subject?"

"Me?" she asked sharply. "How would I have ideas about this? I know nothing about his life. I was not allowed to leave the house. I was sent to my room when he had guests. I only meet wife number one, and Bobby Lee."

"And what about them?" I asked. "Could either of them have killed him?"

She looked shocked. "Kill their benefactor?" Then I saw her considering this. "Wife number one could not kill him," she said. "She is too frail. Besides, he is her protector in a foreign land. With Lee Sing Tai gone, what will happen to her?"

This was true enough. I had witnessed her distress for myself.

"And Bobby Lee? You don't think he is capable of killing his paper father?"

"For what reason?"

"To inherit all Mr. Lee's business empire."

"But surely he will not inherit. He is only paper son. Mr. Lee has relatives at home in China. I heard him say this once to Bobby Lee. They have a big fight and Lee got mad. He said, 'You assume too much. Never forget that you are only a paper son and for me family will always come first. Remember our agreement. I could send you home tomorrow if I wanted to.'"

"Ah," I said. "Interesting. Mr. Lee was threatening to send Bobby Lee home? Now that is a strong motive and he had better opportunity than anyone. Nobody would even question his entering that house. He must have his own key. And he's strong enough to throw a man off the roof."

"Yes, he is strong." Bo Kei turned her face away again and I wondered if she really had been able to fight him off or if he might have raped her.

"And they talked of an agreement he had signed," I went on. "And that paper would have been kept in the big cabinet where Lee Sing Tai kept all important papers. But then why would Bobby have drawn attention to it, and why would he have left it in such disarray? Couldn't he have slipped in and removed the agreement at any time he chose?"

"The cabinet in the corner?" Bo Kei asked, turning back to face me. "But that was always kept locked and Mr. Lee kept the key on a chain around his neck."

"Did he? But when I was there today the key was in the cabinet."

"Then Bobby Lee had to kill his paper father to get the key," she said. "You will tell this to the police. They will arrest Bobby."

"I'll certainly mention it to the police," I said, "but I think they'd have a hard time proving he was guilty. If he found the paper he had signed, he'd surely have destroyed it by now."

"But at least they would then know that Frederick was innocent," she said. "And Bobby Lee is a bad man. It is right that bad men should suffer."

"I'm not sure about that." I laughed. "We can't play God." I brushed a sodden hair back from my face and remembered that I should be hurrying to get ready.

"Listen," I said. "Tonight there will be a party at this house. It is important that you stay upstairs and unseen. A policeman may be present and you don't want to take any risks."

"I will stay in the room," she said.

"I'll bring you up some food before the guests arrive. But now I must go and make myself respectable."

"I think you are most respectable woman already," Bo Kei said.

I had to laugh at this. "There are some who would dispute it, but thank you," I said.

"Thank you, Missie Molly." She gave that funny little bow.

I dried my hair and dressed. I had decided against wearing a costume, although Sid and Gus had tried to tempt me with everything from Marie Antoinette to a Vestal Virgin. Somehow it seemed to be mocking my wedding to dress up in costume at my prenuptial party. So instead I borrowed one of Gus's evening gowns—relics of her former life when she had moved in glittering society. It was a simple affair in gray silk, dotted with pearls, but it showed off my red hair and my curves. I even managed to put my hair up, with the aid of several combs, and was feeling quite sophisticated as I went downstairs to join Sid and Gus. They had taken my pleas not to be too outlandish to heart. Gus was costumed as a water sprite, with lots of trailing green and blue chiffon, and Sid was a wood nymph with a similar costume in green and brown. She wore leaves in her hair, while Gus had a crown of silver starfish.

"You both look spectacular," I said.

"If you hadn't been such a fuddy-duddy we could have made you a spirit of the air and then we would have been complete," Sid said, "but as it is, you look as the future Mrs. Daniel Sullivan should—respectable and demure."

"Oh, dear. That sounds boring."

"My sweet, you are marrying a boring and respectable man. What can I say?" Sid chuckled. "But I'm sure you'll be blissfully happy and that's all that matters."

I thought about this as we removed the aspics and cold salmon from the pantry where they had been sitting on ice. Was I really destined for a boring, respectable life with Daniel? Would he forbid me to attend such functions as this in future? Would he even pressure me eventually to break off my friendship with Sid and Gus? *Rubbish*, I said to myself. I was a strong person and not even my husband was going to tell me what to do. I swept out of the pantry with the platter of salmon, narrowly missing a calamity as it slid across the tilting plate.

The first guests started to arrive—artists and actors, suffragists, and society ladies I had met through my hostesses, as well as people I had never met. Some were in fabulous costumes, while others had chosen more conventional evening dress. Sarah and Monty were of the latter. She looked enchanting in powder blue while he was dashing in white tie and tails. He looked distinctly uncomfortable as he examined the other occupants of the living room.

"Come and try the punch, Mr. Warrington-Chase," Gus whisked him away. "Or would you prefer champagne to start with?"

"Most kind," Monty muttered, looking distinctly uneasy as he was led away by a water sprite.

"Oh, dear." Sarah gave me an embarrassed grin. "I was not at all sure about this and I'm afraid it's going to be a disaster. Monty really doesn't approve of this sort of thing. I tried to persuade him to wear a costume—I suggested that he come as Lord Byron. That's respectable enough, isn't it? I even bought him the wig, but he refused to wear it."

"But they have costume balls in England."

"Yes, but with the right sort of people. It's apparently all right if lords and ladies put on masks and costumes, but not bohemians. I know he only allows me to mix with Sid and Gus because it's such a short time before we sail for our new life at his country estate."

"You must put your foot down and not find yourself under Monty's thumb, Sarah," I said. "Daniel would prefer that I not have Sid and Gus as my friends. He wanted us to take a house in a very different neighborhood so that I could be away from them, but I made it clear that I was not abandoning my friends."

She sighed. "You are so brave. But I shall be far away from friends and moving in a strange society. I won't know how to behave and I shall need Monty to guide me."

"Of course you'll know how to behave," I said. "It's not as if you started life in a peasant's cottage like me. You were raised in a good family, and good manners are the same everywhere in the world. Trust me, Monty's friends will be enchanted with you."

"I hope so." She gave a weak smile.

Monty returned, carrying two glasses of champagne. "Here you are, my dear," he said. He was in the process of handing her the glass when he looked up and said, "What in God's name is that?"

My friend Ryan O'Hare, the flamboyant Irish playwright, had arrived. He was wearing tight black trousers, a frilly white jabot, and a red-lined cape. His dark hair was curled and flicked over his forehead. He looked devastatingly handsome as he held out his hands to me in dramatic gesture. "Molly, my dearest. Come and greet Lord Byron," he said.

I heard a grunt from Monty.

Ryan crossed the room to me, took my hand, and kissed it. "Ravishing, as always," he muttered. Then he noticed Monty standing beside me. "And who is this?" he asked. "I don't believe we've met."

"This is Montague Warrington-Chase," I said.

Ryan turned the full force of his charm on Monty. "Warrington-Chase? English? I believe I once had tea at your place."

"You did?" Monty looked incredulous.

"When I was a child. Osbourne St. George, isn't it?"

"Good God," Monty said curtly. "And what was your name, sir?"

"Ryan O'Hare. The family has a nice little castle in Ireland and I moved in your circles before I was banished."

"Ryan O'Hare. You're the playwright who caused that stir because of the play you wrote about Queen Victoria and Prince Albert."

"What a ridiculous fuss, wasn't it?" Ryan said. "They were horribly stuffy and boring. They needed someone to poke fun at them."

"She was the monarch of our country, sir," Monty said stiffly. "There are limits."

"To hell with limits, I say." Ryan waved a frilly white sleeve.

"As I heard it, you had to flee the country."

"Oh, absolutely. Hunted to the Kentish coast. Almost had to swim the Channel."

"Ryan, you are a terrible liar," I said, slipping my arm through his. "And I should point out to you that Monty is the fiancé of my friend Sarah Lindley."

"Oh," Ryan said, clearly disappointed that his charm was being wasted on Monty. Instead he turned and managed to be charming to Sarah.

CHAPTER TWENTY-FOUR

The gathering became more lively as the evening went on. People ate, drank, and were merry. There were musicians and the carpet was rolled back in the dining room for people to dance. A large pile of presents appeared on the hall table. I kept glancing toward the front door, wondering if Daniel would come. But as the festivities went on, I found I was actually having quite a good time myself, forgetting the way the day had started and the decisions I had made. I was chatting with Sarah when Monty came up to us with a strange expression on his face.

"I've just had the most astounding encounter," he said. "I went upstairs, needing to visit—I mean heeding the call of nature, so to speak." He coughed, uncomfortable at mentioning this subject to ladies. "I located what I believed to be the WC and just as I was about to open the door, it opened and you'll never guess who stepped out—a Chinese girl. I thought for a moment she was one of the guests in a dashed authentic-looking costume, but she was the real thing. Where on earth did she come from?"

When we didn't answer immediately he went on, "Sarah, she's not the girl you told me about, is she? The one at that place where you work who you said was dying of consumption, because she looked quite hale and hearty."

"No, this is a different girl altogether," Sarah said quickly. "That girl is still at the settlement house."

"Thank God. I thought for a moment someone had been injudicious enough to bring consumption into this house. Terribly catching, you know. So who is this girl? I had always understood that the Chinese were not allowed to bring their families to this country, but now Chinese women seem to be springing up all over the place."

My heart was racing. "She was raised by missionaries, who sent her over here," I said, before Sarah could answer. "We are training her to go into service."

"Oh. I see. Splendid idea. I gather the Chinese are frightfully hard workers. She doesn't have any contagious diseases, does she?"

I attempted a light laugh. "No, she's quite healthy."

"She got an awful shock seeing me." He chuckled. "You should have seen her face. Scurried up the stairs as if I was the big bad wolf."

"I told her to stay in her room," I said. "So I expect she thought she'd get into trouble."

"Why is your bridegroom not at your side?" Ryan asked, coming up to us with a glass of champagne in either hand. "Doesn't he realize that you are in danger of being carried off by all the jealous males at this party?"

"Ryan, you still haven't lost your Irish blarney," I replied, laughing. "I'm in no danger of being carried off by you or anyone else and Daniel has to work, I'm afraid."

"Then you'll need one of these to cheer you up." He handed me a champagne glass. "Foolish man to put work before love. I've never done that in my life. Love always comes first."

Monty looked at him with distaste. "So your fiancé has to work on a Sunday evening?" he asked.

"Policemen have to work whenever there is a case to be worked on," I said. "It's something I'm going to have to get used to, I suppose."

"And he's on a big case now, is he?" Monty asked. "Something exciting?"

"I don't really know," I said. "He's not allowed to discuss his work with me."

"I find detective work quite fascinating," Monty said. "I

rather feel I should have been a good detective if I'd put my mind to it. A gifted amateur like Sherlock Holmes. But I should have been careful not to have let my enemy throw me over the Reichenbach Falls." And he gave a self-congratulatory chuckle.

At that moment there was a knock at the front door and Sid appeared, beaming. "Look who has just arrived," she said and ushered in Daniel. "Look everyone, the bridegroom cometh!"

There were suitable murmurs of excitement as Daniel, looking distinctly uncomfortable, was surrounded by outlandishly costumed figures who patted him on the back and attempted to shake his hand.

"How clever," Ryan said, appearing at his side. "You've come disguised as a policeman. Very novel."

"Ryan, you are being wicked again." I went over to rescue Daniel. "I didn't think you'd be able to come," I said as I extracted him from the crush. "It was really good of you. I know how busy you are."

"My conscience got the better of me," he said. "I realized that this party was important to you and I should make some effort to get along with your friends, just as I hope you'll get along with mine."

"They don't always look as strange as this," I muttered as I slipped my hand through his. "And most them are really Sid and Gus's friends. But you're a good man."

He smiled. "How much of a hardship is it to exchange a hasty sandwich at police headquarters for champagne and good food," he said. "I haven't had a good meal in days."

"Come through to the conservatory and you shall eat your fill," I said. "And take a look at that table in the hallway. Wedding presents, I believe."

"For us?" Daniel looked surprised.

"It is our wedding party," I said.

"Good God. We'll need a bigger house to put them in."

"We won't. But we'll be able to entertain more elegantly, which is what you want, isn't it?"

We reached the conservatory and Daniel helped himself

liberally to the fare on the tables. "I must say your friends have really pulled out all the stops, haven't they?" he exclaimed. "What an incredible array of food."

"You know Sid and Gus. When they do something, they throw themselves into it wholeheartedly."

"I rather fear it will make our wedding breakfast seem pale in comparison," he said. He piled a plate. As I was about to go back to the living room he said, "Can't we find a quiet corner? I'd enjoy this food so much more if I didn't have that O'Hare person commenting on the way I eat."

"You have to understand that Ryan enjoys getting a rise out of other people," I said. "Especially members of the establishment like you. Come on, let's sit out here for a while."

We found two chairs in a corner of the conservatory and I let him eat in silence while rain drummed on the glass roof. After a few bites he put down his fork. "I'm afraid I can't stay long," he said. "This Chinese business has just added to my workload."

"Daniel, I really am sorry," I said. "I didn't intend to get involved in anything difficult or dangerous."

"You never do, do you?" he said. "You just seem to stumble into trouble, and then miraculously to stumble out of it again. At least you didn't need rescuing this time and at least you're not in any way involved in the machinations of Chinatown. And believe me, you're well to be out of it, Molly. That Lee fellow was a nasty piece of work. I'm not at all surprised that somebody finished him off. I just hope we can find out who that was before the tongs start hurling accusations at each other."

"So you're going to take over the case, are you?"

"I can't really step on Kear's toes. He's the same rank as I and it's in his precinct, so I should let him handle it."

"But he's got it all worked out in his mind," I said. "He wants it to be Frederick Lee, so he's not going to look any farther. And who knows what kind of methods he might use to make Frederick confess to something he didn't do."

Daniel looked at me strangely. "You sound as if you care about what happens to this Frederick fellow."

"I've only met him a couple of times," I said carefully. "But he seemed such a nice, polite young man. Not one who would murder anybody, especially not someone from his own clan."

"I must say I'm inclined to think it wasn't he," Daniel said. "I went back and took a look at the Lee apartment with the fingerprint expert. Somebody definitely went through that cabinet in a big hurry. Papers were literally stuffed back in all the drawers."

"And did you find any interesting fingerprints?"

"Bobby Lee's were on it," he said, "but not Frederick Lee's. There was also a set of prints that we can't identify yet. And apparently plenty of motives for killing Lee in those little drawers—protection money contracts, IOUs for large sums of money, and who knows what else. Most of them in Chinese, but not all. What seem to be promissory notes from Americans were there as well. I didn't have time to get much of the Chinese translated for me. Just enough to get the idea that a lot of very diverse people owed Lee money."

"Did you happen to come across a document involving Bobby Lee?" I asked. "One concerning his status as a paper son?"

"No," Daniel said. "What are you hinting at?"

"Just a thought," I said. "Mr. Lee had this girl brought over because he wanted a son—a real son. Bobby Lee was no relative really, so he would be supplanted by a real flesh-and-blood son, and apparently Mr. Lee had made it clear that Bobby would inherit nothing when he died."

"How on earth did you learn this?" Daniel demanded.

Of course I'd learned it from Bo Kei. "Frederick Lee told me a little of it after Bobby was so rude to him, then more came out when Captain Kear was questioning Bobby. And I'll tell you another thing that was suspicious. Mr. Lee wore the key to that cabinet in a chain around his neck. Today it was in the cabinet. So I wondered if the body showed any kind of bruising around the neck where the chain had been."

Daniel laughed. "Where the chain had been?—my dear, he was in such a mess that his whole body was bruised and bleeding. But that was an interesting observation. You noticed the chain around his neck when he was alive, did you?"

"Yes," I said, although that wasn't exactly true. But I did have it on good authority from one who had seen him in his night attire.

"So your suggestion is that we look more closely at Bobby Lee?" Daniel said after a pause. "And we hunt for some kind of document that proves he isn't Lee's true son and he doesn't stand to inherit when Lee dies?"

"That is what I am suggesting," I said. "Although I can't see why he wouldn't have had time to remove an incriminating piece of paper before the police arrived."

"The houseboy slept just on the other side of the screen. Perhaps he woke up before Bobby could go through the whole cabinet."

"Then if he knew Bobby had been there, why didn't he tell that to the police when Captain Kear questioned him?" I asked.

"Either loyalty or fear. From what I've heard of Bobby Lee, and from what I know of the ways the tongs operate, the boy could have been afraid of having his hand or ear or tongue cut off."

I tried not to gasp, but my body gave an involuntary shudder.

Daniel noticed. "They are ruthless people, Molly. They have different notions of loyalty and revenge and they regard life as cheap. That's why I'm relieved you had the sense to want no part in this whole sordid business."

I nodded demurely, looking down so that I didn't meet his eye.

"You'd have thought that Bobby would have had opportunities before this to sneak in and remove a piece of paper, wouldn't you? That really must mean that he could never get his hands on Mr. Lee's key or that the paper was cleverly hidden."

"Or that Lee checked at regular intervals," Daniel suggested. "Bobby wouldn't have dared to remove it while his father was alive. He was much too afraid of him."

"So what will you do now?" I asked.

"It's still Kear's case. I'll tell him to get an official translation of everything in that cabinet." He paused, studying my expression. "Better yet, I'll find my own translator and put him to work on it right away. Thank you, you've been a big help." He took a couple of more bites of cold salmon, a swig of champagne, then got to his feet. "I suppose we'd better go and mingle before I have to leave again."

We came out into the hallway. "I know you're suggesting it was Bobby Lee," he said, "but I really want that girl found."

"Girl?" I asked innocently.

"This missing bride. She has an equally good motive for killing the old man. The timing of her flight is just too coincidental for me, and I did notice small footprints when I was up on the roof."

I tried not to glance up the stairs.

"If she was his bride, and his bed was up there, she might well have walked around quite legitimately on the roof," I pointed out.

"But these looked rather fresh, didn't they? And they were at the edge of the roof. At the very least she used the roof as a way to escape, and at worst, she came back that way to kill Lee."

"If you were examining footprints, what did you think about those heavy men's boots?" I asked. "Weren't they equally fresh?"

"Ah, yes. The big boots. I suppose they could be," he said. "It's hard to tell. Lee could have brought in a Caucasian workman to fix a leaking roof. The Chinese don't have that kind of footwear. But to come back to the missing woman—tell me, exactly how far did you get in your search for her?" His voice echoed up the stairwell.

I glanced up nervously, half expecting to hear scurrying feet. "Not very far," I said. "I tried the various missions around Chinatown and while doing so, I found out what was going on and didn't want to return the girl to Mr. Lee."

"I've had men on the lookout for her today," he said.

"Any luck?" I asked cautiously.

"One false lead. We heard of a Chinese girl hiding out at one of those settlement houses. But this one turned out to have escaped from a brothel, and the settlement workers said that she's dying of consumption." He paused and looked at me quizzically. "I wonder how much money I'd have paid for you?"

"Sight unseen, from Ireland?" I asked. "About a couple of chickens and a sack of potatoes, I should think."

He slipped his arms around my waist. "At least two sacks of potatoes," he murmured and kissed me.

CHAPTER TWENTY-FIVE

I was relieved when Daniel finally left the party. He actually started enjoying himself and stayed longer than I would have thought. But in the end he looked up at the clock on the mantel and sighed. "I suppose I had better get back to work," he said. "There may be important developments tonight."

"A big case, is it?" Monty asked. "A murder?"

"Only coincidentally," Daniel said. "But yes, it's a big case, and I'll be mighty glad when it's over. Like Molly and her runaway girl, I find it distasteful."

"Runaway girl?" Monty asked.

Daniel chuckled. "My fiancée gets herself involved in all kinds of queer situations. This time it was tracking down a runaway bride. So if your bride decides to run off before the wedding, just hire Molly. She'll track her down for you."

"Runaway bride?" Monty said. "Wait a second—you don't mean the Chinese girl, do you? Now I remember. Sarah told me about her but I didn't put two and two together. Ah, so that's it." His eyes strayed toward the stairs. Any minute now he would put two and two together.

"Hadn't you better go?" I pulled on Daniel's arm.

"Trying to get rid of me, are you?" Daniel smiled. "But you're right. I do have to go. Where are our hostesses? I should say good-bye."

I didn't start breathing again normally until Daniel was out in the street, and I stood at the front door.

"I'll be in touch when I can," he said. "I hope to have the other case I'm working on sewn up in the next few days. You'll be going back to my mother tomorrow, will you?"

"I should help Sid and Gus clear up first," I said. "And I still need to do some shopping for my trousseau—if you'd like your bride to start off married life with new undergarments."

He looked at me quizzically. "You two have to learn to get along some time," he said. "I thought this would be a good opportunity to do so."

"Don't worry. I'll go back later this week, and I've been trying really hard, Daniel. You'd have been proud of me. When your mother extolled the virtues of every other girl in the county, I bit my tongue and smiled sweetly."

"I'd like to have seen that." He reached out and stroked my cheek. "Behave yourself now. I don't want to find you turning up at any more crime scenes, understand?"

"Yes, Daniel," I said meekly.

He laughed, but as he turned to go, I called after him, "Did you locate the murder weapon yet?"

He turned back to me. "Murder weapon? He was pushed off the roof. Do you want a handprint in the middle of his back?"

"Remember I mentioned the wound to one side of his head? He was struck with some object. If it didn't kill him, at least it knocked him out enough to drag him to the edge of the roof. Isn't it possible that the assailant left the weapon somewhere in Lee's apartment?"

Daniel shook his head, smiling. "Why is it that you and I never have the same conversations as other couples about to be married—about the flowers for the church and the number of guests and the honeymoon?"

"If you'd rather discuss flowers and bridesmaids' dresses, I'm happy to do so," I said sweetly.

"Your problem is that you have become too damned good at this detective stuff," he said. "I'll have one of my men take a quiet look for the murder weapon. Now for heaven's sake go back and enjoy your party and stop thinking about this. And that's an order."

"Yes, sweetheart," I said in my most simpering voice.

He laughed and hurried off into the night.

I heaved a big sigh as I went back inside. The party continued into the wee hours of the morning. Sid and Gus's friends certainly kept late hours, still laughing and drinking with no apparent signs of tiredness as my own eyes kept wanting to close. When at last I dragged myself upstairs I peeked into Bo Kei's room. She was asleep, looking like a peaceful child, her dark hair spilling across the pillow. How could anyone possibly suspect that she could have killed Lee Sing Tai? And if she had dragged his body to the edge of the roof, wouldn't there have been signs of a heavy object being dragged? Spatters of blood on the tar? I wished I could take another look. I had been allowed only the most cursory of examinations last time. But I thought it was unlikely that I'd be able to slip past a police guard without word getting back to Daniel.

My gaze went back to Bo Kei. How long could I go on hiding her? But where could I possibly send her where she would be safe? What if I was charged with harboring a fugitive from the law? Did one go to jail for such things? What would that do to my husband's career? As usual I had let my heart dictate to my head. I would have to learn to start thinking rationally.

"What on earth am I going to do with you?" I whispered to the sleeping girl.

In the morning Bo Kei begged me to find out what was happening to Frederick. However, I could hardly slip out and leave Sid and Gus to the mountains of washing-up. Bo Kei joined in cheerfully and we soon had the house back in order.

"Now you go and save Frederick," she insisted as soon as the last dish was put on the dresser.

I looked at her indignant and innocent young face. She could be forceful when she wanted to be. And the irreverent thought crossed my mind that if they had planned anything together, she would have been the driving force, not him.

"I don't really know what I can do, Bo Kei," I said. "I can't very well show up at the police station and demand that they free him."

"You tell them he is innocent. You make them believe."

"How can I do that unless I can show them who really committed the crime?"

"You tell them Bobby Lee did this terrible thing."

"I don't know that for sure," I said. "I have suggested to Captain Sullivan that they investigate Bobby Lee, so I'm sure he'll do that. Until then, it's a matter for the police so we must just wait patiently."

"I can't wait patiently," she said. "We must help Frederick."

"You can't do anything. You have to stay hidden. You were almost discovered last night when one of the guests saw you."

"I know," she said. "But there was no chamber pot in my room, so I had to go down to water closet. This man, he looked as scared as I felt. He stared at me, then he ran down the stairs."

"Really?" This was an interesting interpretation of events.

"I shall stay hidden," she said. "But you must help us. Find out if Frederick is still in jail. He need good lawyer to help him. Not Chinese lawyer, American man. Make police listen."

That made a lot of sense, although it was unlikely that Frederick could afford to pay for a good lawyer. "I can try to do that much for you," I agreed.

I put on my straw hat and out I went, traveling reluctantly back to Elizabeth Street and just praying that I didn't run into Daniel. I was trying to think if I knew any attorneys. One had been retained for Daniel once when he had been wrongly arrested and thrown into the Tombs. But he hadn't managed to have Daniel released and Daniel was a well-respected person. How much more difficult would it be for a Chinese man? I wondered if they had lawyers within their community. If only I had someone to ask—then, of course, I realized that I did know somebody. Mrs. Chiu would be able to help me.

Yesterday's storm had passed, leaving steaming puddles in the gutters. The sun was beating down from a bright blue sky and the day promised to be a scorcher. Jefferson Market and then Washington Square seemed unnaturally quiet and empty and it took me a moment to realize that it was Labor Day. Other people would be taking picnics to Central Park or heading for the thrills of the new Luna Park on Coney Island. Nobody except for policemen and people like me would choose to stay in the heat of the city. I thought wistfully for a moment about Westchester County. Daniel's mother would surely have a picnic or a croquet game arranged for us. And there would be ice cream and polite conversation. All so safe and civilized. At this moment it did seem infinitely preferable to the distasteful task ahead of me.

I stood outside the Sixth Precinct police station on Elizabeth Street and collected myself before I dared to enter. I wasn't doing anything wrong or stupid, I told myself. I was just finding out whether Frederick was still in jail or had been found innocent and released. Any normal citizen could do the same.

I went in through the glass-fronted door and up to the counter. The same young policeman was on duty.

"I remember you," he said. "You were here the other day asking about something, then you ran off before I could come back with an answer for you."

"I'm sorry," I said. "I had to leave in a hurry the other day. I was late for an appointment. Today I just came to find out whether a man called Frederick Lee was being held in one of the jail cells and whether he has actually been charged with the murder of the Chinaman Lee Sing Tai."

"I don't know anything about that," the young constable said. "He wasn't brought here, I can tell you. But I heard all about the dead Chinaman. Our men had to guard the body. They said he fell off a rooftop—looked pretty gruesome. Said it turned their stomachs."

"Who would know about Frederick Lee?" I asked.

"Well, it's Captain Kear who's in charge here," he said. "I think he's in his office. I'll go get him for you."

I started to say, "No, that's all right," but I was too late. He moved swiftly and I heard the captain's name echoing down a tiled hallway. Almost immediately the captain himself appeared, in braces and rolled-up shirt sleeves, and looked surprised to see me.

"Miss Murphy. What can I do for you?"

"I came to inquire about Frederick Lee," I said. "I wondered if you had officially arrested him and whether he's being held in jail?"

A big smile crossed Kear's face. "So Sullivan is sending you to do his dirty work now, is he? Pretends he's not trying to step on my toes and get involved in my case, so he sends his sweetie to soften me up instead."

"Absolutely not," I said angrily. "Captain Sullivan has no idea that I have come to you. It's just that I met Frederick Lee a couple of times and I found him a thoroughly nice and decent young man. So I just wanted to find out if he was being treated fairly and whether a lawyer had been engaged to represent him."

"It's actually none of your business," he said, "but if it satisfies you, Frederick Lee is being held in the Tombs until we determine his role in the murder of Lee Sing Tai."

"Has he engaged the services of a lawyer?"

"I wouldn't know that."

"So you've dumped him in jail without anyone to advise him." I could feel my hackles rising. "What evidence do you have against him?"

"Motive," he said. "Dismissed from his job the day before. Got too friendly with the master's new bride."

"And did anyone see him entering or leaving the Lee residence that night?"

"Of course not. I thought we'd already established that he came across from the next roof."

"Then why did none of his footprints show up there?"

"Who says they didn't? He's half European, isn't it? What's to stop him from wearing those hobnailed boots to throw us off the scent?"

"Have you found whether he owns such a pair of boots?"

He looked at me scornfully. "He'd have ditched them, wouldn't he?"

"So you actually have no evidence against him," I insisted. "He's in jail because he seems like a good candidate whose arrest would satisfy everyone."

"We're waiting until the bride shows up," Kear said. "She can't have gotten too far. We'll find her, and then when we have them together, we'll get to the truth."

"And if the murderer was someone else?" I asked. "What about Bobby Lee? Shouldn't you be looking into him and his relationship with his father?"

"And shouldn't you be leaving a criminal case to the police?" he said. "If I lodge an official complaint to the commissioner that Sullivan is sending his ladylove to stick his nose into my case, I don't think the commissioner would be very pleased, do you?"

I gave him my coldest stare. "I thought I made it clear to you that Captain Sullivan has nothing to do with this. He would be furious if he knew I had come here."

"Then what's your interest, girlie?" he asked. "Is it just morbid curiosity or are you still involved in this case in some way? Perhaps you know more than you're telling me. Perhaps you actually know who pushed old Lee off the roof."

"Perhaps I just believe in justice," I said. "But you're right. The case has nothing to do with me. I won't bother you again."

CHAPTER TWENTY-SIX

I walked very fast down the rest of the Elizabeth Street, my mind brimming with things that I would have liked to say to the smarmy Captain Kear. No wonder Daniel didn't like him and didn't trust him. I was relieved that I had managed to keep my temper. And of course the moment I was safely away from the police station I had regrets about ever going there in first place. It hadn't been the wisest thing to do. What if Captain Kear really did complain to the commissioner about Daniel? It wasn't that long ago since Daniel himself had been suspended and in disgrace. I shouldn't have done anything to further jeopardize his career.

More disturbing thoughts went through my head as I walked faster and faster toward Mott Street. I had been told that the Sixth Precinct officers accepted bribes from the Chinese community. What if Bobby Lee, or whoever the real killer was, was paying Captain Kear enough money to pin this crime on someone who couldn't defend himself, like Frederick?

If I went to the Tombs, would they let me see Frederick, I wondered. Almost certainly not, and such an act would be bound to get back to Daniel. The only way I could make Daniel take over this investigation was if I could prove Frederick's innocence or find out who really pushed Lee Sing Tai off that roof. And I really had no idea how to do that. But the one thing I could do was to see if I could rally the decent members of the Chinese community to help Frederick. Surely the Chius might know of a lawyer who would take his case?

I felt a growing sense of unease as I entered Mott Street even though the scene was livelier than usual today, with men sitting on stoops, standing outside restaurants drinking tea, or shopping at the stores that were all open in spite of the Labor Day holiday. Again I couldn't see any women among the crowd until I heard a voice blaring from a megaphone and Chuck Connors came into the street with another of his slumming tour groups. Like the one I had seen before, this one was composed of more women than men and their eyes were wide with anticipation as they followed their leader into the forbidden world of Chinatown.

"I am going to show you a scene of such vile depravity that some of you ladies may need to find your smelling salts before we enter," he was saying as he led them to the fake opium den. I have to admit that my curiosity was piqued. What did an opium den actually look like? As they disappeared into a doorway and down a flight of stairs, I acted on impulse and followed the last members of the tour. They were a young couple, the girl clutching her sweetheart's arm desperately.

"Do you really think we should do this?" she whimpered. "What if someone tries to kidnap me? What if we breathe the opium fumes and we're overcome or robbed?"

"I'm here to protect you, Daisy," he said, looking down at her with concern.

"Will we not be putting ourselves in danger?" a woman at the front of the pack asked.

"Don't worry, madam," Connors replied in a low voice. "Those poor wretches we're going to see won't even notice we're here. They are under the power of the drug."

Our footsteps echoed down the narrow stairwell. At the bottom we came into a dimly lit area. Smoke swirled around one hissing lamp, so it was hard to see what lay beyond, but I could make out wooden platforms around the walls. Figures lay on them, some smoking from long pipes, others lying in a stupor. At intervals around the room braziers glowed.

Although I knew it was not a true opium den, I felt a rush of fear. The air was cloying with scented smoke and suddenly I felt that I couldn't breathe. I turned and tiptoed back up the stairs as Connors's voice said in a hushed stage whisper, "They are all in the land of their dreams. For the moment they are happy. They have escaped from their troubles. But the moment the drug wears off, they will have to repeat the process. Once smoked, the drug takes over their lives. They will never escape from it, never be free."

I came out into the fresh air and stood catching my breath, ashamed of my momentary panic. It wasn't like me to be so easily frightened, especially when I knew that the scene had been staged for the benefit of the tourists and the moment they departed the actors would go back to their normal lives. But there was something about the place—some undercurrent of danger that I had picked up. I put it out of my mind and went straight to the Chius' residence.

In response to my knock the door was opened by a tall young man. He was so like Frederick Lee in appearance that I gasped out, "Frederick?"

"Can I help you, ma'am?" he asked, and I realized that the similarity was in the Eurasian features and this boy was younger and skinnier.

"You must be Mrs. Chiu's son who is attending Princeton," I said. "My name is Murphy. I wondered if I might speak to your parents?"

"Who is it, Joe?" a man's voice called from beyond the screen.

"An Irish lady, dad. Mrs. Murphy," the boy called back. "Wants to speak to you and mom."

"From the church or the missions?"

"Didn't say."

"I'll be right there," the man's voice said, and a slightly built Chinaman came around the screen, straightening his ascot.

I held out my hand to him. "Molly Murphy," I said. "I had the pleasure of meeting your wife the other day and I wondered if I could have a word with you both."

"Come in," he said, ushering me through the hallway. "Aileen," he called. "You've got company."

"I'm just finishing up in here," Mrs. Chiu's voice came from the far end of the passage.

"Take a seat. She'll be coming right away." Mr. Chiu escorted me to the sofa. I sat. "If you've come to visit, I'm afraid this isn't a good time. We're just about to go out," he said. Although his words were slightly clipped and staccato, his English was remarkably good. "We take a picnic to Staten Island with friends from church today."

"How lovely. It's a perfect day for a picnic," I said. "I won't keep you long. I came actually because I need some help and your wife is the only person I know in Chinatown whom I felt I could approach."

At that moment Aileen Chiu came into the room, wiping her hands on the apron she wore over her good clothes. "Sorry, I was just finishing making the egg sandwiches," she said. Her face broke into a smile when she saw me. "Why, it's you, Miss Murphy. How nice to see you again. But I'm afraid you've come at a bad time. We're just on our way out. We're meeting friends at the Staten Island ferry. We always share a picnic with members of our church on Labor Day."

"I'm sorry. Of course I won't keep you then," I said. "Perhaps I could come back later today when you get home?"

"We usually stay pretty late," she said, giving her husband a worried glance. "What is this about?"

"You remember the young man you saw me with the other day, Frederick Lee?" I said. "You thought he was my sweetheart?"

"Of course I remember. I used to know his mother before she passed away, God rest her poor soul," Aileen Chiu said.

I took a deep breath. "Well, I don't know if you've heard, but Frederick has been arrested for the murder of Lee Sing Tai. They are holding him in the Tombs."

"Holy Mother of God," Aileen Chiu muttered. "We heard about Mr. Lee being killed, of course, but I don't think we knew he was murdered, did we, Albert?"

"There were rumors going around On Leong, but nobody

knew anything definite," Mr. Chiu said. "So they've arrested Frederick Lee, have they? That's too bad."

"I'm sure he's innocent," I said. "So I wondered if you might know how to obtain a lawyer for him. I don't believe he'll get a fair hearing otherwise. I suspect that Captain Kear wants to pin it on Frederick because he's not connected to one of the tongs."

"Captain Kear. I might have known," Aileen Chiu said, smoothing her hands down her apron. "That man's nothing but trouble. He's given Albert his share of grief, hasn't he, my dear, because Albert won't go along with bribing the police."

"Let's not go into that," Albert said curtly. "So Frederick Lee is being held in the Tombs and you want us to find a lawyer to represent him?"

"A good lawyer," I said. "I just wondered if you knew such a person. I don't know how much Frederick could pay, but I hate to think of him being browbeaten into a confession because he has nobody to speak for him."

"Quite right," Albert Chiu said. "Don't worry, Miss Murphy. I will try to do something about this. I will ask my fellow church members today and if they can't come up with anybody, then I will go to CCBA tomorrow. They will certainly find someone to represent him."

"CCBA? What's that?" I asked

"It is the Consolidated Benevolent Association. It looks after the welfare of Chinese citizens."

"For a price," Aileen muttered.

Albert frowned at her.

"Well, it does," she said defiantly. "You have to pay CCBA if you want to open a business in Chinatown."

"Isn't that just like one of the tongs, then?" I asked.

"Oh, no," Albert said. "It's how the tongs started out. Now they're too busy trying to destroy each other and demand protection money from us businessmen. At least the CCBA is not crooked. They will probably pay to hire a lawyer for Frederick Lee."

"Unless someone in On Leong like Bobby Lee pays them not to," Aileen said.

"Hush, woman. Do not speak of something you know little about," Albert said. "My word is respected in this community. If I ask for help, I will receive help. You need not worry, Miss Murphy. I will do my best for a fellow Chinese."

"Thank you," I said. "I can't tell you how relieved I am."

"How do they know that Lee Sing Tai was murdered?" Albert Chiu asked. "From what I heard, he fell from the roof where he had been sleeping."

"Someone pushed him from the roof," I said.

"How do they know this? Was there a witness?"

"He had a wound to the side of his head," I said. Even as the words came out I realized that I was probably the one who had caused all this trouble. If only I had kept quiet about noticing the wound. If only I had not insisted that Lee Sing Tai had been murdered, then Captain Kear would probably have been happy to let the death be ruled accidental. As usual I had spoken too hastily, without thinking through the consequences, and it was my fault that Frederick Lee was now locked up in the Tombs.

"Is that so?" Mr. Chiu nodded. "So it is believed that someone struck him first and then threw him to his death?"

"You see, I knew it," Aileen Chiu said triumphantly. "I knew there had been a death that night. What did I tell you?"

"What do you mean?" I asked.

"Well, we were sleeping on our roof too," Aileen Chiu said. "And our Kitty woke up and said she thought she saw an angel. So I said to Albert—it's come down from heaven to take somebody, you mark my words. And I was right."

"Your Kitty saw an angel? On Mr. Lee's rooftop?" I asked.

"She couldn't exactly pinpoint it to Mr. Lee's rooftop, but it was one of those buildings farther down the block. Her father thought she'd dreamed it, of course, but she was quite insistent. It was either an angel or a fairy, she said."

"Did she say what this angel looked like?" I tried to keep my voice steady.

"A little dainty spirit thing, like a young girl with white wings, and it flew from one roof to the next."

CHAPTER TWENTY-SEVEN

I ran all the way back to the El station on Chatham Square, driven by my anger. I stood, seething, on the railway platform, waiting for a train that didn't come. Finally it dawned on me that today was a public holiday and the train schedule would be curtailed. I ran down the steps again, not willing to wait any longer, threw caution to the winds, and hailed myself a cab.

I had to get back to Patchin Place immediately. I had to confront her. I didn't stop to think that if she had killed once before, most efficiently, she could do so again if cornered. I was so furious at having been taken in by her. *Poor little Bo Kei—please do what you can to help Frederick. I know he's innocent.* Well, of course he was innocent if she had killed Lee Sing Tai herself. Unless she had persuaded or driven him to help her. She had demonstrated just how forceful she could be. And he was besotted with her. A man will do a lot for a woman he loves, especially if there is only one way for them to be together and that involved hurling her husband from a rooftop.

There was still the question of the big workman's boots. Frederick was a clerk, and his sort didn't wear hobnail boots. But then I had never actually studied his feet. He could have inherited the shoe size of his European mother. He could have worn those boots that night to throw us off the scent. I dismissed that notion right away. Who would be aware that the tar on the rooftop might become soft enough to leave imprints after a hot day?

But if Bo Kei had killed Mr. Lee, she would surely have needed an accomplice to help her carry the unconscious Lee Sing Tai to the edge of the roof. And in my cursory examination I had seen no sign in the dust and dirt up there of a body having been dragged. And what better accomplice than her beloved Frederick? I realized with utter mortification that I had probably been duped yet again.

No, that wasn't quite true. I had made poor judgments. I had assumed that she and Frederick were innocent because they seemed like nice, wholesome young people. And yet Daniel had reminded me more than once that murderers don't look like villains. I came to the conclusion that my anger was directed at myself as much as at Bo Kei.

As the cab came to a halt at the entrance to Patchin Place I felt a sudden spasm of fear. In my mind as I had traveled northward, Bo Kei had become a dangerous monster, not just a frightened and desperate girl. What if she had killed my friends—stolen their jewels and run off? I overpaid the cabby in my haste and teetered in my impractical lady's shoes over the cobbles to their front door. Why, oh, why did they not make sensible shoes for women? I'd willingly have worn hobnail boots. I knocked on the front door, waited for what seemed an age, then let out a huge sigh of relief as Sid answered it.

"Thank heavens," I muttered. "Where is Bo Kei?"

Sid looked surprised.

"What's the matter? You look as white as a sheet. She's sleeping, I believe. Gus felt an urge to paint today, so I moved the Chinese girl into your room, as she said she was sleepy."

The horrible vision in my head transformed into a picture of Gus sitting engrossed in her painting while Bo Kei came up behind her, a heavy object in her hand. I left Sid staring at me and positively ran up the stairs. My bedroom door was closed. I flung it open and a sleepy Bo Kei opened her eyes and looked up at me.

"Missie Molly. You come back. What news?" she asked, sitting up anxiously.

"How could you?" I burst out, my intention to tread carefully with a dangerous killer having been forgotten in the heat of the moment. "You lied to me. You let me help you and spirit you to safety. Do you realize I can find myself in terrible trouble for harboring a criminal? This could put my upcoming marriage in jeopardy."

"What do you mean?" She stared at me worriedly. "What criminal do you speak of?"

"Don't you play innocent with me, miss. You begged me to save poor Frederick because you knew he was innocent. Of course you knew it. All the time it was you!"

She looked as if she was about to cry. "What was me? What have I done?"

"Killed the person who stood between you and happiness. You were seen, Bo Kei. Someone saw you leaping from one rooftop to the next."

"Yes, I did this. On the night that I escaped, more than one week ago."

"No, on the night that Lee Sing Tai was hurled down to his death."

"That is not possible." She looked shocked. "How could I be there? You yourself took me to the house of safety."

"I am told it would be comparatively easy to come and go unnoticed from that house. Maybe you climbed down the drainpipe again. Maybe you got out of your window and crossed the roof to make your escape. You seem rather good at doing that kind of thing."

She was still staring at me in horror. "But I did not kill Lee Sing Tai. I swear this. I also swear that I did not go to his rooftop that night. That man frightens me. I would do anything in my power to stay away from him. Why would I risk going back to a man who would make me his slave?"

"So that you could be free forever, of course. So that you could be with Frederick. While Lee Sing Tai was alive you would never be free, would you?"

"I admit it. I am glad that he is dead," she said in a small voice. "But I swear to you, on all the holy saints of your church, that I was not the one who pushed him from the roof. I was not the one who killed him."

I stared at her, wishing I could read her mind. There was something about the way she phrased that last sentence that made me wonder if she knew who did the actual killing if she didn't do it herself. "You know what I think?" I said. "That you and Frederick planned this between you. You might not have been strong enough to throw Lee off the roof, but Frederick was."

"No, this is not true. Frederick is innocent. He is a good, upright man. He would never do a terrible thing like this, never." She was sobbing now. "Please, Missie Molly. Please believe me."

"I want to believe you, Bo Kei. I wanted to help both of you, but if someone tells me they saw a small, slight figure jumping from roof to roof, the very night that Lee Sing Tai was killed, what am I to believe?"

She went to say something, hesitated, then said, "Maybe what they saw was laundry, flapping in the wind. Plenty laundry on rooftops. Maybe it was someone moving across another roof on their way to bed. Plenty people sleep on roof when weather is hot."

"It doesn't matter. If you and Frederick did this between you, then the truth will soon come out," I said. "He is being held in the Tombs. That is a terrible place. I've been there. If he has something to confess, trust me, he will confess it."

"But what if they make him confess to something that he didn't do?" She wailed. "This happens all the time in China. Men will say anything when police do terrible things like drive bamboo under fingernails or burn with red hot pokers."

I shuddered. "The police here don't do anything like that," I said. "I only meant that those cells are damp and it is frightening to be locked away in darkness. If Frederick really is innocent, then you have nothing to fear."

As I said the words a sliver of doubt crept into my mind. I knew there were policemen like Daniel who were firm but honest. But then there was also Captain Kear, who had made it quite clear that Frederick was the ideal suspect. Might he not resort to underhanded means to make Frederick confess to something he didn't do?

"I do not think they will ever be able to discover who did this crime," she said, looking at me defiantly now. "A man falls from a rooftop. How can they know if he was pushed? How can they say who pushed him if nobody saw?"

"They have ways of finding out," I said. "For one thing, someone had hit him on the head to knock him out. They will find the weapon and there will be fingerprints on it."

"Fingerprints? What is this?"

"Did you know that every person's finger leaves a print of a different pattern? The police now have a way of examining the prints people leave on objects that they touch. Later they take fingerprints from people they suspect, and if one of them matches up, then they know who is guilty. Clever, no?"

She nodded.

"The New York police are among the first to put finger-printing into action."

"But people must leave fingerprints all over their own houses."

"Of course they do. But if a strange print shows up where it shouldn't—on a heavy object that struck Lee Sing Tai, for example—then they will not stop until they have found the person who matches that print."

I had hoped this might scare her, and indeed she did look worried, but then she said, "If Frederick or I had done this terrible thing, you would not be able to prove it by finding our fingerprints at Lee's house. I lived in that place and Frederick was summoned there by his employer. The police would ex-pect to find that we had touched many things."

That was true, of course. I didn't know what else to say. In fact I found myself deeply confused. She wasn't acting as if she was guilty, but then I obviously wasn't as good at ex-tracting a confession as professionals like Daniel. What was I going to do with her? If she had killed Lee Sing Tai, then I certainly didn't want to compromise myself or Sid and Gus for a moment longer. But if she was telling the truth and she was innocent, then I didn't want to hand her over to Captain Kear either. I deeply regretted my rash behavior in bringing her here. When would I learn to think first and not act on impulse? I came to a decision: I would tell Sid and Gus the whole story, as much as I knew it. They were worldly wise, intelligent women. I would let them suggest our next course of action.

"You can go back to your nap," I said, "but whatever you do, don't try to leave the house. Every policeman in New York is looking for you. I want to speak to our hostesses. We must decide what to do with you."

"They will believe I am innocent," she said defiantly. "They are good, kind women."

I was on my way to the door when I heard deep pounding coming from below. Someone was hammering on the front door. Bo Kei leaped to her feet and ran over to me.

"The police have found me," she whimpered.

"Let's hope not. Stay put until I come back."

As I came out onto the upper landing Sid was coming up the stairs. She held a piece of paper in her hand.

"That was a messenger boy," she said. "It's a message from Sarah Lindley for Bo Kei. Not good news, I'm afraid."

She handed me the sheet of paper. It read: I AM SORRY TO INFORM YOU THAT YOUR FRIEND ANNIE HAS JUST PASSED AWAY.

CHAPTER TWENTY-EIGHT

B o Kei was distraught when I told her the sad news.
Her face crumpled and she broke into noisy sobs.

"No, this can't be true," she said. "How did she
die?"

I went to sit on the bed beside her and put my hand gently
on hers. "She was very sick, Bo. She had consumption. People
who catch that disease don't get better."

"No!" She was shaking her head violently now. "She tell
me she not so sick. She says she will soon be well and we
will go away from New York together."

I looked at her with pity. "I'm sure she said that to make
you feel better. She didn't want to upset you with the knowledge that she was going to die."

"But yesterday she was well. She was jumping around and
laughing. Having good time. She has plenty strength to—"
She broke off. "She was plenty strong," she corrected herself.
She stood up suddenly. "I must go to see her."

"You know that's not possible. It's too dangerous for you
to leave the house at the moment. You must stay here."

"But I must. I must make sure her bones are taken back to
China or she will never rest."

"You were raised by Christian nuns, Bo Kei," I said.
"Surely you believe that her soul has gone up to heaven. It
doesn't matter what happens to her bones."

"But Chinese believe bones must be buried with ancestors or ghosts will walk without home." She shook her head, sending out a spray of tears. "All my fault. I should never leave her behind when I come here. I beg you to bring her along, but you say no."

"Bo Kei, I couldn't risk bringing a dreadful disease like consumption into my friends' home. You have to understand that. I was trying to do my best to save you. I should have left well enough alone."

"Yes," she said. "If I had been with Annie, maybe she would still be alive."

"What do you mean?"

"I mean maybe she doesn't die from this wasting disease. New York is dangerous place. Perhaps bad men find her."

"What bad men are you talking about?"

I stared at her. She shrugged. "Plenty bad men in New York," she said.

I wasn't quite sure where this was going. "But she didn't run away from the brothel, did she? She was thrown out because of her disease."

"Yes, but . . ." She hesitated, chewing on her lip. I sensed that she wanted to tell me more, but was afraid to.

It's not your business. Don't get involved. The words boomed through my head. As usual I ignored them.

"I'll go to the settlement house, if you like," I said. "I can find out for you what will happen to her body and where she'll be buried."

"Okay." She nodded, defeated. "You tell them I must know where they bury her, because one day it is my duty, as family member, to take her home to our village in China."

"I'll tell them that," I said, thinking that it was most likely that poor Annie would be buried in the potter's field with all the others who couldn't afford a proper funeral. I went across to Gus's studio and poked my head around the door. Gus was sitting with her back to me, facing a canvas covered in a bewildering array of dots.

"What do you think?" she asked. "I'm trying the new pointillist style. It really captures the essence of the scene, don't you think?"

I actually thought it looked like a child with bad chicken pox, but I nodded politely. "Definitely," I said. "Could I possibly interrupt and ask you to come downstairs for a minute. I want to talk to you and Gus."

She followed me, intrigued. I sat with them in the kitchen and told them everything. "So you see," I finished, "we might be harboring a murderer. I'm deeply sorry I have involved you in this. It's your house. You tell me what you want to do with her. I'm going back to the settlement house now. I can take her with me if you want me to."

"People in this country are innocent until proven guilty," Sid said. "What does she have to say for herself?"

"Of course she pleads innocence, most emphatically— but she would, wouldn't she?"

Sid glanced at Gus. "I think she should stay put for now. At least until we have thought this through."

Gus turned to me. "And I think you should come clean with Daniel. Tell him the whole thing. He may have qualities of which I don't approve, but I think he's fair and straight."

"Tell Daniel?" I felt my stomach twist itself into a knot. I could just imagine what he'd say when he found out that I had hidden the woman the police were searching for.

"He's the only one who can decide what to do with her. We're just not equipped to do so, Molly." She gave me a sympathetic smile. "I know you mean well. I know you wanted to help, but if you really think she may have killed this Chinaman, then we really shouldn't keep on hiding her."

I sighed. "I know. And you're right. I should come clean with Daniel. But I have to tell you I'm dreading the thought."

"Nonsense," Sid said. "You're a responsible adult, Molly. You did what you thought was best. If he doesn't like it, then tough luck." She put her hands on my shoulders. "If you don't stand up to him now, he'll walk all over you. I've seen it so many times—a strong, bright girl gets married and soon she's reduced to a quivering, helpless little jelly, trying to please her bully of a husband."

I had to laugh at this. "I can't see myself ever being reduced to a quivering jelly," I said.

"But if you're frightened of facing him and telling him the truth, that's the first step on that road."

"I suppose I feel guilty because I went behind his back and kept on with the investigation," I said. "But you're right—if we can't face each other as equals, what sort of life do I have ahead of me?"

"Just tell him that. And if he tries to bully you, tell him you'll call off the wedding," Sid said.

I stared at her. "I couldn't do that."

"Molly, he has to know that he is not the king of your little castle—or at least, only if you're the queen."

"I wish I could send you in my place," I said. "But I'll get going right away. Wish me luck."

"Don't stand any nonsense from him," Sid called after me.

It was all right for her. She didn't have to face an angry Daniel. I felt positively sick as I rode the Broadway trolley southward to police headquarters. As the journey progressed, I decided that I really should go to the house on Elizabeth Street first, before I confronted Daniel. I had promised Bo Kei that I would report back to her, and after I had told Daniel the truth, there might not be a chance to fulfill that promise. At least that was my reasoning for putting off the moment when I had to face him. So I set off for Elizabeth Street.

The house seemed awfully quiet as I stepped into the hallway. Someone had been cooking and the odor of fried bacon wafted from the kitchen.

"Hello!" I called and Sarah appeared at the top of the stairs.

"Molly, it's you," she said, coming down the stairs to meet me. "Good of you to come. Such a sad occurrence. She seemed so much better, so much more cheerful, but then I've seen it before, haven't you—that people seem to rally right before they die."

"How long ago did it happen?" I asked.

"We're not quite sure," she said. "I got here around ten o'clock. I was asked to go and collect Annie's breakfast tray. We took her meals up to her so that she didn't eat with the other house residents and risk contaminating them. I went up and tapped on her door, then I let myself into the room. At first I thought she was sleeping and tiptoed across to retrieve her tray. Then something looked strange about her and I took another look. Her eyes were open and she was staring at the ceiling. I touched her and she was cool to the touch—not quite cold, but cool. And I realized she was dead."

"I'm sorry," I said. "That must have been a shock for you."

She nodded agreement. "I've worked here long enough now that I've seen a dead body or two, but one never gets used to it, does one?"

"I agree," I said. "I've seen quite a few dead bodies, but it's always a shock, especially when you had grown fond of the girl and had hopes for her recovery."

"I don't know about that," she said. "One does not normally recover from consumption, but she had seemed so much brighter since the other Chinese girl arrived. Poor thing—I expect it was a shock for Bo Kei, having found a cousin only to lose her again."

I nodded. "She was very upset. She begged me to come and see Annie for a last time and she was emphatic about knowing where Annie will be buried so that her bones can be taken home to China one day."

Sarah sighed. "I don't think we have much control over where she'll be buried. Paupers' graves are—well, paupers' graves. But I'll see what I can do. We have several resident volunteers whose families have clout in this city. Maybe we can bend the rules."

"You're very kind," I said. "Could I possibly go up and see her? Bo Kei will want to know how she looked."

"Of course." Sarah turned back up the stairs. "Please follow me."

Up the stairs we went, one flight, then two. Annie's body was lying covered by a sheet. I tiptoed across as if I were afraid of waking her and gently pulled back the sheet. I looked down at her, then frowned. I had expected her to look pale and translucent, the way people were always described when dying of consumption. Instead of that her face and neck had a purplish hue.

"Was her face that color when you found her?" I asked.

"Yes, it was. I wonder if it was the disease coming out. It's not very pleasant, is it?"

As I continued to stare at her, a thought was nagging at the back of my brain—something Daniel had told me once. He had mentioned skin turning purple when . . . the word *suffocation* popped into my head.

"How was she lying when you found her?" I asked.

"Just like this. Very peaceful, except for the purple skin and the red eyes."

Fighting back my abhorrence, I lifted one of her eyelids. What would normally be the white of her eye was full of little red dots. I released her eyelid and shuddered.

"Sarah, who has been here today? Did anybody from outside go up to see her?"

She looked puzzled. "Nobody. Nobody's been here at all. It's a holiday, you see. It's been especially quiet."

"Who took up the breakfast tray? Was she alive then?"

"Yes, but she was sleeping, so the worker who took up the tray let her sleep. The food hadn't been touched, so she must have just passed away in her sleep."

"How many people are working in the house at present?" I asked. "Do you know them all? Can you vouch for all of them?"

Sarah looked puzzled. "What is this all about? Why the questions?"

I moved closer to her, glancing back at the open door. "I think she may not have died naturally. She may have been suffocated," I said in a whisper.

"You mean she was murdered?" Sarah put a hand to her mouth in horror.

"I'm not sure, but I have been told that red dots on the eye are a sure sign of suffocation and she has them. Has a doctor seen her and signed her death certificate?"

"No, not yet," she said. "But no one in the house could have done it. I know all these people well. We were all fond of Annie. None of them would have any reason to kill her."

"But you said yourself that the door is always open. It

would be relatively simple for an outsider to sneak in and out without being seen."

"I suppose so." Then she shook her head. "Not so easy in the mornings. There is always housework going on—floors being swept, bed linens changed. Someone would have to have taken a terrible risk."

I went across to the window. It was open about four inches. I pushed it up and leaned out. Even the normal clatter of Elizabeth Street was subdued today. Only a few pushcarts and an ice cream vendor. From the far end of the street came the sounds of an organ grinder playing a lively Italian tune.

"Well nobody could have climbed in this way," I said, pulling my head back in and closing the window. "It's sheer brick wall, without even a drainpipe or fire escape."

"I know. This is madness. You must be wrong, Molly. Perhaps her strange color has something to do with her disease."

"We'll know when the doctor comes," I said.

"We may not find a doctor today. It is a holiday, after all."

"Then I must ask Daniel to take a look at her. If what I suspect is true, then her death may have something to do with the murder of Mr. Lee."

"What could it have to do with his death?" Sarah demanded. "Annie was here for a good week before he was killed. And no outsiders knew she was here. What connection could there possibly be?"

"As to that, there was a connection, wasn't there? She had been Mr. Lee's concubine, several years ago, brought from China just like Bo Kei."

"But who could have found out she was here? And why kill a girl who was bound to die soon anyway?"

I couldn't come up with a good answer to this. "Perhaps the murderer thought he was killing Bo Kei. But then nobody knew that she had been brought here either, did they?" I shook my head. "It doesn't make sense, unless . . ."

"Unless what?"

"Unless Bo Kei knows more than she's told me." I drew the cover back over Annie's dead face. "I'm going to find

Daniel and have him question Bo Kei. Perhaps a policeman will get the truth out of her."

"What do you think she could be hiding?"

"That she was the one who killed Mr. Lee. Again it's only a theory and I can't prove it. And she's claiming she's innocent, but I get the feeling that she knows things that she's not telling me."

I touched Sarah's arm. "Don't mention any of this to anyone else yet. Not until Daniel has confirmed my suspicions. If the murderer works here or is observing us, I don't want him alerted."

"You think the murderer could work here or be watching us?" Sarah looked around nervously.

"We can't be too careful at the moment. This is someone who was prepared to take a risk, killing a girl in broad daylight in a house full of people."

"I wish Monty hadn't gone now," Sarah said. "I'd feel safer with a man in the house. We're all women volunteers on today."

"I think you're quite safe. Annie was only killed because someone suspected she knew something they didn't want made public. We'll know more when Daniel speaks with Bo Kei."

I tiptoed out of the room with a backward glance at the form of Annie under the sheet.

CHAPTER TWENTY-NINE

I left the house and started toward police headquarters on Mulberry Street. As I walked, I thought through what I was going to say to Daniel and I realized that I wasn't ready to face him yet. I had too many unanswered questions and I wanted to speak to Bo Kei first. I changed course and continued toward the Broadway trolley. Even if I was going to incur Daniel's displeasure, I didn't want to give up on this investigation now when I could sense that I was onto something. I had no idea what I was onto, but it had been my experience that if a second murder happens, it is usually linked to the first. I already had potential links—Annie had been in Bo Kei's position once as Mr. Lee's concubine. She had been cast out and sent to the ultimate disgrace and degradation of working in a brothel. But that was five years ago. She had already been punished for not having a son, and cast out—so why would somebody want to kill her now?

And yet Bo Kei had feared for her. I remembered how pitifully she had begged me to take Annie with her. She must have suspected that Annie's life was in danger. Which might indicate that she hadn't killed Lee Sing Tai herself. She certainly couldn't have killed Annie since she was helping me clear up the debris of the party when Annie died. It was all quite baffling and I just hoped I might be able to persuade Bo Kei to tell me the truth. At least I'd be able to observe her reaction when I told her that Annie had not died of natural means.

I strode out with determination after I alighted from the trolley. I suppose also at the back of my mind was the desire to present Daniel with a case that I had solved and thus to justify my actions. I entered the house and took Sid and Gus aside to tell them what I had discovered. Then I went upstairs to confront Bo Kei. She was standing at the top of the second flight peering down to see what was going on.

"You saw her, Missie Molly?" she called, her voice quivering with distress. "She is really dead?"

"Yes, I did and—" I stopped short. I was staring at her bare feet.

"Bo Kei," I blurted out, "you have big feet."

"I know." She sounded surprised at this observation. "Big disgrace to my family. Small feet are good. Many girls in China have bound feet, but the missionaries say to my family this is wrong and bad. So my feet were not bound, and they are extra big. My mother say no man want to marry me."

Then whose footprints had made those little indentations at the edge of the roof?

"Bo Kei," I said severely, "it's about time you told me everything that you know. You have lied to me and kept things from me, and if you don't tell me the truth, I'll have the police take you to an American jail."

"But I tell you truth," she wailed. "I say that I do not kill Lee Sing Tai and I do not know who kills him. This is truth."

"Not the whole truth, obviously. You didn't want to leave Annie behind at the house. You were frightened for her—why?"

"She is family and she is sick. I no want to leave her alone among strangers."

"No, it was more than that," I said. A strange idea was forming in my head—a picture of the two girls dancing around together, Annie looking livelier than I'd ever have believed possible. "You thought she might be in danger. Well, it turned out she was in danger. Somebody killed her, Bo Kei."

"Kill her?"

"Put a pillow over her face and suffocated her. Made her stop breathing." I stepped closer, staring her right in the eye, hoping that my greater height would be intimidating. "Why do you think that was? Do you want to tell me the truth now, or are you going to let Annie's killer walk free?"

She looked at me with frightened eyes. "I do not know who might have killed her," she said.

"Then let me ask you this—why do you think someone killed her? Was it someone from the brothel who came after her? Someone who worked for Lee Sing Tai or Bobby Lee? Was someone afraid she would divulge something she knew?"

She shook her head.

"She's dead, Bo. There's nothing you can do to bring her back, but you can help us find her killer. So let me ask you this—I saw small footprints on the roof. A tiny, dainty foot. Were they possibly Annie's footprints? Was she on that roof? Did she go to kill Lee Sing Tai?"

She hung her head. "She make me promise I never tell anyone," she said.

"But she's dead now. Tell me. In this country we punish people for being an accessory to a crime."

"What does this mean?"

"That you knew about a crime and you helped the criminal in some way, even if you didn't commit the crime yourself. Did she kill Lee Sing Tai? Did she?"

"No!" She yelled out the word. "No, she did not kill him." Then she sank onto the top stair and put her head in her hands. "She wanted to. She went to the rooftop with that purpose."

"She was well and strong enough to climb up to a rooftop and then leap from one roof to the next?"

She nodded. "She was not as sick as she acted. She knew if she was sick they would throw her out of the bad-women house—not want her to make their customers sick."

"You're saying she was only acting? She didn't have consumption?"

"Yes, she knew that she had this disease, but not as bad

as she wanted everyone to think. She knew she would die from it one day, but right now she was strong enough to climb up and jump across from one roof to the next. It is not such a big leap if one has no fear. And she had no fear, only anger. She said to me, 'This man must not be allowed to put more girls through shame and misery. He must be stopped now.' And when I tried to tell her not to go, she said, 'My life is over. I will die some day soon. But I make sure this man pays before I die.'"

"She went to kill him—but she didn't go through with it?"

"No," she said. "Because of the ghost."

"What ghost?"

Bo Kei looked up at me as if she didn't want to go on. "When she reached the roof of Lee Sing Tai's house, he was not there but the door that led to the stairs was open. She plucked up courage and started to go down the stairs to his bedroom. As she stood at the top of the stairs she looked down and what do you think she saw? She saw a ghost floating up toward her. That's when she knew that Lee Sing Tai was already dead."

"So what did she do then?"

"Everyone is afraid of angry ghosts. She ran. She jumped across to the next roof and almost didn't make it. When she came back to me she was crying and couldn't breathe. She made me promise that I would tell nobody what she had done."

"This ghost?" I said. "What did it look like?"

"It was a white floating head in the darkness," she said. "It stared up at her with an open mouth but no sound came out. And it had lots of arms and legs, like a demon or a monster."

"And she thought it was Lee's ghost and he was already dead?"

She nodded. "What else could it be?"

"I don't know, but I don't believe in ghosts myself. I'm afraid we'll have to tell this story to the police, Bo Kei. At least it should make them release Frederick."

She gave me a watery smile. "All right. I will tell your good policeman."

"I'm going to see him now," I said. "I will bring him back

here to talk to you and you will tell him everything you know."

"I will get in trouble?"

I shook my head. "No, I don't think so. If what you say is true, then Annie did nothing wrong—except for trespassing on someone's property."

"And they will now believe that Frederick did nothing wrong either and they will set him free?" she asked hopefully.

"Yes, I believe they will set him free."

The smile of relief that flooded her face reassured me once and for all that she had not been involved in the killing herself. And for the third time that day I set off back to Mulberry Street. When Daniel and I were married, I thought, there would be a telephone in the house so that the police could get in contact with him whenever he was needed. Such a useful instrument. It would have saved me a fortune in shoe leather!

CHAPTER THIRTY

As I took the trolley southward yet again I rehearsed what I was going to say to Daniel. I had uncovered valuable information, so he should be pleased with me. On the other hand, I had continued my involvement in this case when he had expressly forbidden me to. The knot in the pit of my stomach returned. He was going to shout at me. Be furious with me. Then suddenly I decided that this wasn't like me at all. I wasn't usually the sort of person who cowered before men. I was turning into the kind of female I despised, the kind who lost her individuality and gumption when she married. What sort of a life would I have if my sole purpose on this Earth was to defer to my husband and make sure I didn't upset him?

Enough is enough, I said to myself. If I didn't stand up to Daniel now, he would dominate me for the rest of my life. He was going to have to accept that I was not prepared to turn into a helpless little wife. I could understand that he didn't want me to continue my career as an investigator because that could be seen as compromising his position in the police department. And he did feel the need to protect me, which was nice. And God knows I'd been in need of protection several times in the past couple of years. But I wasn't going to let him bully me or dictate to me.

Having come to that decision I strode out from the trolley with more confidence. But I have to confess that as I went up

the steps into that austere building, that confidence did waver
a little. Still, I held my chin high as I approached the front
desk.

"I wish to speak to Captain Sullivan," I announced to the
constable who was manning the front desk. "It's most urgent."

"I'm afraid Captain Sullivan's not here at the moment,"
he said. "Will one of the other officers do instead?"

"No, thank you." I felt the relief of reprieve and had to
force myself to continue, "You don't know where I might find
him?"

"No, miss. I couldn't tell you that," he said.

"Even if you did know, you mean?" I stared at him.
"Look, I have some facts for him. It's important that he gets
them as soon as possible. If you won't tell me, may I write a
note and you can ask one of your men to deliver it to him?"

"What's this concerning, miss?" he asked warily.

"A murder case he's working on."

He was still looking at me most suspiciously. "And you say
you have important information for him?"

He was driving me mad. "Yes. Now for goodness sake,
please provide me with a pen and paper."

He did so and I wrote: *Daniel, I need to speak to you immediately about the murder of Lee Sing Tai. I have obtained
valuable knowledge, which I want to share only with you. I
believe there has been a second murder. I will await you
at*—I didn't want to go all the way back to Patchin Place
again—*the settlement house on Elizabeth Street.* It would be
better that he examine Annie's corpse for himself before he
questioned Bo Kei.

I finished up with: *Yours, Molly.*

I only hoped I *was* his after this. I blotted the sheet, folded
it, then handed it to the young policeman.

"I'll see that he gets it, miss," the constable said. He poked
his head through into a back room. "Harry, this note has to
get to Captain Sullivan," he said. "The young lady says she's
got information concerning the case he's working on."

Another constable, this one looking absurdly young and
boyish with a freckled face and strawberry blond hair, came

to the doorway and paused there looking at me with interest. Obviously he then decided I looked respectable enough. "Right you are, miss. I can't guarantee where he's likely to be. Knowing the captain, he could be anywhere." He turned to give his companion a grin. "But I'll find out and we'll see he gets it. What name shall I say?"

I really didn't want them to know I was Daniel's fiancée or they'd think it was some trifling domestic matter such as my needing to speak to him on the color of ribbons.

"It's Murphy," I said, "but the pertinent information is all contained in that letter and it's rather vital that he gets it so that a murderer doesn't have the chance to slip away."

At the word "murderer," the constable's face became somber. "He'll know where to find you, will he?"

"I've put that in the note."

"Then I'm sure he'll come as soon as he can," he said and escorted me to the doorway.

I went out into the street and was about to go on my way to Elizabeth Street when I had an idea. I ducked into a shop front and waited. Sure enough, a few minutes later the freckle-faced constable appeared and set off down Mulberry Street. I followed, at a sensible distance. I had a problem keeping up with him as he was moving along with the large strides of a young man and my shoes didn't fare so well on the cobbles. At the corner of Bayard he turned left. . . . And I realized he was heading for Mott Street. I was in luck. So Daniel had heeded my pleas to find out the truth and get Frederick released. He was still working on the murder investigation, in spite of having told me that it was Captain Kear's territory.

Sure enough, the constable stopped just before he reached Lee Sing Tai's residence. Another constable was standing guard outside.

"Is Captain Sullivan in there?" I heard the first ask.

"As far as I know," the other agreed. "He went in some time ago and I haven't seen him come out yet."

I decided I had been patient long enough. I stepped forward. "Thank you, Constable. I can take it from here," I said.

The constable I had followed from Mulberry looked both shocked and mortified that I had followed him. "But, miss—"

"It's all right. I know the case he's working on and I have important facts that he'll want to receive immediately," I said.

"You do?" I could see him torn between interrupting an angry Captain Sullivan and getting into trouble for letting me interrupt an angry Captain Sullivan.

I decided a small white lie was in order. "He is expecting me," I said. "He wanted me to get in touch with him the minute I heard anything."

I saw relief flood his face. "Oh, well, in that case, miss . . ." He saluted me and hightailed it back up Mott Street. I took a deep breath before going up the stairs to Lee's residence.

The faint smell of incense still lingered in the hallway. On the other side of the screen I could hear low voices. There was no sign of the houseboy. I tapped gently on the wall, then came around the screen.

"I'm sorry to interrupt you, but—"

I broke off in midsentence and froze. Daniel's was not one of the two men's voices I had heard. Captain Kear and Bobby Lee were sitting together on the sofa, heads together in low conversation. They both leaped to their feet as they saw me and I could have sworn they looked guilty.

"I'm terribly sorry," I said. "I was looking for Captain Sullivan."

"Captain Sullivan? He's not here," Kear said.

"But the constable standing guard outside said that he was. He said that the captain had entered some time ago and he hadn't seen him come out."

A quick questioning look passed between Captain Kear and Bobby Lee.

"Well, he's not here now," Bobby Lee snapped.

"I wonder if he could be up on the roof, checking out where the murder was committed or how the assailant got away," I said.

"Why would he be doing that?" Bobby Lee demanded.

"Ordinary murder does not require exalted men like Captain Sullivan who have better things to do."

"Besides," Captain Kear added, "I already made it clear that this was my case and I had the prime suspect in jail."

"I'll just go up to the roof and take a look, if you don't mind," I said. "Just on the off chance he's still up there."

I didn't wait for permission and they didn't deny it. But as I was halfway up the stairs I heard Bobby's Lee's distinctive Chinese accent hissing, "What does she want? Do you think he sent her?"

And Kear replying, "If she hasn't gone in a second we'll get rid of her."

I didn't like the sound of that. It could be as harmless as making sure that I left or it could mean that I followed Lee Sing Tai over the edge of that roof. I hesitated, not wanting to go up the second flight of stairs. But I had to find Daniel and if he wasn't there, that meant that he might also have taken the leap across to the next roof. I certainly wasn't going to follow him on that route.

I went up to the rooftop. It was empty. The brass bed frame was still there, but the bed had been stripped. A strong wind was blowing from the Hudson, making the laundry on surrounding roofs flap loudly. I jumped as a nightgown suddenly billowed out. But there was no sign that Daniel had ever been there. So I came down again. As I crossed the upper landing I thought I saw a flash of movement in Lee Sing Tai's bedroom. I expected it to be the old woman spying on me, but to my surprise I saw Daniel's face. He put his finger to his lips and beckoned me ferociously. I crossed the hallway, and with one swift movement he grabbed my arm and spun me into the room, shutting the door behind me.

"What are you doing here?" he mouthed at me. At least he wasn't using profanity, but he didn't look too overjoyed to see me.

"There's been a second murder, connected to Lee's death," I answered in a whisper. "I wanted you to come and see right away. And why are we whispering?"

"Because I didn't want my presence in this house known to the occupants down below," Daniel said. "Now you've announced to all and sundry that I'm here, I have no choice but to reveal myself. Once again you've successfully managed to wreck what I was trying to do."

"I'm sorry," I said. "But I thought you should know that someone has just been murdered."

"How the devil did you know where to find me—or was it just a lucky chance that you stumbled upon me here?"

"I went to Mulberry Street. I wrote you a note. One of your men was sent to deliver it to you and I followed him."

Daniel shook his head as if nothing about me would surprise him any longer. "There's no point in standing here any longer," he said. "Now that my presence has been revealed, I'd better go down and face the music."

"You could make your escape across the rooftops if you wanted to. I could say I didn't find you," I suggested, wanting to please.

"I'm not risking my neck, thank you. No, there's nothing for it, I'm afraid." He opened the door and went down the stairs ahead of me.

Captain Kear looked up, scowling. "What are you doing here, Sullivan?" he demanded. "I thought we agreed this was Sixth Precinct business."

Daniel had resumed his cocky, almost arrogant appearance. "As to that, Kear, you know damned well that headquarters can take over any case it chooses, if it deems it's beyond the scope of one precinct. But to answer your question civilly, you came to us, asking for forensic help. We have determined that Mr. Lee was knocked over the head with the statue of some god in his bedroom. We've detected traces of blood and hair on the statue—also fingerprints we haven't yet identified, but not those of the man you are holding in the Tombs."

"Then Frederick is innocent," I interrupted, trying to play the innocent myself. "I'm so glad."

Captain Kear and Bobby Lee were both scowling at us.

"So I was just checking the rest of his room for matching

fingerprints," Daniel went on breezily. "It appears he was killed down there and not on the rooftop. Interesting, don't you think? Makes one believe that it would be someone who knew him who would have the nerve to come into his bedroom and feel comfortable walking around his house." He turned to Bobby. "Have my men taken your fingerprints yet, Bobby? No matter, I'm sure they're already in our files from past incidents."

I was impressed at his bravado. Once again he had clearly taken over, asserted his superiority over the other men, and was enjoying it.

"But I must leave you now, gentlemen," he continued after neither of the men spoke. "Miss Murphy has uncovered yet another piece of evidence that I must inspect right away. And I believe that I ordered both this room and the bedroom to be sealed off as crime scenes, until our inspections had concluded. So I'm not sure what you're doing sitting here."

"This is now my place," Bobby said, sticking out his chin belligerently. "I make sure nobody steal from my father's house."

"If anyone did the stealing, I suspect it might be you, Bobby," Daniel said. "Has the cabinet been thoroughly checked yet?"

"There was no need," Captain Kear said. "We had a perfect suspect in jail. If you tell me that his fingerprints are not on the murder weapon, then I suppose we'll have to start from square one again and go through that cabinet. I'll arrange for a translator."

"Notify me when you have him. I want to be there. I take it the cabinet is locked?"

"Yes, and I have the key." Kear produced it from his top pocket, wrapped in a white handkerchief. Daniel held out his hand, took it from him, and inserted it into the cabinet. "We'll leave it there and nobody will be allowed to enter this room. That includes you, Bobby."

"This will be my house, I tell you," he said angrily.

"Only if your birth certificate stands up to scrutiny under American law, and I rather fear that the old lady will be only too happy to testify against you. She's still in the place, I take it?"

"Up in her bedroom. Doesn't come down," Bobby said. "Cook brings her meals up to her."

"That's fine," Daniel said. "The two of them but nobody else, right, Kear? You and I will meet here when you've lined up your interpreter and we'll conclude the last of the fingerprinting."

"If you say so," Kear said flatly, giving Daniel a look of pure animosity.

"Right. Off we go then." Daniel made it sound like an invitation to a picnic. The other men rose reluctantly and went to the stairs ahead of us.

"Come, Molly," Daniel said. Captain Kear was just passing around the screen when Daniel added, "And Kear, I suggest you release your suspect from the Tombs. I think we'll have this case sewn up by the end of the day."

With that he took my hand and escorted me down the stairs.

CHAPTER THIRTY-ONE

The moment we stepped out into the street, Daniel waited until Kear and Bobby Lee went their separate ways, then grabbed my forearm and dragged me into a side alley.

"Now what's this about?" he demanded.

"As I told you, there has been a second murder."

"Why is it you who brings me this message and not one of my own men?" he asked, his face only inches from mine.

"I didn't want to tell anyone else," I said. "Especially not one of Captain Kear's men from the Sixth Precinct."

"You mean the murder hasn't been reported to the police yet?"

I shook my head. "Nobody actually knows it's a murder yet except for the woman who summoned me, and I've asked her to keep quiet until you see the body."

"So who is it?"

"A Chinese girl at the settlement house on Elizabeth Street. The workers there thought she'd died of consumption but I recognized from what you had told me that she'd been suffocated."

"May I ask what you were doing at a settlement house on Elizabeth Street? You are not still working on this case when I made it quite clear to you that it was solely a police matter?"

I could hear the anger rising in his voice.

"Before you get on your high horse," I said, my own voice

rising now, "it was Sarah Lindley, whom you met last night, who called me to the settlement house where she works in a volunteer capacity. Naturally she was upset at finding one of their residents dead." I was rather proud of this explanation, which was nothing but the truth.

"And what does her death have to do with that of Mr. Lee? Is she the missing bride?"

"She was his former concubine who has recently escaped from a brothel," I said.

Daniel's eyebrows shot up at the mention of such subjects coming from the lips of a lady.

"How the devil did you find that out?"

"She told Sarah her whole story when she first came to them, of course."

"And who do you think might have killed her?"

"Whoever killed Mr. Lee," I said.

"And who do you suspect that might be?"

"I thought you knew," I said. "I thought you said to Captain Kear that you'd been going on with the investigation and were about to make an arrest."

Daniel looked around, but the alley was still empty. "That was only to justify my presence in the apartment," he said in a low voice, "and to let him know who is the superior officer."

"So what were you doing there, then? Do you suspect Bobby Lee?"

"It's possible, but I was there on a different matter, about which I can't tell you," Daniel said. "Let's just say that you couldn't have come at a worse moment and I was lucky to get out of it as easily as I did."

"Do you think they were in it together?" I asked. "They seemed awfully chummy when I walked in on them."

Daniel smiled. "I told you—I can't discuss it with you."

"I'm sorry I barged in on you," I said. "I thought you'd want to know about the second murder."

"Of course," he said. "Well, I suppose I'd better go and take a look at the wretched woman, although I'm not sure why you decided there was a connection with Lee's murder."

"I told you—Lee brought her over to America several years ago to be his wife, or rather his concubine. When she didn't produce a son, he sent her to a brothel he owned."

"Charming," Daniel said. "I hope that inspires you to produce a son rapidly." He flashed me a grin before becoming serious again. "But then what current connection could she have had with him? More likely to have been some kind of underworld vendetta."

"Ah," I said.

Daniel was staring at me. "You know more about this matter?"

"Yes, I do." I looked around. "Could we go somewhere else to talk? It smells really bad in this alley and I feel uneasy speaking so close to Lee's residence."

"Very well," he said. "You can walk with me toward Elizabeth Street if you like. First I need to give my constable his orders, then we'll be on our way."

We picked our way past the piles of garbage and back to Mott Street.

"Go on," Daniel said. "What have you found out?"

"I know where the runaway bride is hiding," I said.

"So you *did* you keep working on this matter when I forbade you to?" He gave me a cold stare.

"I don't like the word 'forbade,'" I said. "It implies that you are the master and I the servant, you the captain and I the crew. Well, I'm sorry, but that's not how it's going to be and maybe we should sort this out before the wedding. I want to be your partner, Daniel, not your slave. If you can't see me as an equal, then the wedding is off."

He reacted with surprise, taking a step away from me. "What brought on that little tirade?" he demanded. "I forbade you to continue working on a case because it was now a police matter. I forbade you just as I would have forbidden any civilian involving herself with a criminal case."

"Oh," I said, the wind somewhat taken out of my sails. "I'm sorry, it's just that I've watched enough husbands boss their wives around. I've been worrying about giving up my freedom when we marry—being someone else's wife is a big step. I've seen bright, independent women reduced to simpering idiots doing only what their husbands tell them to do when they become wives."

"Would you really call off the wedding if I ordered you around?"

"Absolutely," I said. "I have a profession. I have good friends. I could live a pleasant life without a husband."

I could see his expression had softened. "But not as pleasant?"

"That remains to be seen," I said. "But I do want to marry you, Daniel. I do love you. It's just that I want us to start off on the right foot."

"And that would also include no deception between us," Daniel said. "I couldn't have a wife who goes behind my back. It has to be out in the open between us."

"Agreed," I said.

"And you will stop working as you promised?"

I hesitated. "We'll discuss that more on our honeymoon," I said. "I understand your reservations and, trust me, I have no wish to live with danger any longer. But I have to warn you now that I don't see my future in sewing undergarments and holding endless tea parties either."

He smiled. "No, I don't see you spending your days sewing, but I expect we'll find something to keep you busy." He paused. "Now we've got our lives sorted out, let's get back to this Chinese woman. Where is she?"

"She's currently at Sid and Gus's house."

"What? You've been hiding her from the police?"

"Don't start getting angry again. This is how it was. She was at the settlement house with the other Chinese girl who has just been murdered. Sarah Lindley told me about her. I brought her to Sid and Gus because I know that Captain Kear wanted to pin the crime on her and Frederick Lee. So I took her to safety until you could talk with her."

"Oh, I see." He nodded. "No, you wouldn't have wanted her turned over to Kear."

I allowed myself a little smirk. I had handled that rather well without telling an actual lie.

"And does this Chinese girl know who killed her friend?"

"Not exactly, but I think we can guess why she was killed. It turned out that the two girls were cousins. The one who had escaped from the brothel was angry that Mr. Lee was putting yet another girl through the degradation that would surely befall her. So she decided it had to stop. She knew how Bo Kei, that's the name of my Chinese bride, had escaped over the rooftop, so she went back that way, intending to kill Lee while he slept on the roof. But when she got there, he wasn't in his bed, and as she started to venture down the stairs she saw what she claimed was a ghost coming up toward her. She was terrified and fled back the way she came."

"You think the ghost she saw was the killer?"

"It had to be, didn't it?"

"But she didn't witness the actual murder?"

"No, but it's pretty obvious that she came face-to-face with the killer and he knew that she could identify him."

"And how did she describe this ghost?"

"A white face floating up above a strange animal shape, with too many arms and legs to be human."

"Ah, I see." Daniel's face lit up. "I knew it. Lee Sing Tai was either knocked out or killed in his bedroom, then the killer carried him up to the roof. She saw Lee's body over the killer's shoulder. That would explain the extra arms and legs."

"Yes!" I agreed excitedly. "Then at least we know that it had to be a man who did this. No woman would have been strong enough to carry a body that way."

"I have a nice set of fingerprints taken from the statue that knocked him out," Daniel said. "Now I just have to find out to whom they belong."

We had reached the corner of Bayard Street. "Look, I don't think you should come with me to the settlement house," he said. "It wouldn't look right to have you with me on a murder investigation. Why don't you go home and stay with this girl until I arrive? I may be a while, as I have some matters to take care of at headquarters first, but I'll come as soon as I can."

"All right, Daniel," I replied. I was delighted that we seemed to be working together for once.

"So Sarah Lindley will be there, will she?" he asked. "And she's the only one who knows that the death could be murder?"

"Oh, yes, she'll be there."

"I thought her fellow wanted her to stop this kind of thing."

"He did, but he relented. His only stipulation is that he accompanies her there and back at all times. He says the neighborhood is too dangerous."

"It is," Daniel agreed. "Only crazy young women like yourself think you can walk around these streets with impunity. Well, good for Monty. I think more charitably of him than I did. So that's why I've seen him in this part of the world."

"You've seen him around here?"

"On more than one occasion. Come to think of it, I saw him on my way to Mott Street today. He was hurrying along at a great clip and didn't see me."

"I expect he wanted to get out of such a distasteful area as quickly as possible," I said. "He always looks as if he's got a bad smell under his nose, doesn't he?"

Daniel smiled. "Not every girl can be lucky enough to land an excellent catch like me."

"Ah, but he's a lord with a huge property," I said. "Sarah will be a lady."

"So there's the attraction." Daniel nodded. "Off home with you, then, and I'll see you when I can."

He put his fingers to his lips to blow me a kiss, then crossed Bayard toward Elizabeth Street.

I was about to head for the elevated railway when a strange idea came to me. Annie hadn't said she had seen a white face floating up the stairs. She had said "a white floating head."

And unbidden, an image of Monty Warrington-Chase flashed into my mind.

CHAPTER THIRTY-TWO

I stood like a statue, staring out across the street. No, that was ridiculous. What could an English aristocrat like Monty Warrington-Chase possibly have to do with Lee Sing Tai? Even as I asked myself the question, a likely answer formed in my head. Monty who looked so unwell recently, who had been seen hurrying toward Chinatown, not noticing either Daniel or myself. I had seen a face that resembled Monty's emerging from an alleyway on Mott Street, and I realized that the man had come from an opium den. So Monty was a drug fiend.

The moment I realized that, I saw how easily he could have killed Annie. He would not have been seen as an outsider at the settlement house. Nobody would have questioned his presence if he went upstairs, looking for Sarah. And of course he had to kill her because he realized that she had seen him, carrying Lee Sing Tai's body up the stairs to throw it off the roof. And I had been partly responsible for her death. If I hadn't brought Bo Kei home with me, then Monty wouldn't have bumped into her coming out of the water closet, and realized that she was not the girl who had seen him at Lee's. That the girl he had seen was the other girl Sarah had told him about—the girl who was still at the settlement house.

I looked across the street for Daniel, but he had already vanished between pushcarts. So what should I do now?

Obviously report what I had deduced to him, but I needed proof. Then it occurred to me that we had proof, in Lee Sing Tai's cabinet. That day when Bobby Lee had opened it and complained that someone had been there, I had glimpsed a signature on a piece of paper, half protruding from one of the drawers. There had been something about it that struck a chord then, but I hadn't been able to place what it was. Now it came to me that I had seen that signature before—when Hermione had shown me Monty's letter to her. There was a particular flourish to the way he formed his M.

I couldn't wait to prove that I was right—what a coup that would be if I could go to Daniel and tell him that I had solved the case. I'd rather enjoy seeing Captain Kear's face too. So I turned back down Mott Street. The constable was standing on duty outside Lee's residence. I went up to him.

"I'm sorry to bother you," I said, "but I think I must have left my gloves up there when I came out with Captain Sullivan a few minutes ago. Would it be all right if I popped up to retrieve them?"

"I don't see why not, miss," he said genially. "Just don't go touching anything or I'll be in the soup."

"Don't worry. I'll be very careful," I said. "I wouldn't have bothered you, but they are new gloves and they cost so much these days, don't they?"

"Doesn't everything," he said.

I gave him a beaming smile and ran up the steps, opened the front door, and moved cautiously around the screen. Then I sprinted across the room to the cabinet and opened it, using my handkerchief to hold the key and then the side of the door. I tried to remember in which of the drawers I had seen the signature. Over on the left, about halfway up. . . . I was conscious of the need to hurry or the constable would come up to see what was delaying me. I pulled open a drawer. It was literally stuffed full of papers—a daunting prospect. Obviously I couldn't go through them all. But the one I wanted had been sticking out. Surely it would have been shoved back hastily when the cabinet was closed. I examined one drawer, then another. I pushed it back, but it didn't seem to go all the way in. On impulse, I pulled the drawer completely out and hit pay dirt. Several papers had been pushed behind the drawer, and one of them contained the signature I had seen.

I held it in my hand. The writing was all in Chinese characters but it was clearly some kind of IOU.

"Perfect," I said, closed the cabinet carefully, and turned to leave.

"I'll take that, thank you," said a low, smooth voice and I turned to see Monty standing by the screen. He came toward me. "You really are a most annoying woman, you know. Give me the paper."

"Did you just owe him money for opium or was he blackmailing you?" I asked.

"The latter," Monty said. "Threatened to tell Sarah's family about my unfortunate habit. Now I'll just take this—" He went to snatch it from me. I stepped aside. "And then off to the border," he added.

"There's no point, you know," I said. "There's a constable at the bottom of the steps. You can't go anywhere."

"I can return the way I came," he said. He took another step toward me. For a second I glanced down at his feet. "Oh," I said. "Climbing boots. Of course. Sarah told me you were a keen mountaineer."

"Sarah talks too much for her own good," he said. "She was only too keen to tell me the whole story of those Chinese girls." He paused smiling as if he hadn't a care in the world. "On second thought," he said, "I think I'd better take you with me. Just in case."

"Don't be ridiculous." I started moving toward the screen. He went to grab me, expecting me to be the usual kind of helpless miss. But I had been well schooled by experience in my profession as well as by my future bridegroom. I delivered a savage kick to his shin, then brought my elbow up to his windpipe. I heard the thin fabric of my dress ripping under the arm but I didn't care. Monty gasped and reeled backward. I only needed that half second to run around the screen and down the stairs.

"He's in there!" I shouted to the constable. "Quickly. The murderer is in there. Don't let him get away."

The constable rushed up the stairs. I stood below, holding my breath. But a few minutes later the constable reappeared. "There was nobody there, miss. You must have imagined it."

"Then he escaped over the rooftop again," I said. "But he can't go too far. He'll have to come down a fire escape on the building behind. Blow your whistle and get help."

He was now looking at me strangely. "Are you sure about this, miss? You didn't just imagine that you saw someone. I don't want to look like a fool if this is for nothing."

"Of course it's not for nothing," I said. "He tried to grab me and I ripped my dress, see?" I demonstrated, not caring that it was unladylike to reveal flesh to a strange man. "And he got into the apartment across the roofs—the way he got in before. He's wearing climbing boots."

"And you say he'll have jumped across to the next roof?"

"Yes, around the corner on Pell Street."

"Right. I'll get help then." He blew his whistle as he headed in that direction. I was very tempted to follow but I saw that there was nothing useful I could do and I certainly didn't want to find myself taken hostage by a desperate man. I should go straight to police headquarters to await Daniel. I set off back up Mott Street. As I passed the narrow arched entrance beside Lee's emporium I thought I saw a flash of something light in the darkness beyond. Surely Monty couldn't have climbed down from the roof already and taken refuge in there? I didn't know where the arcade led, but it didn't seem the brightest move to me, seeing that he could be trapped so easily. I peered into the darkness. Had I really . . . ?

A hand came over my mouth and I was yanked backward. I tried to struggle but the hand clamped over my mouth and nose, making it impossible to breathe. I hadn't realized how strong he was. I was being half dragged, half carried backward down a sort of tunnel. I flailed, fought, and tried to breathe. I could feel singing in my head. Spots danced in front of my eyes and my only thought was one of fury—that I had let this man get the better of me, and that I was going to die before my wedding.

"Damnation," I heard Monty mutter before I blacked out.

I gradually came back to consciousness, like a swimmer coming up from deep water. I was lying on a hard surface in almost total darkness. I lay there, gasping for breath like a landed fish. As I breathed I was conscious of a cloying smoky smell that I couldn't place. My eyes became used to the darkness and I saw a wooden ceiling, only a foot or two above my head. A moment of panic shot through me that I was lying in a coffin. Then I noticed a fire was glowing nearby. As my lungs tried to work properly again I felt something hard and foul-tasting in my mouth. I gasped in smoke, making me cough and retch.

I knew where I was now—an opium den and not the mock kind of Mr. Connors's. The cold hard object in my mouth appeared to be the long stem of a pipe, the bowl of which was propped over a glowing brazier. I saw similar pinpoints of light in similar cubicles around the walls and the darker shape of figures lying in tiers around the walls. I tried to move my hand, but my limbs felt lethargic as if they didn't fully belong to me. If I managed to get my mouth free and shouted for help, would anyone here be awake enough to help me? My eyes wanted to close. I fought the sleep that was overcoming me. Was Monty still here, watching me? Enjoying the spectacle of my being drugged by opium, or had he merely half suffocated me and then left me to give the appearance of an opium addict while he made his getaway?

I had no idea how long I had been unconscious or how much opium I had already breathed in. I was horribly aware of the singing in my head and that my arms and legs were no longer obeying me. If Monty was still watching me, my only course was to breathe as little as possible, feign sleep, and hope that he'd leave.

I shut my eyes and let my mouth droop open, making what I hoped were the snoring noises of one on opium. I think

I may have drifted off because suddenly I was floating, my body completely weightless and my arms propelling me though the bluest of skies with no effort at all like swimming in a warm ocean. Brilliantly green fields were below me, greener than anything I had seen in Ireland, and the air felt sweet and fresh. It came to me that there was nothing to worry about. All would be well.

Except a word hovered at the back of my consciousness. *Daniel. Daniel.* I repeated it and forced my eyes open. *Something I had to tell Daniel.* I tried to sit up and banged my head hard on that ceiling of the bunk above mine. The pain was enough to bring me back to some degree of consciousness. *Daniel. Had to tell Daniel . . .* I tried to get to my feet. My legs felt as if they were remote objects over which I had no control, and I had to cling onto the edge of my bunk while the world swung around me. Have to get out. *Get out,* I muttered. I staggered across to the wall and felt my way around until I came to a door. It took me a long time to find a latch and make my fingers lift it, then to push open the door. I stepped outside, trying to see where I was going, but I couldn't focus on anything. In truth I didn't know where I was. Just two things, darkness and Daniel, echoed through the hollow of my mind.

There was a bad smell in my dark passage and that helped to bring me to some kind of reality, but I still couldn't make my brain function enough to tell me where I was or where I needed to go. I staggered forward, feeling the rough brickwork of the arched wall on my hand. I heard noises ahead—voices, harsh and loud; the chink of crockery; a fiddle played badly. As I stepped out to see what it was, a burst of gunfire sounded right beside me. I leaped back, half fell, and was grabbed by strong arms. I fought myself free.

"Okay, missie. Only firecracker. Firecracker for holiday," a voice said.

Firecracker. My fuzzy mind played with the word. Another burst made me jump again. Danger. Had to get away from here. But I wasn't sure in which direction safety lay. I started to walk. Then I heard a voice.

"Follow me, if you please, ladies and gentlemen. We are now in the heart of Chinatown. There is danger and depravity all around us, so please stay close to me. We wouldn't want the little ladies to be shipped off as white slaves, would we?"

Even in my befuddled state I recognized the voice. Connors. Slumming tours. I was saved. I staggered toward him.

"Mr. Connors, I need help," I tried to say. But the words only came out as a moaning jumble of sounds with no discernible consonants. Instead of offering help, Connors shepherded his group hastily to one side, steering them past me like a herd of sheep.

"There you are, that's one of them," Connors said, his voice booming through a megaphone. "I promised you'd see opium addicts and there you are. You can see how low ordinary white folks have fallen, under the spell of this awful drug."

"No wait, listen," I tried to say, but they swept past me and away.

Then another hand grabbed my arm. "You poor dear woman," a voice said. "Have no fear. I've come to save you. Yes, there is salvation in the Lord. Come back to the mission with me and I'll help you break the bonds of the devil's drug." I could vaguely make out a trim shape of woman in a gray outfit and old-fashioned gray bonnet. "Come on," she said again. "Let me take you to the mission. I promise you won't regret it. The Lord has sent me to find you and lead you on the road to recovery."

I wanted to laugh. I wanted to tell her I was Molly Murphy, private investigator and about to be married to a respectable police captain, but again my mouth made only animal-like sounds. One thing was clear. I didn't want to go with her. Had to find Daniel and tell him . . . I couldn't remember what I had to tell him, but it was important.

She was just trying to drag me away when I heard another voice. "Miss Murphy! Holy Mother of God, it's Miss Murphy, Albert. What has happened to you, my dear? Albert, take her arm. We must get her into the house."

And I was half carried in through a front door. "Are you

sick, my dear? Has someone attacked you? Your dress is all torn."

I tried to tell her with my useless lips, again producing only the incomprehensible words one makes when half asleep.

"Looks to me as if she's been drugged," a male voice said.

"Then we'd better leave her to sleep it off," said the woman's voice. "Wasn't it lucky that the wind got up and we came back from the picnic early, or who knows what might have happened to her?"

Someone put a cup to my lips and I sipped water.

"It's coffee she needs," the male voice said. "If coffee can cure a hangover, it should help with other drugs, shouldn't it?"

They lay me down and tucked a blanket around me. "It's all right, my dear. You're quite safe now," the woman said.

I closed my eyes. Quite safe now. I knew there was some reason I shouldn't sleep, but it had gone again. I closed my eyes and retreated into dreams.

CHAPTER THIRTY-THREE

It was the smell of coffee that aroused me. It crept into the peaceful landscape in which I was residing until my brain formed the word "coffee" and I came to consciousness. Aileen Chiu was standing in front of me, holding a cup.

"I let you sleep it off," she said, "but I guess you'd now like a nice cup of coffee to clear your head."

"What time is it?" I asked.

"A little past nine in the evening."

"That's terrible," I said as memory returned. "I'll be too late."

"Too late for what?"

"To stop him from crossing the border and getting away." I sat up, closing my eyes as the world swung around. "The murderer," I added. "Can you send someone to police headquarters and get Captain Sullivan?"

"Why yes, I'll send my son, Joe, right away," she said, "but what's this about a murderer?"

"The man who killed Mr. Lee. He dragged me into an opium den and drugged me while he got away," I said.

"Jesus, Mary, and Joseph," she muttered, crossing herself. "You poor dear. What an experience. You're lucky to have escaped with your life."

"Yes, I am," I said, realizing as I spoke the words how true they were. I was alive and soon Daniel was going to come and all would be well—except that I'd slept so long that Monty

Warrington-Chase would be in Canada and nobody would bother to pursue someone who killed Chinese people. At least Sarah would be safe now—an awful thought struck me. Had he taken her with him?

I sipped the coffee, feeling normality returning. I was conscious of voices, a door slamming; then I lay back again until I heard a voice I recognized. "Where is she? Is she all right?"

And Daniel burst into the room. He dropped to his knees, enveloping me in his arms. "Thank God," he murmured, burying his face in my hair. "Thank God. I was going out of my mind with worry. I've had men combing the city for you." And then as he held me away I saw that his eyes were moist with tears. "Where the devil did you get to? I thought I told you to go straight home and wait for me."

"I intended to," I said. "I was on my way home when he grabbed me."

"Who grabbed you?"

"Monty Warrington-Chase," I said. "He committed both the murders, Daniel."

"Monty? What the deuce did he have to do with Chinatown?"

"Opium addict," I said. "Lee Sing Tai was blackmailing him and threatening to tell Sarah's family."

"He told you all this?"

"I figured most of it out for myself," I said. "I actually found the piece of paper with his signature on it, but I suppose he must have taken it when I was unconscious."

"He knocked you out?"

"I think he tried to kill me, but then someone was coming or his conscience got the better of him, and he dumped me in an opium den instead," I said. "You must stop him, Daniel. He said he was going to the border. That must mean Canada, I suppose."

"How long ago was this?"

"I'm not sure. I don't know how long I was asleep, but it must be several hours. The Chius found me in the street and brought me home with them. I wanted to tell them to find you, but I was so drugged that I couldn't form any words."

"I'll tell the constable outside to get things moving, and I'll arrange for someone to take you home," Daniel said. He was gone for a moment, then came striding up to me. "Just a minute. You found the piece of paper with his signature on it? Where did you find this paper?"

"In Lee's cabinet," I answered, realizing that I should not have mentioned this fact.

"You went back to Lee's place?"

"Only because there was a constable standing outside the door, so I knew I'd be safe," I said. "I hadn't realized that Monty came in across the roof."

"Molly, what did I tell you?" Daniel was glaring at me now.

"Two seconds ago you were crying and thanking God I was still alive," I said. "Now you're looking at me as if you could kill me."

"Did it occur to you it's because I love you?" he said. "If anything happened to you—well, I don't want to picture life without you. And yet you continue to put yourself in harm's way."

"I don't put myself in harm's way deliberately," I said. "Harm's way just seems to find me."

"Not any longer," Daniel said. "If you don't behave yourself from now on, we'll go and live with my mother. There. How's that for a threat."

"Terrifying," I said, managing a smile. I took a deep breath. "I'm really sorry about all of this, Daniel. I knew I shouldn't get involved from the beginning. I thought I was helping, but I wasn't."

"I don't know about that," Daniel said. "You've solved my case for me. We'll have men watching all border crossings so we've a still good chance of catching him."

"But if he's taken that signature with him, you'll have no proof."

"My dear girl, I told you, I have a nice set of fingerprints on that statue. If Monty's match—well then. There we are. The courts have never yet allowed us to admit fingerprints as evidence, but they'll have to soon. And at very least you've stopped your friend Sarah from marrying him."

"Poor Sarah," I said. "She might really love him. I know how I'd feel if you turned out to be a drug fiend or a murderer."

Daniel actually laughed. "That's one thing you can say for me. I'm a straightforward kind of guy. What you see is what you get."

I looked at him with love in my eyes. "That's just fine with me," I said.

I arrived back at Sid and Gus's to find a beaming Bo Kei with Frederick beside her. He had been released that afternoon and they were already planning what they should do next.

"I will be forever in gratitude, Missie Molly," Bo Kei said. "You have given me my life and my happiness."

Well, at least I'd done something right. They were going to go back to Canada where they felt that Chinese people had a better chance of leading normal lives. This made me think of Monty crossing the border. Had the police been too late to catch him? Would the Canadian authorities return him?

We didn't learn the truth until a few days later. Monty had been apprehended trying to sail out of Montreal on a ship bound for England. He had died of a drug overdose that night, whether intentionally or accidentally we'd never know. Given his position in society, it would have been unlikely that he would have had to face a harsh punishment for the crime of killing Chinese. He might even have walked away a free man. Sarah was with us when Daniel came to tell us the news.

"I'm glad he's not going to prison," Sarah said. She sat staring down at her hands, her face betraying no emotion. "I know that addiction causes people to do all kinds of wicked, reckless things. Poor Monty, I believe he tried to tell me about it once, in a subtle way. He said that he'd fallen from his polo pony in India and broken his ribs. The pain had been so great that they'd fed him a constant supply of morphine. I suppose the addiction started then."

"I think you're being too kind," Sid said. "You're well rid of him, Sarah. Now that you're no longer engaged we can tell you that we thought him a selfish, arrogant brute who would have made your life miserable."

"Why didn't you say this to me before?"

"Because we know that people fall in love with the most unsuitable types," Gus added. "And if you really were in love with him, it was not up to us to stop you."

Sarah gave a sad sort of smile. "I don't think I ever was truly in love with him. I can't have been because I felt such a sense of relief when I heard he had fled to Canada. And I'm not heartbroken that he died. Now that I've had time to think about it, I'm sure he didn't love me either. He was only marrying me for my money."

"That's the same with Molly and me." Daniel patted my hand. "I'm only marrying her for her money."

"So you're off back to Westchester tomorrow for the final wedding preparations, are you?" Sarah asked.

I nodded. "Final fittings on my dress, that kind of thing. If you think you could bear it, I'd like you to come to the wedding too."

"I'd like to, if only to see Sid and Gus dressed as bridesmaids." Sarah managed a smile.

"I'll have you know that Gus and I will be the most demure and correct bridesmaids in the history of weddings," Sid said. "You wait until you see us in lavender."

"I must be going." Daniel got to his feet. "I only came to tell you the news and I have paperwork to finish tonight if I want to be free to come with you tomorrow to my mother's. Ladies, I bid you farewell." And he bowed correctly.

I walked with him to the door. "How is it that you have time to come with me? I thought you were working on a big case you couldn't tell me about."

"I was." He paused. "It is concluded, satisfactorily as far as the commissioner is concerned, in spite of you, Miss Murphy."

"What did I do?"

"I was ordered by the commissioner to look into corruption in the New York City police—a task I found most repugnant, as you can imagine. Spying on my fellow officers and turning them in. I can tell you, that goes against the grain; but I had no choice in the matter. I obey orders. As you can imagine, a good deal of my attention was focused on the issue of accepting bribes. I was spying on Kear and Bobby Lee when you barged in on me. They were about to conclude a lucrative deal. Luckily I was able to nail him anyway—something I don't regret too much, as I couldn't stand the man. The commissioner hopes that a couple of examples like this will put the fear of God into the rest of the force. We shall see. On a policeman's pay it's all too easy to accept bribes and sometimes it's expedient to work on both sides of the law."

"But you'll never do that," I said.

"If I did, you'd never hear about it." He laughed. Then he took me into his arms and kissed me.

The next day when I went back to Mrs. Sullivan's house I took little Bridie with me. When I went to Cherry Street to deliver the wedding invitation, Seamus had let me know that he wasn't planning to attend. Had to be near the docks in case the ship decided to sail, was how he put it, but I got the feeling that he'd feel out of place at a fancy wedding in Westchester County. So he said his good-byes to his daughter and she trotted off with me, holding my hand and scarcely a look back at her father and brother.

To my relief Mrs. Sullivan made her quite welcome, indicating she was pleased to have a flower girl in the bridal procession after all. She set about making a dress for her and was delighted that Bridie proved a quick learner with her needle. "Why she's better at it than you," she said, looking up at me with triumph in her eyes. "I think she'll make a splendid little helper for my maid."

I was sure she would, but I had other ideas by this time. I took Daniel aside when he came up to see how we were getting along.

"Listen, how would you feel about starting married life with a child in the house?" I asked him.

He looked at me suspiciously. "Are you trying to tell me— because we haven't . . . for some time."

I laughed. "Not ours. I was thinking of Bridie. I'm sure she'd be fine with your mother, but I'm thinking she'd be a grand little helper for me, especially when the babies come, and she could continue her schooling."

"But my mother's grown quite fond of her," he said. "And I think we should get off to a better start with just the two of us on our own. Later when we're settled, we can discuss it again if you like."

So now Bridie had people actually fighting over her. I could see that Daniel's mother liked having someone to look after again, which was just fine with me. I suspected that Bridie would not end up as any maid's helper. She would be spoiled and would learn to play croquet with the local young ladies.

During the next week I had plenty to occupy me, so that I had no time to think about crime and detection and specifically what had just happened to me in Chinatown. My days were filled with the minutiae of arranging a wedding, from ordering the ham from the butcher to the flowers for the church and the final fittings on my wedding gown. None of it seemed real until I awoke one morning and realized it was my wedding day. I looked out of my window to a perfect blue sky. Mrs. Sullivan had arranged a hearty breakfast, but I couldn't eat a thing. While I was still toying with my boiled egg Sid and Gus arrived from New York, dressed so conventionally that I hardly recognized them.

We went up to my room and they helped me into my dress. It was all creamy silk and lace, and when I looked at myself in the looking glass, I hardly recognized myself. I was no longer the Irish tomboy—I was an elegant woman, about to be married.

I saw Mrs. Sullivan standing in the doorway, watching me admiring myself. She looked pleased and proud. I went over to her and gave her a hug. "Thank you, it's wonderful," I said.

"You look grand," she said, going quite pink. "I only wish that my dear husband had lived to see this day."

So wonders would never cease. She actually approved of me. Then a second wonder happened as Sid and Gus came back, having turned into demure young ladies in dresses of lavender silk.

"The carriage has come," Bridie called, looking out of the window. "And it's beautiful and it's got two white horses, like Cinderella."

In truth I felt like a magic princess. The others went down and I stood alone in the room, still looking at my reflection. In an hour's time I'd be a married woman, Mrs. Daniel Sullivan. I'd have given up my freedom. I'd no longer be hunting people through Chinatown or the Lower East Side. I'd be expected to behave sedately and do the kind of things wives did. For a second I felt a twinge of panic. Then I thought—was it really such fun to be risking my life on a daily basis, not knowing where my next dollar was coming from? And was Mrs. Daniel Sullivan such a bad thing to be?

"Molly, come on, we'll be late," Mrs. Sullivan called from the stairs.

"Coming," I called and went down to meet my future.

I climbed into the open carriage and we rode to the church, my veil blowing out behind me in the wind. The organ was playing as I went up the path to the church, with Bridie walking ahead of me. The organist switched to the wedding march. There were so many people in the pews, and as all those faces turned toward me, I was suddenly overcome with shyness and self-consciousness until I spotted Daniel. He was standing there by the altar in his dark suit, his unruly hair combed into submission, and he was staring at me with a strange look of wonder on his face, as if he'd just seen me for the first time. And he looked so handsome he almost took my breath away.

"This is the man I'm going to marry," I whispered and almost had to pinch myself. Mrs. Daniel Sullivan wasn't a bad thing to be at all.

I started to walk up the aisle toward him, hardly conscious of Bridie ahead of me or Sid and Gus following just behind. As I came close to the altar, Daniel held out his hand to me. His eyes were smiling.

The next bit was something of a blur. Then we were walking down the aisle together, my hand tucked through his arm and people were throwing rice as we stepped out into the bright sunshine.

"Well, Mrs. Sullivan?" Daniel said. "I've finally tamed the wild Irish girl."

"Don't you believe it." I laughed.

Then it was back to the house for a magnificent spread of food and toasts and champagne. I had always known that Daniel moved in society, but I was surprised at the number of distinguished people who were attending. Daniel introduced me to aldermen and members of the Four Hundred. Even Mr. John Wilkie, head of the Secret Service with whom Daniel had recently worked, had come up from Washington. Actually I had worked for him too, unbeknownst to my bridegroom!

"So you're giving up your profession, are you?" he said as he came to congratulate us. "I must say I'm disappointed. Such a waste of talent, Sullivan. I was hoping to recruit her."

"You'll do no such thing," Daniel said. "I am delighted I can finally stop worrying about her and know that she's safely at home."

The reception line moved on. For a while I had felt like a stranger at my own wedding until I realized that I did know quite a few of the guests. There were several of Daniel's fellow officers, including my friend and female detective Mrs. Goodwin. I was delighted to see old Miss Van Woekem, the distinguished lady who had taken me under her wing when I first arrived in New York. Sarah Lindley had come, looking rather pale and sad, but giving me a kiss and a brave smile. "It was for the best, wasn't it?" she whispered to me. I nodded.

And then I looked up as an amazing figure came flying toward me. It was Ryan O'Hare, wearing a floor-length black cape over a white suit.

"You didn't think I'd let the small matter of a lack of invitation keep me away, did you?" he asked, taking my hand and kissing it. "I've never been known to miss a good party

in my life. Besides, I can see that this one needs livening up.
I may give one of my recitations—'The Boy Stood on the
Burning Deck,' perhaps?"

I started to laugh. "Oh, Ryan, I'm so glad you're here," I
said.

If Daniel didn't feel the same way, he was gracious enough
not to say anything. As we moved through the crowd together
I heard Daniel's mother's voice. "Yes, she is such a dear girl,
isn't she? I'm so lucky to be getting such a daughter-in-law."

After the toasts and the cutting of the cake the party
slowed down as guests stood around the lawn in the balmy
evening air.

"Ah, so there you are, Mrs. Sullivan." Mr. Wilkie came up
to me. "Come for a stroll with me and show me those lovely
rosebushes."

We walked across the lawn together.

"You know, I can't see you settling down to domestic bliss,"
he said.

"I'm going to have to learn how to," I replied.

He leaned closer to me. "When you come back from the
honeymoon," he said in a low voice, "there's a little job I'd
like you to do for me. Oh, and no need to mention it to Daniel." He put his finger to his lips and moved back into the
crowd, leaving me staring after him.

"Ah, there you are," Daniel called, coming toward me. "I
thought you'd run away from me already." He put his arm
around my waist. "They all seem to be having a good time,
don't they?"

I nodded. "Your mother has done a wonderful job. It's magnificent, Daniel."

"Let's leave them to it. I think it's time you and I slipped
away together, don't you?" he murmured.

He took my hand and led me back toward the house.

HISTORICAL NOTE

Everything I have written about Chinatown in 1903 is accurate, including Chuck Connors's slumming tours, the overzealous missionaries, the opium dens, and the lack of Chinese women. Congress passed the Exclusion Act in 1884, hoping to drive those Chinese who had come for the Gold Rush and the building of the railways back to their homeland. The act decreed they could never become citizens, even if born here. They could not bring over their wives and families (certain rich merchants got around this). However, in the Census of 1900 there were over three thousand men living in Chinatown and only thirty women. Of course there could have been more women, including the small-foot wives hidden away, and there were definitely Chinese prostitutes in the brothels on the Bowery.

In spite of the Chinese being sober and hardworking, they were universally mistrusted and considered to be a threat. Misconceptions about their customs and lifestyle continued well into the century, which is why Chinatowns have endured for so long.

HUSH NOW, DON'T YOU CRY

October 8, 1903

We should not have come here!" I shouted over the howl of the wind. Rain swept in great squalls off the ocean, snatching the words from my mouth. It was not a night to be standing on a clifftop in complete darkness. Our umbrella had given up the unequal struggle with the storm on the way from the station and now lay in a rubbish bin, its ribs sticking out like a large dead spider. Daniel had deposited it there despite my protests, stating that it was past all hope of repair.

It was a long walk from the station and not one that should have been attempted on a stormy night. But we had little choice. The directions we had been given were for a delightful afternoon stroll along a cliff path, with blue ocean below us. We had not anticipated that Daniel would be delayed with a last-minute problem at headquarters and that what the locals called a nor'easter would arrive at the same time as ourselves.

After changing trains in Providence, then again to a branch line in Kingston, we finally pulled into Newport station, at almost ten o'clock. There was not a hansom cab or any kind of conveyance to be found. The town appeared to be battened down in anticipation of the coming storm. We'd set off bravely enough under Daniel's big umbrella but once out of the town center, heading toward the clifftop footpath the full force of the wind had turned the umbrella inside out and ripped it to shreds in minutes.

"Damn and blast it," Daniel had muttered, no longer apologizing if he swore in my presence now that I was married to him. "We should have waited for the morning. I should not have listened to you."

"What, and missed a whole day of our honeymoon?" I demanded as I struggled to take off my new hat. It was a jaunty little concoction piled high with ribbons and lace and I certainly didn't want to lose it over the cliff. I stuffed it into my carpetbag, probably not doing it much good in the process but at least preventing it from sailing off into the ocean. "Cheer up. I'm sure it can't be far. Newport is only a small seaside town, isn't it? Just a few cottages, I was told."

Daniel had to chuckle at this and put an arm around my shoulders. "You wait until daylight and then you'll see the extent of the cottages."

In my mind's eye I pictured a long road like the one leading into Westport in Ireland, with simple whitewashed cottages stretching along the side of the road facing the sea. It would be nice to be spending my honeymoon in a place that reminded me of home, I had thought when Daniel told me of this opportunity.

The walk turned from an annoyance into a frightening experience. We tried to follow a dark little street called Cliff Avenue, but it ended in a pair of high-locked gates, forcing us back to our original route along the cliff—not what we would have chosen on a dark night. No lights shone out through the storm and we could hear the pounding waves crashing onto rocks below us. That cliff path seemed to go on forever and even I began to doubt the sense of wanting to reach our cottage tonight. Luckily the wind was blowing in from the ocean or I should have worried about being swept over that unseen cliff edge to our deaths.

"Are you sure this is the right way?" I shouted, grabbing on to Daniel's arm. "Are there no roads in this place? Is this cottage not on a proper street?"

"Obviously," Daniel said tersely. "But it never occurred to me to ask for foul weather directions. I assumed there would be a cab if we needed one."

I peered into the blackness. "There are no lights. We can't be near any cottages. Surely the whole population of Newport doesn't go to bed by nine o'clock?"

"It's October. None of the cottages are likely to be inhabited at this time of year," Daniel shouted back. "They are only used in the summer."

The thought of being the only people in a remote seaside village had seemed desirable when Daniel had presented it to me, our original honeymoon plans having fallen through when Daniel was summoned back to work two days after our wedding. I had borne this with remarkable patience for once, understanding that this was to be the lot of a policeman's wife. I think Daniel had been impressed by my stoicism and had promised me that we would escape from the city as soon as his work permitted. So when the offer of a seaside cottage had come up, he'd jumped at it. Of course October was a little late in the year for beaches and bathing, but we had other activities in mind anyway. And this part of the country often experienced what they called an Indian summer, with glorious sunny days and glowing fall colors. Just not this year, it appeared.

"Nearly there, I think." Daniel propelled me forward, his arm still around my waist. "Then a bath and a hot drink will soon bring us to rights. Ah, this way. I believe we follow this wall and it will lead us to the gate."

As Daniel took my hand and guided me away from the cliff path, there was an ominous rumble of thunder overhead. A few moments later a flash of lightning lit up towering wrought-iron gates. Daniel felt for a latch but the gates refused to open.

"Blast and damnation!" he shouted. "These infernal gates must open somehow." He shook them in frustration but they refused to budge.

"They knew we were expected today, didn't they?" I asked. "I don't see any lights." I was soaked to the skin, my teeth chattering now, my hair plastered to my face, and my clothes clinging to me. All I wanted was to get indoors to a fire and a cup of tea.

"I don't understand it. I know the family is not usually here at this time of year, but there has to be a caretaker on the property." Daniel snapped out the words. "But we have no way of alerting anyone, unless we walk back into town and see if we can reach the place by telephone."

This suggestion didn't seem too appealing. "Everything seemed to be closed for the night in town. Besides we can't walk all the way back," I said. "We're already soaked to the skin. I don't suppose it's any good shouting."

"No one would hear us with this infernal racket going on."

Thunder growled again and once again the scene was illuminated with a lighting flash. It revealed a long driveway behind those gates and in the distance the great black shape of what seemed to be an enormous castle. I stared in amazement.

"I thought you said it was a cottage."

"I wanted to surprise you," Daniel replied in an annoyed voice. "The wealthy who own summer homes in Newport call them cottages but they are actually mansions. This one is called Connemara."

"Holy mother of God," I muttered. "We're not getting a whole mansion to ourselves are we?"

"No, we've been offered the guest cottage on the property. If only we can find a way in." He rattled the gates again angrily.

I had been experiencing a growing sense of anxiety. It wasn't just the howl of the storm and the flashes of lightning. God knows I'd seen enough storms on the West Coast of Ireland. It was something more. "Daniel, don't let's stay here," I blurted out suddenly. "Perhaps we should go back into town after all. There is bound to be a hotel or inn of some sort where we can spend the night. The house clearly doesn't want us."

Daniel gave me a quizzical smile. "The house doesn't want us?"

"I'm getting this overwhelming feeling that we shouldn't be here, that we're not wanted."

"You and your sixth sense," Daniel said. He was still prowling, staring up at the gates and the high stone wall. "You'll feel differently when we're safely inside. I am determined to find a way in, even if I have to scale that wall."

A great clap of thunder right overhead drowned out his last words and simultaneously the world was bathed in electric blue light. I was staring up at the house and I saw a face quite clearly framed in an upstairs window. It was a child's face and it was laughing with maniacal glee.

I let go of the bars of the gate as if burned. "Come away!" I shouted. "We shouldn't be here."